Margaret Yorke lives in Buckinghamshire. She is a past chairman of the Crime Writers' Association and her outstanding contribution to the genre has been internationally recognised. She won the Swedish Academy of Detection Award in 1982 for the best crime novel in translation.

in memory of

Belinda MacDougall

A QUESTION OF BELIEF

Margaret Yorke

WARNER BOOKS

A *Warner* Book

First published in Great Britain in 1996
by Little, Brown and Company

Copyright © Margaret Yorke 1996

The moral right of the author has been asserted.

A CIP catalogue record for this book
is available from the British Library.

ISBN 0 7515 1850 6

Typeset by Solidus (Bristol) Limited
Printed and bound in Great Britain by
Clays Ltd, St. Ives plc

Warner Books
A Division of
Little, Brown and Company (UK)
Brettenham House
Lancaster Place
London WC2E 7EN

A Question of Belief

1

HE'D LEFT HER everything: the house, and the mortgage, even the car, because that would be found where he had abandoned it near the river. She'd think he'd jumped in, and after a while his death would be presumed and she'd get probate. Did that take seven years? There might be complications but she would be able to carry on a normal life. He didn't think she'd hurry to report him missing. She wouldn't want him back. By the time she took action, or the car was found, he'd be far away.

He'd made no plans. He had no goal. He was a broken, defeated man and he did not know what else to do. At least she would be free of him, free from the shame.

At first, when he was released on bail before the trial, he had planned to kill himself, but that would have been too easy. It would have been a confession of guilt, but then she and everyone else he cared about believed he'd done it.

Andrew, his student son, had said, 'Surely there are other ways, Dad,' almost with pity, but contempt had been there, too. The boy had been mocked by his friends, and so had Jackie, his daughter, who was still at school. It had been worse for her, because they had always been so close.

'I can't expect you to understand, only to believe in me,' he'd said, and had made a move to hug her, but she had drawn back from him in revulsion. That was what had killed his final hope of support.

Lesley, his wife, had at first accepted what he told her had happened, but when he was dismissed from Lavery's, the large store where he was a departmental manager, she had changed her mind.

He'd been given no opportunity to defend himself before it went to court. There was no internal enquiry, and at that stage taking legal action would have meant risking a huge financial loss if he failed. He had consulted a solicitor who had pointed out the hazards.

'It seems you've got no proof,' he said. 'It's her word against yours. You'd need witnesses to testify on your behalf.'

He had tried to find them, but none of his colleagues was prepared to be involved, though one or two showed sympathy, and even regret.

'You'd have been safe if you'd gone along with it,' said Bob, from soft furnishings. 'That's what I did, and after a bit she let me go.' He'd grinned, sheepishly. 'It was all right,' he said. 'An experience.

Taught me to be more careful in the future.'

'What if Polly'd found out?' he'd asked, horrified. Polly was Bob's wife.

'She didn't,' Bob had answered. 'And if you tell her,' he'd added, suddenly menacing, 'I'll say you made it up to get yourself off the hook.'

But then she'd gone to the police, made it public.

Disappearing now, he'd got some money – not a lot, because if he took any out of the bank account, suicide would be discounted. He had almost a hundred pounds, saved from his social security payment; his watch, which he could sell; and he took the radio from the car because that was what car thieves went for and it would look as if the abandoned vehicle had been pillaged. He left it unlocked, with the keys in the ignition.

It was to be a long time before the thought of revenge occurred to him.

Autumn seemed to be lasting for ever. Frances Dixon could not remember when the trees had displayed such brilliant shades of gold and russet, and for so long. Throughout October the leaves hung upon the branches, reluctant to give up their hold, and sunlight shafted down among them for days on end. She savoured it. Such moments were for treasuring.

She spent many hours working in her garden, planting still more bulbs, though in the years since she had lived at Badger's End she had naturalised hundreds under the apple trees. It was partly because of its name and partly because of its garden that she had bought the house nearly ten years ago, in an act of defiance. It was a square Edwardian stone house with a slate roof: not beautiful, but sound.

'It seems solid enough,' her daughter Hazel had grudgingly admitted, when brought on a voyage of inspection, permitted by her mother only after the contract had been signed. Frances had sold her house in Hertfordshire quite easily and at a good price; she had lived there for a long time, and she moved before the recession sent prices down.

Hazel had thought her mother, who was sixty-two years old at the time, mad to move so far away, at her age.

'What will you do if you're ill?' she had demanded.

'Call the doctor,' Frances replied. 'As I should here, if I were bad enough.'

'Your friends,' her daughter had said. 'It's hard to make new ones at your age.'

'What friends?' her mother had asked, with asperity.

In recent years, many houses in the neighbour-hood had changed hands and were occupied by younger families. People Frances had known had moved away or died, but Hazel had grown used to having her mother close at hand, a captive baby-sitter on whom her own successful career in public relations had depended. If any of Hazel's three children were ill, or the au pair proved unsatisfactory, Hazel enrolled her mother to hold the fort, never even saying that she didn't know how she would manage without Frances's support.

But when I was raising you, I had to do it, Frances longed to scream at her, forced by her daughter to abandon a planned theatre visit, or a supper party for those few of her friends remaining in the area, because one of Hazel's children had to be collected from the station, or because Hazel's sister, Arabella, a physicist married to another physicist living in Cambridge, had a rush of work or a domestic crisis and sent an appeal. Frances loved her grandchildren, but there were so many of them – Hazel's three, Arabella's five (and who knew if there might not be more) and three stepchildren from her husband's previous marriage. In school holidays, the daughters never seemed to think their own mother needed a break too as they made plans for her to look after their families. When she retired, and wanted time to learn to paint or follow interests of her own, she was completely at their mercy and it had all become too much.

If I'm not near, they can't send for me, Frances had decided one day after she fell and broke her wrist. The pain was intense, and she felt weepy. I'm tired of being brave, she recognised, while managing to be stoical on the way to hospital.

Luckily it was her left wrist. Frances was right-handed. She had plenty of time to reflect as she patiently endured the weeks in plaster waiting for it to heal.

Frances had been widowed when she was forty, and she had brought up her two daughters on her own. It had not been easy, and now she felt she was rearing her grandchildren as well. She had deeply loved her husband, who was a freelance travel writer, and when he died suddenly of a heart attack while caught up in a riot in South America, he left her little in the way of insurance: only enough to clear the mortgage. At the time, though, that was a considerable boon; rising and falling interest rates had not affected her. She had already returned to part-time teaching, for he was often away and, apart from the increased income, working occupied her mind. She was thankful that her own career left her free in the school holidays; if either of her own girls were ill in term-time, there was a woman she could call upon to help and who would look after them when Frances went out in the evenings, which wasn't very often.

Hazel and Arabella seemed unable to find such people. Perhaps they no longer existed, or perhaps neither of them understood how to treat those who worked for them. Certainly, au pairs turned over at a rapid rate in both households. Hazel's was orderly, running to strict timetables with everything minutely planned, while Arabella lived in academic chaos, even squalor. Since both had had the same upbringing – a sort of halfway house between the two – Frances had decided that environment was not the most important factor in development, though it must be an influence. Genes were responsible for many aspects of an individual's disposition. Her husband had been volatile, often disorganised, intensely sensitive; she was more pragmatic, less prone to sudden whims and enthusiasms. She sometimes wondered how their marriage, cut short so suddenly, would have endured; it had been a passionate and fulfilling partnership, and she still missed him, thinking of him every day of her life. Would their natures have polarised through the years? Would they have irritated one another, or would they, as she liked to think, have drawn closer, become more like each other, less extreme?

She would never discover.

Life in Chingbury was very different from what she had known before. Badger's End was on the outskirts of the village, which, when she moved in, was still small, but as the years passed it had expanded. There were now some small clusters of modern houses where people lived who worked as far away as Swindon.

Frances had spent the first years taming the garden, learning as she went. She had always enjoyed keeping the small plot behind the Hertfordshire house in order; it had a lawn, where the girls had played badminton, and there were small borders where she put bedding plants and grew roses; there was never time for more. Now, the fresh air and the freedom – even the rain, and the occasional snowfall – were a benison to her. For at least a year she revelled in the knowledge that if she wanted to make the trip to Bristol to the theatre, or to the nearer cinema, she could go, without having to change her plans at the last minute. She did not miss her family at all. She'd really only seen them, she concluded, when they needed her: the sudden trips she'd had to make to Hazel's house, and the late drive home or early morning departure ready for her own work had been very taxing as the years had gone by.

Soon after breaking her wrist, while she was staying with Hazel – not because of her own injury but because Hazel had a product launch – she had heard Hazel say to a friend, who had come to show her some fabric samples for proposed new curtains, that she didn't know how they'd cope when Frances went gaga.

'How will you know when she has flipped?' asked the friend, who was an interior designer.

'Oh, she'll start losing things and she won't know the name of the prime minister,' said Hazel. 'There are tests.'

Ice-cold fury filled Frances as she overheard these words. She walked straight out of the house and stormed round the streets muttering angrily beneath her breath, and did not return for two hours, then had to apologise to Hazel for alarming her by her unexplained absence. She had not stayed long enough to hear Hazel's friend reprove her for her heartlessness and tell her she was lucky to have a mother; her own had died and was much missed.

'My father died when I was eight,' said Hazel, but she didn't win that round because her friend then reminded her that Frances had brought her up alone when there was very little help for single mothers, even widows, whereas now it almost paid a woman not to marry.

The two women made up their tiff over some wine. Hazel, after all, was single now, though her ex-husband paid proper maintenance for the children.

It might do them good to spend more time with him, Frances had sometimes thought, stifling guilt lest she seem to be abandoning them. But they were all now in their teens, the two elder ones at university.

She'd always rather liked her son-in-law; she'd found him more congenial than Arabella's physicist. He was a systems analyst, and he had taken off with a secretary from his office.

The friend had gone when Frances returned after going to a pub for a whisky. As soon as she went back to Hertfordshire she had telephoned the estate agent, any earlier doubts about the wisdom of her plan dismissed.

She had never once regretted what she had done. She made friends, slowly, over time; they were not like old friends, who knew one's history and to whom long spells without contact made no difference because threads were picked up and links renewed as if the last meeting had been only days before. She had had to make an effort, joining a painting class, a gardening club and going to local fine arts lectures. Gradually, over the years, she had dropped out of these activities, spending more and more time in her garden, by now knowledgeable herself. She visited other gardens, too: notable ones within a day's driving distance, and once every year she went on holiday which took her to gardens overseas not normally open to the public. Like-minded travellers made up each group, mostly women, but there were a few men too. Some of the women were themselves garden designers; what a fine career, Frances thought, and wondered if Charlotte, the granddaughter she thought needed her the most, would ever consider doing that. Perhaps she would like to go with her grandmother on the next garden holiday? But perhaps not: perhaps she sought young company and a sunny beach.

Frances was spending some of these glorious October weeks paying late visits to gardens which she went to every year. Soon they would close down until the spring.

This Saturday, she was setting off for Singleton, a manor house some thirty miles away. She'd have her lunch there, in the Orangery.

Denis Smith sat in the back of the Ford Transit van. He felt quite excited, setting off for a day in the country, and being paid for going. The van had been driven out of London by Orlando, but at the service station where Tessa had met them, she had taken over. It was clear that she was now the boss. She was quite a looker, Denis thought, with her red curly hair and pale skin, and blue eyes like he imagined the sea must be. He'd never seen the sea.

Denis had come along with Biff, whom he'd met while they were both doing community service – Denis for theft, Biff for trying to set fire to a pet shop.

'Them little animals, all cooped up. It ain't right,' he'd said to Denis. Biff was broad and strong, with dark curly hair worn rather long, a snake tattooed on one arm, and *Save the Apes* with a representation of St Francis on the other. As they painted a community hall together, he told Denis about St Francis talking to the animals and how harmless beasts were used in animal experimentation and were hunted for pleasure. 'It ain't right,' he repeated. 'Them as does it are like animals.'

Denis said, rashly, 'But you want to save animals.'

'Yeah. Stands to reason, they can't save theirselves,' said Biff. 'Besides, sometimes you get paid,' he added, irrelevantly, as it seemed.

'Paid? What for?' asked Denis.

'For helping them out. Making a noise. Throwing smoke bombs. Letting the dogs out,' said Biff. 'It depends. It's a laugh, anyway.'

When Denis agreed to go on Biff's next excursion, he learned that they were to receive fifty pounds each for the day's activities, and meals. For Biff and Denis, neither of whom had ever had a steady job nor tried very hard to get one, this was novel. Denis hadn't thought too much about their destination, or the ethics of their cause. It was something to do, and Biff, now, was his mate. This was good, because Biff kept others off his back. Denis was not good at fending for himself, and when he begged, his takings were sometimes stolen by other, brasher beggars. His flat, when the social found him one, had been invaded, too, by squatters, and it was Denis who, in the end, had moved out because they were into drugs and fighting. At the moment he was sleeping in a shed at the back of an empty shop in a derelict area where the recession had hit hard. Biff spent a night there now and then, when he had nowhere better to go. Denis didn't know where he was at other times. It was better not to ask people about their movements.

Biff said that their next project – he called it that – was to free animals kept caged and used to test drugs. He didn't know the location. Tessa and Orlando always kept the targets secret until they were on their way, in case the news leaked out.

When they reached the service area where Tessa joined them, she was waiting in a black VW Golf. She got out and opened the back, and Orlando helped her transfer several bags and packages which they stowed in the transit, having told the others to form a screen to hide their actions from onlookers. As well as Biff and Denis, there were Steve and Jet, who were already in the van when Orlando collected Denis and Biff from a roadside in Hammersmith, where they'd gone by Tube. Biff had paid, saying he'd get their fares back from Orlando.

Denis wondered what was in the bags and bundles. He saw something dark and shiny, like the barrel of a shotgun, but it was stowed away in an instant and he hoped he was mistaken. He hadn't reckoned on getting mixed up with anything violent. Letting rabbits out of cages wasn't even criminal damage, was it, if you did it peacefully? He was unaware that the holdalls contained empty bottles, tins of lighter fuel, and dry rags, and that there was a crowbar.

Biff had brought a rucksack which held cans of beer. He seemed to know all the others well, telling Denis he'd been on several trips with them and reminiscing about how they'd freed some sheep who were going to be sent to market, and how they'd set fire to a factory where drugs tested on animals were packed.

Steve and Jet held hands in the back of the van and seemed more intent on one another than the present cause. Denis didn't take much notice of them, and Biff concentrated on Tessa and Orlando, talking loudly, discussing the passing traffic, until Tessa told him to keep quiet and let her concentrate. Orlando, who wore shabby jeans and a drab khaki jacket, seemed ordinary enough but he talked a bit posh, and so did Tessa, though she said very little at first. She drove fast, aggressively.

Orlando was not his real name. He'd been christened Roland like his father but had turned it around when he created a new identity for himself after his mother failed to return from a holiday in

Greece; she had decided to stay there with a man called Spiros who ran a car rental business. Roland senior had consoled himself with a series of affairs with much younger women, but had not remarried, devoting most of his energies to increasing his already considerable income. In due time he had launched his son on a career as a banker. By day, Orlando wore a dark suit and sleeked back his fair hair with gel. At weekends, his spare hours were, when she agreed, spent with Tessa, or working on her behalf as she hunted down those who, in her view, oppressed dumb animals.

Sitting behind Orlando in the van, Denis felt that he was on the brink of a whole new existence, all thanks to Biff.

Denis was eighteen, and had been in care for most of his life, moving between various children's homes and several sets of foster parents until, after his sixteenth birthday, he was deemed independent and expected to fend for himself. This was when he was placed in a council flat, a boy alone, to be eventually forced out of it by other boys. Rootless and quite frightened, he had drifted round amusement arcades and cheap cafés, meeting other youngsters like himself, none with effective parents or a secure adult in the background. They hid their fears beneath a brash bravado. Some were into drugs and Denis had tried that, but beyond the odd smoke, he wasn't interested. Besides, it cost money and he had none. He'd had a job for a while, sweeping up at the back of a pub, but it was only part-time and after a few days he was sacked because he had put the rubbish in the wrong bin.

'Can't you read?' the exasperated landlord had demanded, when for the third time Denis had mixed dust, grime and general detritus with tins, and had, accidentally, caused some waste paper to catch light.

Denis couldn't, not properly, just a few words here and there.

'Anyway, where's your sense?' the landlord had added, not waiting for an answer. 'Can't you see what's what?'

After that, Denis had started begging, and had done quite well in subways and in shopping centres, though you had to watch out for the police. He was sleeping rough when he was arrested, with another youth, for breaking into a newsagent's. Denis had kept watch while his companion robbed the till. He'd admitted, then, to other thefts, things he'd sold for cash, but he didn't mention the coat he was wearing at the time of his arrest. He needed it. He was listed as being of no fixed address, and he almost hoped to be sent to a young offenders' prison. If so, he would be housed, fed and clothed and told what to do. His friend, who had a history of past crimes and was older, did go down, but Denis, still under eighteen at the time, was spared.

'Lucky for you,' said Biff, when he heard this story, minus the bit about not being able to read. Denis, small and fair-haired, with blue eyes and scarcely any growth of beard, might have had a bad time inside.

Protecting Denis made Biff feel good, and when he met Tessa and Orlando at a demonstration, his life acquired a purpose.

Biff had gone to the demonstration with no convinced opinions; he'd seen the protestors gathering, with their banners, and attached himself to their ranks. It was all about sheep, sending them abroad for slaughtering. Cruel, people said, and how would you like to be cramped up in a truck without food and water? Biff had found himself marching along near Tessa; her red hair was tucked up under a woollen cap and he saw it only later, when they were all drinking beer outside a pub. Orlando – her bloke, as Biff thought of him then – had bought it for them and included Biff and some others in the round. He'd eagerly agreed to go on more demonstrations with them when he discovered that Tessa and Orlando went on small private expeditions and wanted back-up, for which they were prepared to pay a fee, and later he decided that he must introduce young Denis to the team. Orlando seemed to run it, and Biff took Denis to meet him one evening. It meant going up West, and meeting at a pub. Denis enjoyed himself. He said very little, sipping his beer and nodding when Orlando asked if he was available at weekends and at short notice.

Orlando thought he seemed a pleasant enough youth, and he was small and slight, which could be useful for wriggling under wire and taking risks which neither Orlando nor Tessa was prepared to run. Tessa maintained, on some occasions, that they needed extra bodies, to provide a diversion from their main attack. Jet and Steve, whom Orlando had recruited earlier, were convinced animal rights defenders; these two, Biff and Denis, were more opportunist, but this made them no less useful. Tessa would be pleased with Denis, he decided.

Biff was the go-between. He telephoned Orlando, who had a mobile phone, to make arrangements.

Parting from them, Orlando gave each of them ten pounds for their evening's expenses, and went back to his flat. He would spend the evening sketching posters for Tessa's crusade against the drug barons. She said they still did dreadful things to mice and rabbits, testing out their theories.

You had to, didn't you, before you tried them out on humans? That was what Orlando thought, but Tessa meant more to him than just her theories, and if going along with them earned him her favour, he was prepared to do it. Besides, there was a lot to be said for using more natural remedies, like herbs and flowers, as in ancient times.

Their next trip, Denis's first outing with them, was to thwart the efforts of a team financed by a major drug company which was engaged in some long-term research into, among other things, the causes of nervous diseases. Some of their experiments, it was alleged, were cruel and unnecessary.

Orlando had organised his part in the expedition with meticulous care. The van was hired from a garage he had not used before and he arrived on foot, having travelled there by public transport. Once or twice there had been violence on these trips and it was wise to leave no trail.

They were travelling west. Denis, sitting behind Orlando, could see some traffic ahead of them but very little more. The doors at the back of the van were solid. He hoped they'd soon arrive. This was boring.

After a while, they turned off and began to travel along narrower single carriageway roads. Orlando had a map out and was consulting it. He and Tessa seemed to be in some disagreement about the route they should be taking, and Biff and Denis heard her say, quite sharply, 'This is the way we're going, Orlando. This is my campaign.'

'That's Tessa for you,' Biff said airily, to Denis, who, free from any responsibility for himself, just nodded.

Soon they turned off again, and now they were in what was just a lane. Staring past Orlando's head, Denis saw a lot of green bushes, like in parks, and there were trees with leaves on, brown and a sort of orange. Nice. They were travelling quite fast when suddenly towards them came a car, a small blue one. They'd had it, Denis thought: there was going to be a smash. But Tessa had jammed on the brakes and started blasting on the horn.

There were no seat-belts in the back. All four of

them were catapulted forward, but unhurt. Tessa paid no heed, revving the engine while the blue car reversed away. What if it hit something coming up behind, Orlando thought, and called out, 'God, Tessa, look where you're going, can't you?'

But Tessa was advancing on the retreating car, blasting her horn and flashing her lights as she did so.

'It's only some old bat,' she said. 'She can bloody well get out of my way,' and she continued to move forward until the blue car reached a passing spot where the road widened. It drew in, and Tessa accelerated, roaring past Frances Dixon with a final loud blast on the horn.

'She's as much right on the road as we have,' Orlando growled, lowering his head to avoid recognition by the other driver in case she filed a complaint.

'Don't be so wet, Orlando,' Tessa said.

She always chose confrontation; negotiation was a weakness, in her view. He found this strange and disconcerting, but it made her more exciting.

Now that they had survived the encounter, Denis felt elated. This was better than hanging round street corners waiting for something to happen.

Something was happening.

Of those in the back, only Denis and Biff really saw the other car.

2

WHAT SHOULD HE call himself?

Walking away from his car, giving it a final pat because it had served all the family well for years, Philip Winter contemplated being reborn under another name. He could be Tom Harris, he thought: that was a straightforward sort of name, and, indeed, he remembered that the science master at his school had been named Harris. He was a genial man who wore hand-knitted cardigans and had a pretty daughter. But was adopting a false identity an offence? And what about social security: he would not be able to obtain it without proof of identity. He could say he had lost his papers – had them stolen. You read about fraud all the time, and while he was at Lavery's, he'd witnessed some of it. Maybe he would be able to manage without state aid or documents. He could try.

He felt a huge sense of loss as he set off, leaving his past behind, and he was afraid, but the fear was no worse than the horror which had preceded it, and now he had shed his responsibilities. He had no problems except his own survival, and he didn't care a great deal about that.

He turned away from the river, intending to go to the nearest station and catch the first train out of it that travelled north. It was a beautiful October afternoon, warm enough for summer. After a prolonged wet and chilly spell, the weather had turned glorious and the bronze leaves still clung to the trees he passed as he walked towards the centre of the town. He had never been here before, which had seemed a good enough reason for visiting it now.

Unless someone stole his car, the police would notice it and make enquiries. They'd start looking for him here, maybe in the river. How would Lesley feel then? Would she be sad, or relieved. When they didn't find his body, would she be anxious? He couldn't imagine her reaction, and at the moment, he simply didn't care. Walking on, he came to a long distance bus station. A coach was about to leave, and he saw that it was heading west. On impulse, he boarded it.

'All the way,' he said extravagantly, offering a twenty-pound note. Some change would come in handy.

He took a seat near the back, a man of forty-two, dark-haired, wearing a trench-coat and dark trousers: no one special. He spoke to no one, gazing out of the window as they bowled along, and when they stopped in Salisbury, he got off, though the coach was going on to Bournemouth. It was dark now, and he had nowhere to spend the night. Should he spend money on a bed and breakfast place? He walked around the town, trying to decide, but it would use up precious funds. He could spend most of the evening in a pub if he nursed a drink, and he did this, making half a pint last for two hours, then going out into the street again. Eventually, he found a bench seat and stretched out on it for the remainder of the chilly night. His spirits fell as the temperature dropped and he thought how much one took for granted: even when the world had turned against him, until now food and shelter had not disappeared. He did not sleep.

When daylight came, he started moving once again, trying to restore his circulation. He must have a cup of tea and something to eat. That needn't cost a lot. Then he'd resume his plan of heading north, and he'd spend no more money on his travel. He would hitch a lift.

Walking round the streets, he couldn't find an open café, so he headed towards the outskirts, hoping at a major road junction to pick up a ride. The weather was still fine, but, so early, it was cold, and cars whizzed past him as he walked on, thumb extended when a vehicle passed by. At last a man in a pick-up, with a dog in the back, took him to a main crossroads, and there he waited for a long time before a tanker driver stopped for him, saying he liked a bit of company. You met all sorts of folks on the road, he said, but he never gave lifts to girls. They meant trouble – they could be running away from home, or on the game, or looking for prey.

'What do you mean by that?' asked Philip.

'You may be trying to persuade them to go home,' said the driver. 'But they'll still cry rape and land you in a lot of strife.'

'I believe you,' Philip answered, fervently.

The driver wanted to know where he was going and why he chose to hitch. It was surprisingly easy to invent a reason, Philip found. He said his car had been stolen, with all his money which was in his jacket. He'd gone to the toilet at a service area, he said, and had locked the car but that hadn't stopped two lads from taking it away.

'Didn't the police offer to run you home?' the driver asked.

'I haven't told them yet,' said Philip. 'I'll do it when I get home. My wife's away,' he added. 'Otherwise I'd have rung her.'

What an unlikely tale, thought the driver.

'It'll probably be on video, at the service area,' he pointed out. 'I hope you get it sorted.' He thought his passenger might have walked away from some serious problem, even a police court. Obviously he'd slept rough last night; you'd only got to look at him, with his crumpled trench-coat and his bristly chin. Still, he seemed harmless enough, and the driver, who had seen his share of life's difficulties, probed no further. It wasn't his business. If the police were after the guy, as seemed most likely,

23

they'd soon find him. He put a fresh tape in his stereo and they drove on to the accompaniment of a country and western medley. After a while, Philip fell asleep.

The tanker was heading north. Philip woke when the driver stopped for petrol.

'Got to have a rest now, mate,' he said. 'You can hang on if you want, but you might like to find yourself another ride.'

He'd had enough of this passenger, who had proved to be poor company, and he didn't want to see him on a wanted poster and feel obliged to mention they had met. The man had a car radio in his raincoat pocket; the driver had noticed it when he slumped over to slumber in a more comfortable position than his original upright pose. Maybe it was stolen.

'It's all right. I need a bite to eat,' said Philip, who had woken feeling rather faint. He'd had no food since breakfast the previous morning; just the beer last night, and a packet of crisps he'd bought to go with it. 'Thanks anyway,' he added.

He'd slept heavily as they drove along: he'd no idea where they were or how far they had travelled. For months now, ever since it happened, he'd been sleeping badly. Perhaps, as he had severed his connections with the past, he'd be able to sleep properly again.

Before eating, he went to the men's toilet, where he washed his face and hands. That made him feel better. Food here was expensive, but a good meal should last him all day, so he bought egg, chips and sausages, with baked beans, and had a pot of tea. The place was very busy and he had to queue. He hoped he wouldn't see the driver in the cafeteria; he ought to spread himself around, obtain another lift from someone else.

He supposed you could live here if you had nowhere else to go. These places stayed open round the clock; there were food and shelter, and cloakroom facilities, though no showers. Philip smiled at the idea. It wasn't so way out. Why shouldn't he spend the day here, and even the night; then leave? He'd wait, anyway, until the driver who had brought him had moved on. Money was going to be the problem. He had been receiving unemployment benefit since losing his job. Perhaps he could go on getting it elsewhere; didn't those New Age travellers who camped at Stonehenge and such spots go on drawing it, with special arrangements made to give it to them, regardless of where they were? They couldn't be actively seeking work: it was a weird system.

He'd been able to find no other job because each employer wanted to know why he had left his last one, and required a reference, which Lavery's were not prepared to supply.

Maybe he could find work where he would be paid in cash. He could do gardening, but the season was about to end. He could decorate – he was a dab hand at paper-hanging. He wasn't much of a carpenter – simple shelving fixed on brackets and fitting hooks were about his level.

Musing, he drank his tea. Who were all these people round him? Where were they going, and why? He wondered about them, idly watching the shuffling customers with their trays. What an anonymous sort of place. He couldn't sit here all day long; he'd have to walk around, and at least buy a paper.

Philip rose and went out to the shop, where he bought *The Times* which was selling at a lower price than most tabloids; there was a lot to read in that, though much of it, he thought wryly, would be very dull.

He found a seat near the video games installed for recreation, but before long the noise wore him down, so he went back into the restaurant area and sat at a table. No one challenged him; he did not need to buy another cup of tea. Eventually, however, he grew restless and decided he must move on. He'd try to get to a town, where he could sell the radio, which was a nuisance in his pocket; he felt he must conceal its bulk, and that made him look guilty. If anyone became suspicious and asked him where he'd got it, a truthful answer might not be believed: he could find himself accused of stealing his own car radio.

He trudged along the exit route, still carrying *The Times*. He'd take the first lift he was offered and see how far the driver was going; it would be difficult for him to be dropped except when the vehicle was either turning off or stopping. He was in the hands of fate.

It was better than being at the mercy of an unjust justice system.

He had to wait for some time, but at last a man in a plumber's van stopped for him. He was leaving the motorway at the next junction.

Philip did not stay with him to the end of his journey: at the roundabout after the slip road he alighted, uttered his thanks, and headed off in a westerly direction while the plumber turned the other way.

He could walk along this road, unlike the motorway. The exercise was good, and he stepped out, often forgetting to turn and display his upturned thumb to passing motorists. No one stopped for him. People in cars didn't like giving lifts. The setting sun was brilliant in the autumn sky, a ball of fire sending streaks of light across the hills. On the fringe of the Lake District, this was a beautiful part of England and one he had driven through but never visited. He hadn't really meant to come here: he'd been aiming in a general way at the north, perhaps Liverpool or Leeds – nowhere precise – but chance had carried him to this point. There must be a town or village soon, he thought, plodding on, and feeling thirsty. His left heel was sore; his shoes were comfortable, but they were not meant for walking long distances. He could have dressed more appropriately for this enterprise, but when he left home, he had no plan except to get away. Now, he was determined to leave no trail, to disappear.

After Philip had walked for three or four miles, with traffic passing him regardless, he heard another vehicle coming up behind him and saw it was a bus. His economic resolution vanished and he hailed it. To his relief, it stopped, and he took a ticket to the town advertised above its windscreen. By the time it dropped him in the centre, it was dark. He pulled his trench-coat collar up and set off to explore. He had to find a bed for tonight. Tomorrow he'd sell the radio. How soft he was, he thought; only a few hours ago he'd been fantasising about spending the night in that service station, and now here he was, longing for a shower and a clean bed. He wondered how easy it would be to pick up some casual work. While he was waiting for his trial he had done the whole house over, painting every room, and had spruced the garden up so that not a weed survived and all the plants and shrubs were staked and trimmed. Lesley would not have to give it a thought until the spring; he'd even laid the mower up. He might try job-hunting in the morning; there would be notices in shop windows in a place like this. He rubbed a hand across his chin, rasping the stubble. He ought to get a razor; no one would employ him with several days' growth adorning his chin. He could, however, grow a beard: that would save trouble, and act as a disguise in case he was reported missing and his photograph was displayed. Lesley would have an old one somewhere, from a holiday, or there was his passport. They'd been to Corsica last year, all four of them; this year, there had been no trip abroad because he was a man condemned before his case was heard.

How would Lesley manage, with the mortgage to pay? She could get a better job; she was capable of it. If he were reported missing, she might get help towards it; you read of bankrupt men in mansions whose mortgages were paid and who were granted legal aid. The houses were in their wives' names, no doubt. She could find a lodger, a student or a teacher; she'd think of something. She'd survive.

His own indifference shocked him, and, seeing a café open, he went in and ordered tea and a toasted cheese sandwich. That would do him for the evening. After that, he'd look for a room. Would anyone take him, with no luggage? He'd even left *The Times* on the bus.

The first place he tried turned him down. The woman who opened the door looked him over thoroughly and then decided she had no vacancies and had forgotten to move the card from her window. He thanked her and moved on. One advantage of this area was that there was no shortage of boarding houses. He tried another in a different street, and this time was accepted.

'My car was stolen, with my case inside,' he said here. 'That's why I look rather untidy, I'm afraid. Luckily I had my wallet on me,' and he displayed a twenty-pound note. 'I'm sure you insist on payment in advance.'

He was well spoken and his clothes were good,

but that was no testament to honesty and he had already told her a false tale; however, the woman welcomed him, lent him a pair of her husband's pyjamas and found him a new toothbrush. Philip was amazed. How gullible some people were: tell your lie confidently and it would be believed. He must remember that. It was what had made him a victim: that woman had lied and had been believed, and he, telling the truth, had been pilloried.

His room was small but spotless. He had a hot bath in which he luxuriated, and he washed his socks, shirt and boxer shorts in the basin, using the toilet soap. He squeezed the excess water out of them in his towel, something he remembered seeing his mother do, and then hung them up in his room. There was no radiator but there was a coin-operated electric heater. He fed it a pound and hoped that would provide enough heat to dry them overnight.

He was tired, but was too wound up to sleep. He lay under the covers with the events of the past two days running through his mind like a film. It seemed an incredible dream, but then everything that had happened since he was first accused had had an unreal quality; he had felt that none of it could really be happening to him. After a while he dropped off, only to wake at four o'clock in the morning. He got out of bed to test the moistness of his laundry and found that his socks were still damp, so he put another pound in the meter. The money was disappearing, but he couldn't go on in wet socks. He'd better buy another pair. Some things were essential. Then he went back to bed where again sleep eluded him. There was a pile of tattered magazines on a table so, giving up, he selected an old *Reader's Digest* and began reading it. Concentration was difficult, as he had discovered during the preceding months. His eyes traversed the pages but his brain absorbed only random sentences. His mind kept returning to what had brought him to this moment.

How could she do it? How could she tell such lies so brazenly and watch the destruction of him and his family? What harm had he ever done her? He knew he had not convinced the jury of his innocence, but they did not believe beyond reasonable doubt in his guilt. He might have gone to prison: at least he had been spared that, but perhaps it would have been better if he had been convicted; there would have been an appeal, possibly a further investigation. Someone who, like Bob, knew the truth might have had enough courage to speak up for him. Over and over again he recalled his own actions, trying to remember a word or gesture that she could, in all fairness, have misconstrued, but he failed. As for raping her, he had not touched her; it was she who had seized hold of him.

He couldn't even picture her face now; his imagination refused to yield it to the eye of memory, but he would never forget his own daughter's horrified stare.

'Dad, you didn't,' she said, when at last she

understood the accusation against him.

'No, I didn't,' he had told her, but he had not convinced her. If she lost her trust, who else would believe the woman had lied? Certainly Lesley did not.

'You made a pass, at least,' she had said, and had looked at him with contempt. 'Why choose her?' she'd added, and in vain he had said that his was not the choice; it was the other way round.

'I've never heard anything so pathetic,' Lesley, bitterly hurt herself, had said.

They'd met, he and Lesley, when he was doing business studies at a polytechnic. Lesley was taking A levels; she wanted to be a teacher but this had never happened because they married before she could go to training college, and then Andrew was born. She took a secretarial course when Jackie was seven, and since then had had various office jobs. At the time of his arrest she had been, for some years, personal assistant to the director of a lighting centre. She'd kept her job; her boss had been sympathetic about the difficult situation she was in and he would not add to her problems by making things hard for her at work – not that he could have dismissed her because of her husband's failings. Some of the staff, though, had made snide remarks.

His accuser was a Lavery's customer, one who had had an account for years and spent large sums there every month. He'd admired her; he was prepared to admit that. She was chic and confident, and she knew what she wanted, or seemed to, at first. She'd buy items of glass or ceramics, then return a few days later to say that they were not suitable and she wanted to change them. Philip never noticed that Bob disappeared when she came into the department; in any case, Bob's station was across the floor; he managed soft furnishings. She always asked for Philip to serve her, and indeed, one of the assistants used to tease him about it.

'Your girlfriend's here,' he'd say, when he was in the office. 'Wants your special services,' and he would wink and leer. How ironic that reaction turned out to be.

Philip took no more trouble over Mrs Sandra White than any other customer; all were entitled to receive his full attention. She was known to the sales staff: a well-dressed woman in her forties. She wore expensive scent, which Philip noticed when she stood close to him inspecting some object she contemplated buying, but so did many women shoppers. Philip knew nothing about her private life; she paid with her Lavery's account card and once their transactions were concluded, he never gave another thought to her. There were other customers he found more attractive, but beyond a mild occasional lustful urge, soon suppressed, he did not fantasise about them. He was married and he had no wish to stray; he did not even flirt.

So he was out of his depth when the accusation came.

How could she do it?

It was all because he'd turned her down, his

solicitor, who believed him, had explained. Ulti-
mately the jury had given him the benefit of the
doubt, apart from two of them, who had found him
guilty, and so he had escaped imprisonment. After
he was dismissed from Lavery's, when her complaint was made, there was a murmur among the
staff that he had been unlucky, and one of them,
Betty, spoke up for him in court. She was called as
a defence witness and was questioned about his
manner with female customers. She had declared
that he was always courteous, never familiar, and
that she had noticed nothing untoward, but none of
the men came forward. Philip suspected that some,
like Bob, might know more about Mrs White than
they cared to disclose. His solicitor found it
interesting that it was a woman who had testified
for him.

Mrs White had not called the police until a week
after Philip had, she alleged, raped her. By then it
was too late to prove scientifically that he had had
sexual intercourse with her, but a hair from his head
had been found on her clothing, and she had
marked him. Colleagues had observed the scratches
on his face, and Mrs White maintained that they
were made by her in her struggle to escape him.

It was he who had fought her off, not the other
way around, and it was he who had been a
simpleton when he found her purse left on the
counter after she had finished shopping on that fatal
day. Her account and credit cards were inside; there
was no mistaking whose it was. They'd paged her,

34

but with no result; she had already left the store. Instead of handing the purse in, Philip, thinking she would be anxious about its loss, had telephoned her himself, and she had been so grateful, almost tearful, as she thanked him and asked him to be good enough to bring it to her himself, on his way home.

Foolishly, he had agreed. It would help her, and was not much out of his way for she lived only a few bus stops from the store. He missed his usual train home, which Lesley remembered; she also remembered the scratches on his face, which he said he'd got when he walked into a sharp protrusion in the storeroom. But Lesley gave no evidence: a wife is not obliged to testify against her husband.

Mrs White had opened the door of her flat – the main door to the street worked in response to an entryphone – and she had urged him to come in. Without giving it a thought, he had obeyed, the purse still in his hand. Then she had offered him a drink, and again, he had accepted, feeling that to refuse would seem ungracious. After all, he'd gone to some trouble on her behalf and naturally she wished to express her thanks. She'd poured him out a glass of wine, making him shed his coat, which she'd laid on a chair in the hall.

As they drank their wine, she had talked about the loneliness of marriage to a man whose work often took him overseas. They'd divorced, she said: it was hurtful to admit he'd found a younger second wife.

Philip had muttered a few sympathetic words and was about to leave when she made her proposition.

'You could visit me,' she said. 'I'll be here every Wednesday evening.'

'But why?' he'd asked, naively.

'What did you think she meant?' prosecuting counsel had enquired.

'I didn't know at first,' he said. 'Then she made it clear.'

'In what way?'

'She offered sex.' He had just managed to utter it. 'She said she wanted it.'

'And what did you say?'

'I tried to be polite. I thanked her but said that I was married.'

'What did she say then?'

In fact, she'd laughed loudly, opening her big mouth to show a lot of large white teeth, making him think of a shark. 'So what?' she'd said.

'She said it need not make a difference,' he told the court.

'I put it to you that you are inventing this. The truth is that you threw yourself upon the complainant, as she has described,' said prosecuting counsel.

'No,' he had almost shouted. 'I'm telling you the truth.'

Philip's own counsel, with agonising patience, had extracted his version of events from him. He had been sitting on the sofa holding his empty wine glass, preparing to move, when she leaned over, took the glass from him and set it down, then laid one hand on his thigh and thrust herself against him, pinning him among the soft pile of cushions at his back. In the same instant, her mouth was glued to his and she was trying to force her tongue between his lips. She almost succeeded, so great was his astonishment. He pushed her away, while still striving to be civil.

'You're making a mistake, Mrs White,' he had said. If he could only get to his feet and reach the door, he thought, his reactions those of many a woman in a similar predicament.

'But you like me,' she had said, still clinging to him, so that her cashmere sweater deposited shreds of wool on his suit jacket, as was later proved. He brushed it every night before he hung it up, but a few persistent fibres, not visible at a glance, had remained.

'Of course, Mrs White,' he agreed. 'But as a customer.'

'A very special one,' she had insisted. 'You've made that clear, by bringing me my purse.'

'You asked me to,' he said, fending her off, the muscles in his outstretched arms quivering under the strain. It was so silly and undignified. Why couldn't she just release him? Somehow, he managed to scramble up, and it was then that she sprang at him, scraping her nails down his cheek, trying to wind herself around him as he shrank back from her.

He was determined to escape, and he reached the

door, grabbing at his coat, while she was caught off balance. She picked the empty wine glass up and flung it at him, and as he ducked it hit the wall and shattered. Later, she said that this had happened as she attempted to defend herself.

Counsel for the defence had suggested that she had left the purse behind deliberately, thus creating the opportunity for the scene that ensued.

The complainant had denied this vehemently.

'I couldn't know that Mr Winter would offer to return it himself,' she said.

'But the accused said that you asked him to,' was counsel's response.

'That's his story,' she replied.

No one had overheard his telephone conversation with her: there was no way to prove the truth of either account. It was a question of belief.

The judge, summing up, had been very fair, and some journalists said that it should never have come to court, but the case was no more fanciful than other incidents where accused men had been convicted on evidence which was just as slight.

Mud sticks, thought Philip; that was so true. Though acquitted, he could not get his job back; Lavery's believed the customer. Although he had been with them for twelve years, rising in a steady manner through the hierarchy, they would not even offer him a position in a provincial branch. To sue for wrongful dismissal would be to invite further publicity and cause more pain within the family, with no sure outcome. It could involve the loss of what little he had left, for it would be a civil case and it might go against him.

'You'll find another job,' his solicitor had consoled him.

But three months later he had not, except for a brief spell helping in a bar where very soon someone had recognised him and, despite the outcome of the case, the landlord had not appreciated the subsequent taunts and comments. The male customers' remarks were crude, but a number of professional women used the bar and they did not want their drinks served by someone with a tarnished reputation. So it had gone on, until now.

I ran away, he told himself, sitting up in the hard bed in his lodgings. I'm a coward. But his action would, in the long run, make things easier for Lesley and the children. Now they could stop watching every remark they made, and he no longer had to endure their guarded glances. Andrew's studies would cease to suffer; he would get his degree next year, and soon Jackie would follow him to college, unembarrassed by her father.

He tried the *Reader's Digest* again. Its jokes were often entertaining, and he managed to see the humour in a few of them as he leafed through the pages until he heard his landlady going downstairs.

Not shaving still seemed strange. He'd always been so spruce, going to the store, where beards were not encouraged, nor long hair. He'd had an almost pink and white complexion, with his greying hair slicked down, setting off his fair skin.

He'd been a handsome boy, tall and willowy, and had stayed slim. Now he was really thin; he had lost weight during the long waiting time before the trial, and had regained none of it.

He washed and put his clothes on. His socks were dry now, and warm. He had always dressed well: his appearance had been important in his job, where the staff were expected not only to be smart, but to have clean fingernails and unscuffed shoes. Now, he seemed to be going in reverse.

His landlady provided him with a splendid breakfast – bacon, two fried eggs, fried bread, a sausage and a tomato; he ate every crumb. This would have to be his pattern: one large meal a day, and an evening snack. His stomach would adjust. As he finished off with toast and marmalade, he realised that he had not eaten with such pleasure for months. So escape had done him good already.

While he ate, the landlady's husband consumed a similar feast, washed down with several cups of tea to Philip's one. Then he was ready to depart for his day's work. He was a builder, at present renovating a pub near Lancaster.

On impulse, Philip asked him for a lift.

'I'm going to Blackpool,' he invented – but why not go there? It was a large resort; there might be work, though perhaps not out of season.

The man agreed to take him on.

'You never had no car stolen, mate,' he said, when they were in his van, bowling back the way Philip had come the night before. 'You're on the road.

Maybe on the run. What have you done?'

'Left my wife,' said Philip bluntly.

The man laughed.

'Well, as long as you've not robbed a bank,' he said.

'I haven't,' Philip said. 'I'm nearly skint. I need to find a job.'

'I'd give you one, if I could,' said the builder. 'But there's not much going in my line just now. I've got this contract to help out a mate. What'll turn up next, I don't know.'

They parted near the town centre, and immediately Philip set out to sell the radio. It took him quite a while, but eventually a second-hand dealer gave him twelve pounds for it. It was a disappointingly small sum. He decided to keep his watch until another time. Then he went seeking notice boards advertising job vacancies. By evening, he'd found nothing, though he had just missed a position as a van driver and another as a storeman. Both openings had been filled when he arrived at the addresses. Once again, he spent the evening in a pub nursing a single beer, until it was closing time. Then he found a bus shelter where, after some youths who were in it had, at last, departed, he spent the rest of the night.

In the morning, although there might have been other opportunities in the town, he decided to move on. Cold and hungry, he resolved to accept the first lift that came along, regardless of the driver's final destination. He'd be warm in the cab of a lorry, and he would be going somewhere.

3

'**W**HERE ARE WE going today, then, Tessa?'
Biff had dared to ask, when she had calmed
down after nearly causing a collision with that blue
Viva.

'We're going to harass a guy who makes blisters
grow on mice and rabbits,' Tessa said. 'And we'll
free the creatures, if we can.'

'Who'll feed them, then?' Denis asked. 'When
they're let loose, like?'

'Give me strength. They're wild animals,' said
Tessa. 'They'll live off the land.'

In one of the children's homes where Denis had
spent time, they'd had some rabbits which had
eaten dandelion leaves and lettuce. He supposed
they'd have that sort of stuff round here. In the end,
the rabbits had had babies, which were eaten by the
mothers. Some of the children had found it quite a
laugh but Denis had been sickened. Afterwards, he
dreamt his own mother had eaten him.

When they parked to stretch their legs and hear Tessa's plans for their protest action, he saw dandelions among the grass at the roadside. She'd pulled off the road into a lay-by beside a group of trees, alongside a field in which there were some cattle. One of the beasts lowed loudly, and Denis, who had been planning to climb the gate and relieve himself in the shelter of the hedge, abruptly changed his mind.

'Won't hurt you, chum,' said Orlando, who had noticed his recruit's startled movement. 'Only a moo-cow.' He clambered over the gate himself and began shooing the young heifers away.

'For God's sake, Orlando, stop that,' called Tessa. 'We don't want some snotty farmer coming along to see who's upsetting his precious herd. We don't want to be noticed.'

Denis thought they'd been noticed already by the old dame they'd nearly driven off the road, but he kept quiet. Tessa's attitude was weird. She was so keen on saving animals, but she hadn't given a rap for the old woman, and she didn't seem too keen on this bunch of cows. He had no time to pursue this line of thought because Biff had begun unloading the cans of beer he'd brought and started to hand them round.

'No drinking,' ordered Tessa.

'Too late,' smirked Biff, who had already opened a can. This was a bit of all right. He was enjoying himself, and he could see that Denis was having the time of his young life. Biff, in the role of benefactor, felt good. He accepted the cans Steve and Jet were meekly handing him in obedience to Tessa's ban, finished his own, dropped the can where he stood, undid his fly and urinated proudly into the grass beyond his feet. After a short pause, Denis walked a short way along the road and turned his back modestly as he relieved himself. Steve followed him. Orlando had returned from the field and, when all the males were back in the van, Tessa and Jet climbed the gate, followed inquisitively by the heifers.

'Nice name, Jet,' said Biff, while they were absent.

'It's not her real name,' Steven said. 'She just likes it.'

Orlando felt it suited her. She had black hair and wore a lot of eyeliner, and a dark, almost black lipstick. She was very small and rather quiet, and she always dressed in black. He thought she had braved the field of heifers only because she did not want to seem afraid of them in front of Tessa. Tessa was the sort of person who inspired courage in her companions; he adored her.

Back in the van, Tessa addressed her troops.

'We're going to split up,' she said. 'Biff and I are going to spy out the land. We'll collect you four later, at a meeting place on the other side of that hill.' She gestured vaguely westwards. 'Orlando will be in charge of you.' She pulled a map from the pocket of the shabby waxed jacket she wore and showed it to Orlando, pointing out a route to him. 'I'll drop you at the start of the track you can follow which will bring you out near a crossroads where Biff and I will find you.'

Biff puffed out his chest. He'd been selected as her partner in a most important task. Great. He waited with impatience for the others to leave, so that he could sit in front beside her. He, not Steve, who was a student and had passed exams, was her choice.

While they drove off, Orlando, not pleased at the role allotted to him, led his little force up a rutted track. Jet's boots pinched and Steve complained of being out of breath as Orlando shepherded them along with bracing remarks about how it couldn't be much further, and when they reached the crossroads, there would be a garage with a shop where they could buy drinks and ice creams or Mars Bars. He felt like a teacher with a pack of awkward children as they spread out in single file. Only Denis did not complain; he was in paradise. He had never seen so much empty space before. There were low rolling hills, with clumps of trees here and there, and otherwise nothing but grassy downland, still green but with yellowing patches, and it seemed you were allowed to walk where you liked. There were no cows wandering around, but they met three people on horseback. He was quite alarmed as they cantered past. The only horses he had previously encountered were police horses deployed to keep order in a crowd. These riders, however, waved, and one called out, 'Hi, isn't it a lovely day?'

It was. There was a curious smell, and, sniffing it, Denis asked Orlando what it was.

Orlando laughed, but not unkindly.

'It's fresh air, you nit,' he said. 'Haven't you smelled it before?'

Denis hadn't; not like this. And he hadn't been called a nit before: dork, jerk, and much worse, but never a nit. Orlando was a weird guy, but he was all right.

'Not such a lot of it,' he answered.

He looked around. He could not see a single house. If he'd been alone, he thought he might not like it; he'd feel sort of naked. But with Orlando striding on in front, looking round now and then to see if the others were following, and Jet and Steve, hand in hand, behind him, he felt protected. They trudged on, and when they reached the summit of the hill, below them stretched a panoramic view. In the distance, on the skyline, were tall buildings which were part of some industrial area, but closer, beneath where they were walking, was a straggling village with many-coloured roofs and a church spire rising from among some trees. It was wild, thought Denis: this was his utmost term of approval.

Orlando, while they walked, was wondering what Tessa had in mind, choosing Biff as her companion. Why had she offloaded the rest of them? Couldn't they all have done whatever reconnoitring she had planned? It was true that she couldn't have left Biff and the other three to find their way over the downs, but was this walk really necessary?

He supposed it was doing them all good, in the sense that they were getting exercise, and Denis seemed entranced. Poor kid, he'd clearly never been to the country before, but though he seemed to like it, most townies, according to Tessa's father, wanted to introduce urban conditions into rural areas, banning cocks that crowed and braying donkeys. At least none of these three would get out of hand and behave badly, if they had to wait for Tessa when they reached the meeting place. Some of the demonstrations Orlando had been on with Tessa had developed into alarming events, when he had been afraid for his own and her safety, as bricks were thrown and obscenities yelled by sweating angry mobs who surely had lost sight of their original grievance. But the more timorous Orlando felt on these occasions, the better Tessa enjoyed it. She yelled with the rest, and grew excited. Sometimes, afterwards, she let him go to bed with her, and that reward made up for all his fears.

She'd never marry him. He asked her to, at intervals, but when she laughed and refused, he was just a mite relieved. She was like a mettlesome horse which was difficult to control; he couldn't do it: could anyone?

She rather wrecked your palate, though, for other flavours.

When Tessa dumped the others and swept Biff off

with her, he was sure she wanted sex. He didn't believe her story of wanting to spy out the land. She seemed to know her way about these confusing lanes and narrow roads; the map had been needed only for Orlando's sake. Biff had supposed that Orlando was her lover. Perhaps he was, and she wanted to make him jealous. He had seemed a bit put out when they left, but not really angry, not like Biff would be if anyone tried to cut him out with a girl, but Biff would soon sort out a guy who tried that on. He flexed his muscles under his grey sweatshirt. Biff was a real man.

However, they were not driving off to a quiet spot like where they'd parked before. Tessa was turning on to a main road, and she drove fast towards some tall buildings in the distance. Her gloveless hands, on the wheel, were pale and slender; he'd noticed that she bit her nails. She looked as if she couldn't iron a shirt, much less drive a van which had a fault in its timing which Biff longed to fix. He loved tinkering with cars, and had a record of convictions for taking away and driving without consent. In the end he'd been sent on a course where lads like himself were taught mechanics and rebuilt old heaps to discourage them from re-offending. It had almost cured Biff of stealing cars; he felt obliged to get his kicks from other sources now; but he was still besotted with engines. He'd often thought he'd like to work in a garage, but he hadn't tried to find a job in one. Maybe, when he got bored with this animal lark, he'd give it a go.

Tessa had parked outside the gates of a large complex of buildings.

'That's where it all happens, Biff,' she said. 'In there, all sorts of terrible experiments go on. Animal genes are mixed with other genes to create monsters. Helpless rabbits are given dreadful diseases from which they die in agony.'

Apart from being clothes, Biff didn't know what genes were. Wasn't Jean a girl's name? His mum had had a friend called Jean. Biff hadn't seen his mum for years. When he thought about her, he remembered her with a pile of ironing, thumping away among clouds of steam. He looked at the high fencing, the gate with the security barrier and the manned guard room.

'We can't get in there to free them animals,' he said.

'No, I'm afraid we can't, not without a small army and a lot of weapons, and some master keys,' she said. 'I just wanted to have a look at the place. That's all. We're going to go for the man behind it, Biff. He's our target.'

She slid the van into gear and drove on towards the town which lay beyond the complex. On a Saturday afternoon there was a lot of traffic; she tapped her fingers on the wheel impatiently while they waited for some lights to change. Then she turned away from the main shopping area, driving down to a bridge over a river, which she crossed. She carried on up the hill on the further side, past a park and into a street of large, detached houses with trees and shrubs around them: a thieves' paradise, Biff thought, automatically eyeing the homes which were well sheltered from the passer-by. Tessa halted outside one of these.

'That's it,' she said. 'Hop out, Biff, and see if anyone's at home. I'm sure you can do it. Don't let them see you. They might be in the garden. I'll wait for you at the corner.'

Biff was out of the van in an instant, delighted at the importance of his role. Tessa watched him in the van's rear mirror. He'd disappeared almost at once. She wondered if any nosey neighbours were observing them. She had seen Neighbourhood Watch stickers on lamp posts and windows as they drove through the streets, but that scheme's efficiency depended on who was around at a given time. On a Saturday afternoon, people were often out: playing golf, shopping, visiting friends, taking children to theme parks or whatever families did.

She hoped Biff wouldn't get caught. If he didn't reappear in ten minutes, she'd abandon him.

But he did. He emerged from a gateway close to where she'd parked, having crossed intervening fences. He swaggered up the road towards her, grinning.

Tessa started the engine and drove off as he tumbled in beside her. She did not speak for several minutes, until they were back in the open countryside beyond the town. Then she stopped and faced him.

'Well?' she said.

'It's a great place,' said Biff. 'No one's in, but

there's some rabbits in a cage thing at the back. Pets, like. There was kids' washing on the line – small size stuff – you know.' He gestured with his hands. 'Lots of grass, too,' he added. 'Flowers, and that. And veg. Cabbages. There's a kind of office place, too, a hut. It's got stuff inside that I – that's worth a bit. Computers.' He'd been going to say, stuff that he could sell, but bit it back.

'An office, you said?' Tessa asked.

'Yeah. I suppose so.'

'Well done, Biff,' said Tessa. 'We'll go back there after dark.'

'There's a dog,' he volunteered. 'It barked at me. It's shut up in the house. There's an alarm,' he added.

'That's all right. We're not going inside,' said Tessa.

'I let the rabbits out,' said Biff. 'I thought that's what you wanted.'

'Did you, Biff? That wasn't really in the plan,' said Tessa.

'It was easy.' Biff was pleased with himself. 'They had such simple catches on their cages. They ran down the garden straight away. I expect they'll eat up all the cabbages.'

'I expect they will,' said Tessa, wondering if this display of initiative was going to thwart her scheme. It needn't, she decided. It might act as a diversion.

She looked at her watch. Orlando and his troop could not have reached the rendez-vous so soon;

she'd sent them on quite a trek. She drove up the road and through more residential streets until they had left the town behind and were in the country. Now they were travelling along a lane, one that was almost as narrow as where they had met the old woman in the Viva. Suddenly a cock pheasant ran into the road in front of them and Tessa swerved violently to miss it. She stopped and got out of the van to make sure that it had not been struck. There was no sign of it.

'What was that bird?' Biff asked. He'd followed her out of the van, and saw that she looked white and shaken.

'It's OK,' she said. 'I didn't hit it.'

'What was it?' Biff repeated. 'Was it a bantam?' He'd heard of them; they were sort of cockerels.

'No – no, it was a cock pheasant,' Tessa said. 'Beautiful, isn't he?'

'Certainly is,' said Biff, who had been impressed by the bird's size and his bright plumage.

'Imagine shooting him, for kicks,' said Tessa. 'That's what people do. Could you? Isn't it cruel?'

Biff had been on the point of making some crack about how, if they'd hit it, they could have roasted it over a camp fire, but he saw that Tessa would find such a remark out of order.

'Dunno,' he said, knowing that if he had a gun, he'd do it; no question about that. 'Suppose I could if I was starving,' he temporised.

'They're bred just to be killed,' said Tessa, now accelerating hard.

Biff grabbed the side of the van. He thought about offering to drive, but decided not to risk offending her.

So are cattle, bred to be killed, he thought; and sheep, and pigs. Would they exist, otherwise?

'You one of them vegetarians?' he asked. But he knew she wasn't. He'd seen her eat sausages and chips, after they'd been on that trip to Folkestone to blockade a ship that was exporting sheep.

'That's different,' Tessa said.

Biff couldn't see it, but he didn't argue, because now she had turned the van up a track like the one where they had left the others. This, though, led to a copse and was more secluded. She parked beneath a tree.

As she turned to face him, Biff understood that his first suspicions about why she had chosen him had, after all, been correct.

They moved into the back of the van, where there was more room. She was like a tiger, Biff thought, appreciating every move.

Afterwards, he remembered how upset she had been about the pheasant's narrow escape, and yet was unmoved by the earlier near collision with the Viva, when its driver, and even they, themselves, could have been hurt, and maybe killed.

Funny, really.

4

ORLANDO AND HIS band were waiting for them at the service station when they reached it just as dusk was falling. He'd bought drinks and snacks, as promised. Denis had noticed that he had a wad of notes in his wallet. They perched on a wall near the shop and pumps, eating Twix bars and drinking out of cans.

'We'll wait till dark. Then we'll move in,' said Tessa, and she drove them to the spot where she and Biff had parked half an hour earlier. She never looked at him as she ordered all of them out of the van and told them to light a fire.

'There's plenty of wood, and it's dry,' she said.

'Won't someone see us?' Denis whispered to Steve, as Jet and Orlando set to work with a cigarette lighter and some bits of paper from the van. They doused it with a very small amount of lighter fuel that had been loaded from Tessa's car, and it flared alarmingly, but some of the twigs caught, and, nurtured carefully, soon it was burning well.

'It's OK out here,' Steve reassured him. 'They'll think we're campers. Let's find some bigger sticks. Pity we haven't got some potatoes to bake,' he added. 'Still, I suppose they'd take too long. Tessa'll want to be off as soon as it's going well.'

'How can you cook potatoes on a fire like that?' asked Denis.

'Stick them in the embers,' Steve replied. 'They're great.'

Denis was amazed. This was, so far, the best day in his entire life, and the fire was brilliant. No wonder so many people wanted to live like this, go travelling around.

Steve was right about Tessa. The fire was blazing well, and they were all crouched round it, faces lit up by the flames, when she spoke.

'Right,' she said. 'We'll be off now. We can't free the animals, unfortunately, because the place they're in is so well guarded, but we can cause some grief. We're going to lob some petrol bombs over the wire. We'll get them ready now, so hold them carefully. We don't want an accident in the van. It's quite a short drive – you saw the place when you were walking over the hill.'

She made the preparations, putting fuel in three milk bottles, then stuffing rags into their openings. All of them except Denis had seen this done before, but only Tessa had ever thrown one. They were silent, driving towards the town, and on the outskirts Tessa parked beside the research complex, well away from the gate and the security control. There, she gave Jet, Steve and Denis cans of spray paint and told them to spray slogans on the boundary wall. Jet and Steve knew what to write: MURDERERS, SAVE WILD ANIMALS, WHAT PRICE KILLING MICE? Denis, illiterate, sprayed crosses and squirls, and, for fun, a swastika, but Steve blotted that one out. Meanwhile, Biff lit the petrol bombs and lobbed them over the wall. Tessa had told him he was the strongest, able to throw the furthest.

Like a javelin athlete, Biff did his best. Orlando could scarcely bear to watch: what if one exploded before it was thrown? But none did. They could not reach the buildings but the alarm went and the group piled back into the van. An approaching siren wailed as they sped off towards the town and the house where Tessa and Biff had been earlier.

'The man behind those experiments lives here,' Tessa told the others.

There were lights on now, in the house.

'You're not going to attack him, are you?' Orlando had to make his protest. If this was Tessa's plan, she was going too far. Tessa did not give him a direct answer.

'I think he'll come out,' she said. 'I think he'll hear about the attack we've just done at the research place and he'll go over there.' She drove down the road and stopped the engine.

'You take the wheel, Orlando,' she instructed. 'Be ready for a quick getaway when I come back.' Then she got out of the van, went round to the rear, rummaged in the bundles, and removed a shotgun. She thrust it under her coat and went walking back towards the house.

As Orlando slid behind the wheel, there was silence in the van.

'She going to kill the guy, then?' Biff asked nervously. Judging by the lights, the family had probably come home.

'Oh no,' said Orlando bracingly, but he could not be certain, with Tessa obviously on such a high.

They waited for what seemed like hours, but nothing happened, apart from several cars going by, and a woman with a dog. Then they heard two shots. All of them in the van held their breaths, waiting for uproar and for Tessa to come running back, but no windows were thrown open and there were no screams. Then they heard two more shots, and soon Tessa did appear, walking quietly towards them. She calmly put the gun back in the rear of the van, got in beside Orlando and told him to drive on. He already had the engine running and the noise masked the sound of the burglar alarm coming from the house she had just left.

She smelled of petrol and she was smiling in a way that alarmed the already scared Orlando. What had she done?

He knew that their best plan was to put distance between themselves and this area. He headed for the country once again. Denis was amazed at how quickly they left the busy streets behind. Soon they were driving along narrow lanes once more, with just the headlight beams piercing the darkness. When they'd put their camp fire out, he'd been startled by how dark it was around them: no street lights; no moon yet; and no stars.

They stopped in a quiet spot. Tessa wanted to take over the driving.

'Comfort interval,' she sang out, when Orlando had pulled in, drawing the van off the road into a gateway. She reached over and turned the lights off. 'Everyone back in five minutes,' she said.

Once again the night was black. Denis, tumbling out, blinked. He couldn't see a thing except the pale outline of the van. Jet bumped into him; then she and Steve, arms linked, went up the road together. Denis almost fell over his own feet, edging forward on the grass beside the road. His eyes began to adapt to the lack of light and he saw Orlando go round to the back of the van and open the door. He did something to the gun, wrapping it up, Denis thought.

He'd better have a pee, while he had a chance. He stepped forward, feeling with his outstretched toe for obstacles, not worrying now about concealment. Biff came up behind him.

'She shot something, Tessa did,' he said, 'Or someone.' His tone held admiration, only slightly tinged with disapproval. 'You heard them shots, Denis.'

'I thought it might be a car backfiring,' Denis said, but he hadn't, really.

'Let's hope that's what the neighbours thought,' said Biff.

What had she shot, though?

Orlando was asking her the same question. He was standing with her by the bonnet of the van.

'I haven't murdered anyone, you idiot,' Tessa said to him. 'I fixed his equipment. That's all. Broke some windows in his office and torched it. I don't care if it burns his whole house down. That'll stop him harming animals.'

Orlando didn't know whether to find her wonderful or terrifying. She was a bit of each, he knew.

'Hope no one saw you,' he said. Surely a neighbour had heard the shots?

'I don't think they did,' she said. 'And in case you're wondering, there was no one at home. The house lights must be on time switches.' She did not mention the security lights.

She'd seen the rabbits. They hadn't gone far. Two large brown ones were crouched among the vegetables; two more scampered over the garden when the lights came on. She'd shot both of them as they ran; the first pair were sitting targets. Then she'd set fire to the workshop shed. She'd kept back one of the cans of fuel used in their earlier attack, stuffing it in the large pocket of her waxed jacket. After breaking the window, she had poured its contents through the gap and dropped a lighted piece of paper into the room. The fluid had soon caught; the rest was left to chance. There were sure to be papers in there; a strong draught might fan the flames and she had broken every pane of glass. Then, as the alarm rang and the dog in the house started barking, she walked away. It would not do to be seen running.

'We'd better disappear,' said Orlando, who could not believe that no one had noticed the van parked in the street, if not Tessa and the rest of them. But it would be difficult to describe her accurately; her red hair was thrust up under a woollen cap, and coats like hers were universal.

'Yes,' she agreed. 'Get the others.'

She started the engine and switched on the lights, and the other four turned and ran towards her.

'They're afraid we'll abandon them,' she said, and began laughing. She was still laughing as she drove away.

When they reached the service area where she had left her VW, Orlando handed each of them a fifty-pound note.

'Keep quiet about where we've been today,' he told them, after Tessa, the gun and other gear returned to her car, had driven off. 'No one's been hurt.'

Criminal damage was the offence they had committed; that was all. Tessa was the arsonist.

He dropped the four of them outside Hammersmith Tube station. Then he returned the van. He'd paid in cash when he hired it, and he hadn't used his own name. Biff, some months ago, had obtained a stolen driving licence for him, a private deal between the two of them, and worth it, to Orlando, for protection.

Tessa still hadn't explained why she had fired the shots.

5

TESSA SLEPT LATE on Sunday morning.

She had not reached her parents' house in a Cotswold village until the small hours, having told them she was going to a party. It was true. After parting from Orlando and the others, she had been to a club where she had danced and drunk a lot of wine. She could never wind down after a raid or demonstration; on a high of excitement, she sought more thrills and ran more risks, eventually driving herself home fast, and dangerously. She met no police patrol car on her journey, nor another reckless driver.

Tessa was a solicitor with a city firm whose practice was mainly civil litigation. She enjoyed being overtly on the side of the law, and covertly defying it. So far, neither aspect of her life had intruded on the other; only Orlando had a place in both her worlds. They had met when her firm acted for a client of his bank; entranced, he had listened to her proselytising when he took her out to dinner. Tessa had admitted him to her private life because she needed an emotional prop. He was no threat; she could manipulate him as she chose, and he was eminently presentable: her parents were always pleased when she brought him down for a weekend. His presence in her life mollified them.

On Sunday morning Tessa's parents went to church while their daughter still slept on. Tessa's father, who was a judge, read the lesson, while her mother thought about Clive, their son, a barrister whose wife had left him for a sculptor, taking their two small children to live in Cornwall, where her lover had a studio. She'd hated life in London. Clive had accepted that, and had been willing to commute; they'd just found a house near Amersham and were about to move when she had fled. She'd met the sculptor on a family holiday, it seemed, and somehow, in spite of the distances involved, their romance had culminated in this crisis.

Had Clive been unkind to her, his mother wondered, having sung and appeared to pray; she stretched uncomfortably in her seat while the vicar spoke of tolerance. Surely not: Clive was a decent man, if unimaginative. Now, because they lived so far away, it would be difficult for him to see much of his two daughters, who were only four and six. As their grandmother, she would keep in touch, sending them postcards and presents, but they might as well be in Australia, she sometimes felt. If only Tessa would settle down: that would be some compensation. So often, in repose, her face wore a discontented expression and she was very tense. Millicent Graham knew very little about her daughter's private life but from time to time she had brought Orlando with her for a weekend. However, her interest in him was far from serious; Millicent knew he was only a passing fancy in Tessa's eyes. A woman with a job like hers, in a thriving firm, could combine motherhood with a profession. Millicent, who had never wanted to do the same, nor, as a young woman, been forced by circumstances to contribute to the family income, thought too much was demanded of today's mothers as they strove to juggle their various roles, and they expected a great deal from their husbands or partners, and from life itself. Millicent had expected to be loved and respected, and she had never doubted James's faithfulness. If she were to find out now that he had a mistress, she would be devastated. If he'd had one in the past, she didn't want to know. She thought briefly of his tubby body, his reddish, greying hair, his small but undeniable paunch, with amused affection. He was no Adonis, nor ever had been, but he had a first-class brain and his conversation still interested her. When they met again, after a separation of only the working day, she always felt a glow of pleasure: nothing sexual, simply comfort. He went to church because he saw it as his duty; she usually accompanied him, because she saw that as hers. Millicent had a degree in Modern Languages; she kept up her

French and German by reading, and now acted as a guide at a mansion owned by the National Trust, where this ability was useful when she escorted groups of foreign tourists round the building.

They walked back from church with a couple whose daughter was a research scientist.

'Someone chucked fire bombs at the laboratory last night,' Jenny's mother said. 'And there were a lot of slogans painted on the walls. Jenny went over there this morning, though there's no damage done. But her boss's house was attacked, too. He's got a study workshop in a shed; it was set on fire, and his children's pet rabbits were released and shot. Luckily the family were all out.'

'Oh no! Oh, how awful! Who was it?' Millicent asked.

'Animal rights activists, they say. The slogans were that sort of thing.'

'But to shoot the children's rabbits! That's hardly in accordance with their creed, is it?'

'No, but some of these groups have been infiltrated by anarchists,' said James Graham. 'The raids are used as an excuse to stir up trouble.'

'We all want to cure disease, and that's what they're trying to do in Jenny's lab. But these people seem more intent on causing harm. They don't mind injuring humans,' said Jenny's father.

'The suffragettes were militant,' said Millicent. 'Women might have been denied the vote for far longer if they had been less extreme. Such actions certainly attract attention.'

'Are you saying this effort last night was justified?' her husband asked her, knowing this was not her view but he liked to draw her out.

'Of course not, dear. There is an order of things in nature. Beatrix Potter has a lot to answer for,' said Millicent.

In their various ways, all were disturbed by the news. Jenny's parents feared she could be hurt in some future demonstration; the attack on Dr Frost's house was proof of that. The raiders could not have known in advance that no one was at home. The judge sighed over the impossibility of dealing effectively with those who might be arrested for such actions; they saw themselves as martyrs.

It was a beautiful day. His duty done, James Graham changed into shabby corduroy trousers and a worn sweater, and went out to give the lawn yet another final mow. Each autumn, he and the part-time gardener would decide when the grass had been cut for the final time, and annually James would squeeze in just one more trim on a dry autumn day.

Tessa's VW was parked outside the house. She'd arrived too late to bother with putting it in the garage. She had had it for three years; he imagined it was still in a reliable condition. He did not like to think of her driving around in a car that might let her down, though now, of course, she had a mobile phone. He might wash it for her after lunch. He had to break off from his mowing when Millicent called out that the meal was ready. Tessa was in good spirits after her long sleep and entertained them with an account of a meeting during the previous week at which she had out-manoeuvred a defaulting creditor and obtained substantial damages for her clients, though whether they would ever be paid was another matter.

After lunch, James resisted the temptation of a snooze with the Sunday papers. He was engaged on a case which required him to study some documents before going to court the next day, but he finished the mowing first, cleaned the machine, and reminded himself to lay it up for the winter the following weekend without fail. Then he went to ask Tessa for her car keys. He would have to move the Golf on to the concrete area near the tap before he could wash it.

'Don't worry, Dad,' she said, when he explained his plan. 'I know it's dirty. I'll put it through a machine when I pick up some petrol. Thanks, though.' She smiled at him, got up, and ruffled his faded red hair with a small hand as she passed. 'I'm leaving soon,' she added.

'Very well,' he said. 'I suppose you should get ahead of the traffic.' He had hoped she would stay for an early supper; they had so little chance to talk. He was sorry to be absolved from his beneficent act; he found washing cars soothing, and you saw results. Besides, he liked things to be clean and neat; the smooth lines on the long lawn gratified his eye now, as he took a last saunter down the garden.

Returning to the house, he went to his study and

picked up the papers relating to his current case, while listening with half an ear for sounds of Tessa's departure.

He heard her come down the stairs and followed her outside. She opened the passenger door of her car and put her bag – a soft holdall – in the back.

'Aren't you going to stow that out of sight?' he asked. 'Much safer, when you stop.'

'But I won't stop, except for petrol, and the carwash,' Tessa answered. 'I'll be with it at all times. Silly old His Honour fusspot.'

'I'm glad you didn't bring any work down this weekend,' he said. 'The rest will have done you good.' Like him, she sometimes had to study papers in times allegedly off duty.

'So am I,' she answered, and kissed his cheek.

She drove off, leaving her father unaware that her car contained, stowed out of sight, evidence, including a gun, of her participation in last night's raid.

She took Orlando home with her the next weekend.

The attack on the home of the research scientist and the deaths of the pet rabbits had attracted considerable coverage in the tabloid press. Well-wishers sent more rabbits for the children, who were pictured holding them. Guy Frost had pleaded for the media to go away in return for one photo call, hoping that another topic might soon divert their interest.

WHO ARE THESE PEOPLE? headlines asked, pointing out that the arson attack had to be connected with the fire bombs thrown ineffectually at the laboratory.

Though paint had been sprayed there, no cans were found at the site; Tessa had ordered her team to carry them away and dump them. She suspected that some of her recruits had pasts which could mean their fingerprints were on file. Not even Orlando saw her pocket one that Biff had handled.

Millicent mentioned the incident.

'What a cruel thing,' she said.

Orlando waited for Tessa to defend the actions of the animal protestors, though he knew her parents were unaware that she was one of them. She didn't.

'Talking of newspapers,' she said, 'had you seen that Philip Winter's disappeared? Isn't he the man who came up before you on a rape charge, Dad?'

James had seen an item in *The Times* about the discovery of the man's car beside a river, and the subsequent search by police frogmen for the body. It mentioned the missing man's recent acquittal on a rape charge.

'Yes,' the judge agreed. He remembered the case very clearly. In his opinion, it should not have come to trial; the evidence was weak and depended on the woman's accusation. Why should a hitherto respectable man suddenly act in such a fashion? The defence had not managed to blacken his accuser's reputation by allegations about her past, and the woman had walked away unscathed, but not appeased. At least the defendant had not been unjustly sentenced; juries often showed great good sense, though this one acquitted him more for reasons of doubt than certainty of the man's innocence.

Over dinner, they discussed the case, the rights and wrongs of anonymity for the accuser – the so-called victim.

'That man was a victim this time,' said James. 'How tragic it will be if he has committed suicide.'

'The woman who accused him has a lot to answer for,' said Millicent. 'I wonder if she knows about this?'

'She'll see it in the paper, as we've done,' said James.

'It seems most unfair that he was named and she wasn't,' said Millicent. 'And he lost his job, poor man.'

'Mrs Sandra White, of Belvoir Mansions,' Tessa said, and her father frowned at her.

'How did you learn who she was?' asked Orlando, amazed.

'Plenty of people knew her identity,' said Tessa dismissively. 'The man must be a prize wimp to get himself in such a mess.'

'I feel sorry for him,' said Orlando, who had read about the case. Sexual harassment was a lively topic of discussion in his office. Signals could so easily be misinterpreted. He was wondering if Tessa would make it clear as to whether he was to remain in the spare bedroom tonight or slip along the corridor to hers. He knew she enjoyed flouting the conventions beneath her parents' roof.

She'd certainly turned the conversation away from their lawless raid with great adroitness, he reflected wryly.

6

WHEN PHILIP HAD not returned home on the day he disappeared, his wife, Lesley, was only irritated. Why had he not told her that he planned to go away?

The last months had been a nightmare. On the evening of the alleged rape, he had come home two hours later than his usual time looking dishevelled, with his hair untidy and a large angry scratch, now crusted over, on his face. He said he had scraped it on a protrusion in the store room, but in all his years at Lavery's, such a thing had never happened before. She was sure he had been in some sort of fight.

'You've been drinking,' she declared. 'Were you mugged?'

He wasn't tough; he would have been easy prey for two or three determined youths – even for one. Like so many other commuters, he wore a trench-coat over his dark suit, and did not, at first glance, look particularly prosperous, merely clean and neat, an average businessman; but all such men were targets, for they carried money, credit cards and driving licences, items of value to any thief.

He told her no more, and the police did not come to see him until after Sandra White had lodged her complaint. Philip had maintained, at first, that their visit concerned some problem at the store, but then he was dismissed, and so she had to learn the truth.

He wasn't given time to state his case at Lavery's, and that was most unfair, but Lesley began to fear the complaint was justified. Perhaps he hadn't really tried to rape the customer – that did seem most unlikely – but he might have tried it on. Why go round to her flat if he didn't fancy her? He often served her personally, in the shop; that was confirmed at the trial by his colleagues, called as prosecution witnesses. She was surprised, though: Philip was not sexually voracious, nor was he prone to anger; petulance was more his line when things went wrong. The whole thing seemed incredible, but when police enquiries continued, and he was taken in for further questioning and tests, she began to wonder, for serial rapists, she had heard, were often mild-mannered men at home, with what were, on the surface, normal family lives.

But he wasn't a serial rapist: he was accused of raping one wealthy customer, whose name he had revealed to her.

She hadn't gone to the hearing: she couldn't, even

to show support for him; it was too painful. His solicitor was disappointed by her decision, implying it would not help his case if she failed to back him up. She was afraid that she would learn the truth in court, hear details of their intimate life discussed, and, in a sense, be tried herself. Afterwards, she could not accept that it was, in fact, the truth which had been established when he was acquitted. He'd been lucky. Everyone said that. The delay in reporting the assault was in his favour, and the absence of strong evidence; after all, he didn't deny that he had been to the woman's flat.

There was no celebration, no champagne and back-slapping. On the night of the verdict the evening meal was fish pie with green beans, followed by apricot fool, eaten in near silence, the only conversation being stilted exchanges between Andrew, who had come home from college to support his mother, and Jackie, as they discussed prospects for the next test match series. Andrew was keen on cricket and Jackie was fond enough of him to take an interest. Lesley ate in silence. When the washing up was done, Philip left the house to go for a walk. It was his habit, now, to do this every evening after supper. Lesley had no idea where he went, and in her worst moments she imagined he was stalking women.

The truth was that he could not bear to remain in the sitting-room with her, pretending to watch television, knowing what was in her thoughts and how she doubted him.

And now he seemed to have escaped more positively.

He'd taken his car, which they had agreed must be sold to bring in some money, and to save on its insurance and upkeep. She had her own small Fiat in which she went to work. Even after his acquittal he could not get a job, apart from odd spells of casual employment.

Then came the day when, while Lesley was at work, Jackie was at school, and Andrew was back at college, Philip went off in his car and, by nightfall, was still out.

'Where's Dad?' Jackie asked, at breakfast the next morning.

He was never late, appearing, wearing his white shirt and a tie as on any working day, but with a pullover. He did the tidying up and most of the housework now; it was the least he could do, since he was not earning, he had said, though in fairness Lesley did admit that he had always been helpful in the house.

'I don't know,' Lesley answered. It was pointless to pretend that he was sleeping in; if he'd gone away, Jackie would have to be told.

'Has he left us?' asked Jackie.

Her mother shrugged. He'd left no note, or if he had, she hadn't found it. Didn't departing husbands do that, except when they stormed out in a rage?

'Has he packed his stuff?' asked Jackie.

'I haven't looked,' said Lesley. 'I expect he'll be

back soon enough, or he'll ring up. You get off to school and don't worry.'

'I'm not worrying,' said Jackie. 'He'll do us all a favour if he's gone.'

Her bitter tone shocked Lesley, but she knew that Jackie had had to endure a lot of mockery at school after her father's arrest and trial.

'Has it stopped now, at school? That nasty talk?' she asked.

'Yes,' said Jackie, although it was not strictly true; to some she was a heroine because it was so awful for her to have a father accused of such a crime, but the general feeling was that he had been lucky to get off because he was, most likely, guilty.

Jackie, trying to be just, had said that the case had not been proved. She had gone to court, skiving off school to do so, watching from the gallery, seeing her father pale, tense, and diminished, being pitilessly cross-examined, yet standing firm, never contradicting himself. Despite the shame she felt, Jackie wanted to believe him, yet why should that woman lie about something so serious? Why get him into such a lot of trouble and make him lose his job? He must have done something wrong, if not what she said. After all, it couldn't have been much fun for her, having to talk about her divorce and being asked about her past lovers. She declared there had been none since she parted from her husband, and none had been discovered by the defence. Anyway, what difference did that make? Lots of people got married more than once, and had several boyfriends; making out a woman was a slag was what always happened in a rape case, Jackie knew. His arrest was the most dreadful thing that had happened in her life. If he was not an honest man, nothing was safe. Her heart told her he was innocent, but her cool and cynical head wanted to know why, if so, he had got himself into such a mess. Why was he in the woman's flat at all? Maybe he'd only tried to kiss her, but that, in itself, was disgusting.

He'd said he went there to return the purse. Why not just hand it over at the door, and leave?

She went off to school resolved not to wonder where he was; he'd spoiled enough of her life already and she would not let him wreck the rest. Lesley, having discovered that he had packed nothing, also decided, although anxiously, to forget about him for the moment.

It was Jackie who grew worried first, although she tried to hide it. Despite her angry, cruel words, she began to imagine fearful things and to feel guilty. Had her unforgiving attitude driven him away? Memories of happier times came, unbidden, came into her mind, and she wondered what had transformed him from the kind man who read stories to her when she was small, and made endless sandcastles when they went to Cornwall in the summer, into the ravening beast described in court.

He'd never been anything but kind to her.

Was he dead? Had her hostility driven him to

suicide? People didn't just vanish, did they? She knew that teenagers ran away from home after quarrelling with their parents – often over nothing – but it was the children who left, not the fathers. Fathers left because of marriage problems.

Well, there were marriage problems. Her mother hated him, just as Jackie thought she did. Both believed he had come on to that woman, even if it hadn't gone as far as she had alleged. It was gross. He didn't know what it had been like for her, having to hear the comments other youngsters made. It was the girls who were the worst; some of the boys had been quite cool about it, saying her father was unlucky, picking the wrong person if he wanted an affair. But he shouldn't have been after an affair. Her mother, for her age, was quite nice-looking; she hadn't let herself go. He didn't need to look around, or if he must, couldn't he do it in the normal way and get divorced? Not that Jackie would have liked that, either, but it wasn't crimi-nal.

But he'd got off. He hadn't gone to gaol. It kept coming back to that. If only she could know the truth for certain. When, after two days, he still hadn't come home, nor been in touch, she asked her mother if he could be with his parents, who lived in Kent. Lesley agreed that he might have gone there; they, naturally, had been deeply upset about the trial, but were staunch believers in his innocence. His mother had been quite unwell as a result of her anxiety and distress; it was possible that he was with them. She telephoned them, approaching the reason for her call indirectly, saying she had rung to ask how they were. If Philip were there, they would assume she had rung to speak to him; she need not ask for him, outright.

But he wasn't there. Instead, they asked how he was, so Lesley reported that he was all right – out just now, or he would have spoken to them. If they thought that odd, it was too bad; she could do no more.

Where else could he be? She tried to think of friends whom he might visit, but there were few who were his exclusively. In the end she rang Betty, from Lavery's, who had given evidence for Philip. She had no news of him, nor, as far as she knew, had he been to the store since the hearing.

'Oh dear,' said Betty. 'Poor Philip. He didn't do it, you know, Lesley.' He'd told her all about it – described Sandra White's assault on him.

'Her tongue – ugh!' he'd said. 'It was like a persistent snake. Sometimes I think that I can taste it still.'

Betty had noticed that Mrs White never wanted a female assistant to look after her, but the younger men, though keen enough to attend to younger women customers, all avoided Mrs White. Philip, however, was a simple soul, and he became the fall guy. After Lesley's call she was worried. Philip's life had been destroyed by that woman's accusations; what if he had gone that step further and ended it?

The next morning Lesley told the police that he

had disappeared. A constable came to the house and took details about his car. It was rather soon to list him as a missing person, she was told, and even if he were found, all she would learn was that he was safe, not where he was.

'What if he's dead?' she asked, voicing it at last.

'Well, if his body turned up, we'd tell you then. You'd need to identify him,' was the blunt answer. 'We'll look out for his car. It'll probably be noticed, if we ask all forces to watch out for it.'

'He hasn't any money,' Lesley said. 'Well, he had his wallet on him, and he'd got a cash card.'

The officer took details of their bank account and later the same day was able to tell her that, to date, Philip had not withdrawn any money. At least he hadn't cleaned the account out and fled abroad. He hadn't got his passport with him, though; when he was remanded on bail, he had had to surrender it, but it had been returned and was in his desk.

The next day, his car, the keys still in it, was found beside the river, and a full-scale search was undertaken.

'We should have stood by him,' said Jackie, now in tears.

But Lesley saw it differently. To her, his flight was confirmation of his guilt.

7

W HAT DID YOU do when you had absolutely no money at all?

Philip could not apply for unemployment benefit without producing papers of some sort: doing that would reveal his identity and previous address. It was strange to be so rootless, and quite frightening. He wondered how soon Lesley would report him missing. Maybe she wouldn't bother, but if the car was found, she'd have to take some notice. The best solution would be if it were stolen; then she could claim on the insurance and they could all forget about him.

Since leaving the Lake District, he had followed a serpentine course, taking lifts, not caring where they were going. After several nights at Blackpool, on the front, he'd gone south again, and had spent one night in a men's hostel, something he hoped not to repeat. He was husbanding his money, using it in small amounts for food, and he had bought a spare pair of socks, and a pair of shorts. In Swindon, in a charity shop, he bought a second shirt, and these few belongings went with him everywhere in a plastic Safeway carrier. If he was going to sleep rough, he'd need a sleeping bag, and that would be expensive. Cardboard boxes, he thought, like those living on the streets in London: he'd seen such people daily in his working life. How could you carry a cardboard box around? Could you leave it somewhere, while you spent the day job-hunting or in the library? The library was warm and there were comfortable chairs, and plenty to read; you could doze there, quietly.

He had applied for several jobs. He could drive a van – he had his licence, which was clean. He could sweep up, could serve in a bar, could stack super-market shelves. But no one took him on. Some were sorry, saying he had just missed a chance when an earlier applicant had been successful. They didn't take to him, Philip decided: was it his appearance? His beard was coming in quite grey; it made him look much older, and it was still sparse: he hadn't had to trim it yet. His shirt, rough dried, was always clean; didn't he look respectable?

Then he saw the report about his car. It had been found, and he was officially missing. He'd bought a tabloid newspaper, which he took into a café where he had soup and bread; that would be his hot meal for the day. He'd started filling up a small mineral water bottle with water from a public washroom, and carrying that around with him, and he looked for cut-price displays where he could buy cheap biscuits. Reading the tabloid, he saw a picture of himself dating from the trial, and a report that his wife and daughter were too upset to talk to newsmen. Frogmen were searching for his body, Philip read: he felt as though the news referred to a stranger, not himself. He acknowledged no remorse about his family's alleged distress: it was not him they cared about, simply themselves and this added notoriety.

If they'd stood by him, he wouldn't be in such a state now. What about trust, and duty: all those things that people thought were so important in relationships; where were they in his case? He would not let himself contemplate his parents' possible concern. He left the paper on the table, and walked off.

He wasn't wanted by the police. Anyone who thought they recognised him would not feel bound to report the sighting. If he let his beard grow longer, and his hair, he'd be extremely well disguised. Perhaps he'd pass as a poet, Philip thought, and then reflected that more likely, if he went on sleeping rough, he'd be taken for a down-and-out.

And he would be one.

Frances Dixon had heard about the attack on Guy Frost's house on the radio news the morning after it happened.

She was horrified. Nothing like this had occurred

in the area since she moved to Chingbury. Darsing-ford, where the Frosts lived, was where she went for shopping which could not be done in the village. It had been a market town and had now expanded to include some industry on its perimeter, with housing for those who worked there. There had been burglaries and muggings in the town, and car thefts, but very little violent crime, and this was different: this was terrorism, setting fire to the home of a man who was working to benefit mankind.

It seemed that the family had been out when the attack took place. Perhaps it would not have happened if they had been at home because the arsonists could have been discovered. Whatever the facts, it was wicked and cowardly, and Dr Frost had lost valuable disks and papers which were destroyed. The damage had been confined to his workshop in the garden shed.

But why kill the pet rabbits, when the protestors were proclaiming that they were defending animals?

The police seemed to think that this was strange.

Frances was not a churchgoer, and she met no one on that Sunday, which she spent working in the garden. It was one of the days on which she spoke to nobody. Since tucking herself away in this isolated spot, such days happened fairly frequently and sometimes she made a note of them, just for interest. Once a month she rang each daughter; sometimes they rang her. She sent each grandchild postcards now and then, all of them on the same day so that no one got forgotten. Now that they were growing up, they stayed with her less often, but sometimes one of Arabella's brood would come for several weeks in the summer. There was a tennis club in Chingbury, with two hard courts, where they could play, and at Friar's Court, where Dorothy and Hugo Ware lived, there was a pool, which the Wares let the youngsters use on visits. Friar's Court was an old stone house which had been part of an abbey; now, some of the outbuildings had been turned into units where people ran small businesses, among them a man who restored furniture, a potter, and a printer.

Frances had been offered the use of the pool, but she was a poor swimmer, and found that keeping her large garden orderly gave her enough exercise.

Earlier that summer, she had met the Frosts at a party the Wares held for their daughter, who had recently married a man who already had a small son and daughter from an earlier marriage. The Wares were wishing that she was not taking on this pair of stepchildren, who lived mainly with their mother but would spend some weekends with their father.

'It can work out,' Frances had consoled them, thinking of Arabella, who had made a success of her role as a stepmother but was, perhaps, less successful with her own children.

'It's so difficult in any case,' said Dorothy Ware, a large woman with wavy iron-grey hair. Her husband was a retired general who had been persuaded to write his memoirs. This kept him busy, and would be a useful historical record even if the result never reached a wide public.

Frances had met the Wares through their mutual interest in gardens. The Wares had seven acres of land surrounding their house; four of them formed a paddock, where from time to time a neighbour's two ponies grazed, and the rest was cultivated, some of it as a small arboretum. The general liked trees, had carefully selected those to plant, and had naturalised hundreds of bulbs beneath them. Snow-drops, daffodils, narcissi and bluebells flourished in their chosen areas; Frances loved to walk there.

She remembered the Frosts. They had struck her as a strong family: the craggy-featured father, a balding, thick-set, sturdy man, and the rather plain wife who wore glasses and had a sweet expression on her face as she kept an eye on the two young children, a girl and a boy, who played card games together on a rug on the grass and, when that bored them, chased each other round the garden.

Thank goodness only property and the rabbits had been hurt, but what an extraordinary thing to do: to shoot the pets.

For no particular reason, she remembered the near collision she had had in the lane the day of the attack: the white van which had come much too fast towards her and the aggressive driver who had almost pushed her backwards as she reversed away. Their encounter was at least twenty miles from the complex and the Frosts' house, and hours before either incident. They could not be connected.

What a pity the demonstrators did not use their energy to draw attention to human hardship, Frances thought, as, like Judge Graham forty miles away, she mowed her lawn.

Biff and Denis knew nothing about the shot rabbits. They never bothered with the paper, or any other form of news dissemination. There was no television in their world. They went on several other protests, not about animals but for causes which Biff had heard needed support. He got a buzz from the crowd's mood, the chanting and the movement as they massed together with the police walking along beside them, ready for a riot to break out. He'd seen policemen knocked to the ground and kicked. He wouldn't do that himself; the penalty if you were caught was much too high; but a sort of fury could get hold of you and make you want to hunt them down.

Denis was not so keen on the urban demonstrations, though they were something to do. He kept hoping for another trip to the country. Often, lying in his corner of the dingy hut where he slept, light entering through cracks in the boarded-up windows, he thought about the space and the darkness of the night. He would remember the field with the alarming cattle by the gate: their wet noses and their sweet breath puffing at him when at last he plucked up the nerve to go near them. They'd soon returned, after Orlando had scared them off.

Orlando hadn't minded them at all.

Biff had been in the country before. When he was quite young he'd been sent to a centre where he had cleared ditches and put up fences and climbed nearby hills. The food had been good, and they'd had some laughs, but he liked a bit of noise and people round him. Tessa and Orlando's raids were small stuff, in his view; he preferred being part of a large active crowd. The pay-offs, though, were better with Tessa, and he'd always go with her again. Besides, last time he'd had his bonus; that was what she'd called it, afterwards. He knew that if he told Denis what had happened, he wouldn't be believed.

Soon, the anti-hunting expeditions would be starting.

'That's real,' he told Denis. 'You chase them dogs and you chase the toffs on horses. It's great.'

Denis was ready to believe him.

Early in November, they went on such a demonstration, joining hunt saboteurs in a minibus where they sang anarchic songs on the way to a village where a targeted hunt was to meet. Biff and Denis had no major role to play; they were supporting actors in a cast which included people with canisters which they planned to spray around to confuse the hounds and lead them on a false trail.

The two were told not to be violent.

'But you can use your initiative,' they were advised.

Denis, sitting by a window in the minibus, tried

to understand the purpose of their protest. He knew that Tessa and Orlando thought it cruel to make mice and rabbits ill by dosing them with drugs or giving them diseases, all in the name of science. Now he had to accept that it was cruel to chase a fox with a pack of hounds which would tear it to shreds and eat it. But foxes ate chickens. Biff had told him that; he'd seen the results when he was sent to the country institution. Now, the people round him in the coach were talking about chasing the riders and the hounds. He heard a girl boast how, the previous season, her actions had caused a horse to take fright and stumble, throwing the rider who was taken to hospital. 'Stretchered, he was,' she said, with satisfaction. The horse had cut its leg and was led off bleeding. Hadn't that been cruel? Denis was puzzled.

People quietened down when they reached their destination. They were dropped outside the village, where they met some local demonstrators who, knowing the area, suggested how they should be deployed in groups. Some were sent to block a road down which the hunt would have to go to reach a wood where a fox might be found. Other demonstrators, favouring the hunt, stood peacefully about with placards proclaiming that banning hunting would throw hundreds out of work. WHAT ABOUT FISHING? said one sign.

This year, the police had new powers of arrest, so the saboteurs' strategy, now, meant avoiding the actual meet, where intruding could be trespass. No one wanted to end up in the back of a police van.

The two groups of demonstrators faced one another like troops before a battle, the protestors often dressed in black or combat gear, the supporters more conventionally in anoraks or waxed jackets, most of them country dwellers, some of whom earned their living from the land.

There came the distant sound of a horn and the crowd began to stir. The hunt had moved off from its meeting place and was approaching. Denis heard the clatter of horses' hooves on the tarmac of the road, and the murmur of voices, but none of it was loud, not until the group around him started chanting. Suddenly, sticks appeared in people's hands and Denis saw that Biff now held a cudgel. Where had that come from? The hunt supporters had fallen back on to the grass verges, allowing hounds and riders to pass, but the protestors formed a solid phalanx facing the oncoming hounds and the field behind them. Denis, bemused and rather frightened, saw two men in red coats riding enormous horses from whose nostrils plumed puffs of steamy breath. The men carried whips with long thongs which trailed beside them. One kept talking in encouraging tones to the sea of pale creamy hounds which billowed around his horse's hooves. An occasional yelp came from a hound, but they were mostly quiet. Behind, bobbing up and down in their saddles, was a mass of riders, men, women and children, most of them in black or navy coats, but there were a few splashes of scarlet here and there and some tweed. All of them wore dark hard hats. Denis felt panic. What if this huge army chose to charge at the protestors? They'd be bowled over, savaged by the hounds and trampled by the horses, as at a riot when the mounted police rode in. Denis had seen that happen, and it was scary. What if these riders used their whips on the demonstrators? He wanted to turn back, but he couldn't because of the press of people round him who were shouting now.

Suddenly the hunt turned aside, into a field where, miraculously, a gap in the fence had appeared. Tipped off in advance, two men had cut the wire and moved a couple of posts to let the field stream through before they reached the demonstrators.

Frustrated and furious as their quarry galloped away, the protestors set off in pursuit across the field, waving their sticks in the air and screaming. The weather had been dry for weeks, so the ground was not unduly wet, but where the horses had gone, it was churned up in places, and some of the demonstrators were inadequately shod for their chase. Denis, in his shabby trainers, stood back beside the hedge to let the protestors sweep past him, and he saw the hunt spread out, the hounds in front with the huntsman and the whipper-in, the other riders following in what looked to him an orderly manner. He caught his breath. It was a colourful and splendid sight, and the only cruelty he had seen so far was the expression on the faces of his companions.

Along the road, now, came a line of vehicles and cycles carrying the foot followers of the hunt. Meanwhile, the two original men, aided by two more, were swiftly repairing the gap they had made in the wire fence.

Biff was among the group of protestors who had surged into the field behind the horses; the rest regrouped to decide on their next tactic, which was to circumnavigate the wood so that they would be ready if a fox was flushed out on the further side. Denis sauntered after them, in no hurry.

The day was cold and crisp, the sky a brilliant blue. In London, unless it rained or was very windy, you scarcely noticed the weather; here it was so different. This was why he had come, he decided, inhaling deeply. On either side of the lane stretched fields, woodland, and this great, amazing space. Imagine living here, among all this emptiness! You'd soon get used to the quiet. It was quiet now; the cars following the hunt were all drawn up with their engines switched off. Denis walked slowly, letting the demonstrators round him overtake him; these were the local dedicated campaigners who plodded on with grim expressions, anxious lest the violent element among the imported saboteurs got out of hand, for to some of them the cause was immaterial; it was the chase that was the lure.

Denis found himself walking up a track towards a wood. He hesitated, then tagged along among the other stragglers. It was rather like the trail on which Orlando had led them on the day of that raid; then, they'd ended on the downs. They'd passed some downs on the way here today but Denis hadn't known where they were going; he couldn't read the road signs.

Now, from ahead, came excited yelps and deeper barks, then a great babble from the hounds. It was a bit like music, Denis thought.

'They've found a fox,' said a youth, brushing past him. Rushing on, he produced a horn from his own pocket and blew on it, unmelodiously but loudly. 'This'll call them off,' he promised, halting to blow the better.

Denis could not see the main pack of hounds but there were about forty riders waiting quietly at the edge of the wood, some of the horses fidgeting impatiently but most standing still, ears pricked, listening. The horn was blowing now – not the youth's, but the official one – as the cry of the hounds hit a crescendo. Denis thought he'd like to see them chasing after the fox. This wasn't like a night at the dogs; he'd been greyhound racing a few times and it was exciting, but this was different: this was real. There was more point to this than running round a track chasing a dummy hare.

Biff suddenly appeared beside him.

'Phew!' he exclaimed. 'This is great!'

Denis had forgotten about him. He was walking slowly now while ahead others were running, many of them yelling.

'I hit one of them,' Biff told him proudly. 'I hit one of them big horses.'

Denis stared at him. Hadn't he come on this trip to save foxes, not hurt horses? More figures were converging in the wood as those who had entered from other directions met. With various rallying calls and shouts, they formed themselves into a straggling line and set off after the hunt; the hounds, in full cry, were streaming across the country on the far side of the wood. Biff joined the pursuers, and Denis's slow walk grew even slower. The noises he heard now were not the hunt, but the yells of the demonstrators. He heard the youth blow his horn discordantly and hoped the hounds would take no notice. The protestors were upsetting it all. They were wrong. They were hunters too.

When at last he emerged from the wood into another field, he saw a drab crowd of people trailing towards a distant gate where a line of vans was drawn up. They began clambering into the vehicles, preparing to move to another position for a fresh assault; this was local transport they were using. Denis thought he saw Biff among them, but it was difficult, at such a distance, to distinguish individuals. Would Biff be going in a van when they had come by minibus? Denis did not know that this transport was provided by the local organisations, anxious to keep forces mobile. He did not care where they were going. He went back towards the wood, intending to make his way to the village where the minibus had dropped them. Presumably it would return there later to collect them for the homeward trip. He did not hurry. Time had never had much importance for Denis, and today it mattered even less. He was alone in the wood now. The paths and rides had been churned up as much by the protestors as the horses, few of which had come this way since .most had been outside the wood in sight of where the fox broke cover. A hen pheasant ran in front of him. What a big wild bird, thought Denis. Then he saw a grey squirrel race up a tree trunk. It crouched above him, watching him over its front paws, its whiskers twitching, not at all afraid. Denis had seen squirrels in a park, but never as close as this.

The wood was settling back to normal. On another day, Denis might have come across beaters and obstructed a shooting party, but not now. With the departure of the hunt and its followers, peace returned, and with it came that strange quiet he had noted before. It was broken only by the soft sound of his own footsteps as he moved on. He had been rather fearful of the silence on the expedition with Orlando and the rest; now, it did not worry him. No one was going to drag him into a scrap or a brawl, and there was no traffic to dodge. What would it be like to live here? The wood didn't seem to belong to anyone. Couldn't he build a hut? There were plenty of trees and bushes around; it should be simple to use branches and make a den. Long ago, with some other boys, he'd played on a patch of waste ground near the foster home he was in at the time; they'd had a hide-out there. He'd almost forgotten about it. That had been one of the better times. The foster mother had read stories to them. He'd cried when he left to go back to a children's home. He thought he'd been moved on because he'd been naughty, not realising that it had only ever been a stop-gap placement. After that, he had often behaved badly on purpose, seeing that being good made no difference.

What could you eat, if you lived in a wood? It would be cold at night, but he could light a fire. He'd slept out often enough; that wouldn't bother him, though here there would be no warm grating to give out heat, and he had no big cardboard box. Once, when an old dosser had died, he'd taken the man's sleeping bag and had used it until someone stole it from him when he'd gone off to the toilet. Even the toilet wouldn't be a problem in a wood.

People came round to those sleeping on the streets with soup and sandwiches, if you were lucky. Sometimes they brought blankets. That wouldn't happen here. Denis wondered if he could catch rabbits, or some of those big birds, and cook them. How did you get the feathers off, and the fur? Would they sit quietly enough for you to pounce on them? He'd got a knife. He could use that to kill them. He thought about it, walking back towards the village. Then he saw the fox. It took him a moment to realise what it was – the rather muddy animal, bigger than a cat, which slunk across the road ahead of him and went into the field. He watched it lope towards the wood from which it had been driven earlier in the day.

That was good, then. It had escaped the hunt. In fact, this wily fox had crossed a stream and the hounds had lost its scent as it doubled back, surviving to be pursued another time. The hunt, meanwhile, had moved to a different covert where it found a second fox, losing many of the saboteurs this time as the chase moved fast and in a direction they had not anticipated. Hanging about in exposed fields with no action bored the maverick brigade, denied the chance to disrupt the sport and hurl abuse. The more conventional objectors tended to go home when they had made their point.

Biff had forgotten about Denis, for he had fallen in with some new friends. He had already met some of this mob when he went on a march protesting against a recent government bill some people found objectionable. Biff had no idea what it was about. Unfortunately, out here in the wilds, there were no handy snack bars or chip shops to get a bite. Tessa and Orlando, on their trips, always organised the feeding of the troops – that was what they called it. On these bigger demonstrations you had to think about yourself.

As the day wore on, he grew hungry, and at last one of their group called up their minibus by mobile phone. When they were all aboard, it was agreed that they would stop for refreshments at the first possible opportunity. Denis was only one of several stragglers who missed their transport home.

'They should have kept with us. That was the instruction,' said one of the organisers, a woman in a waxed jacket and wellingtons, wearing a green hood. 'They must get back as best they can. They can hitch a lift.'

Biff hoped Denis would not get lost. The kid was useless on his own. Still, he had to learn. He'd turn up. Biff moved up in the bus to sit beside a long-haired girl he'd noticed earlier. He might try his luck there.

He didn't get very far with her on the journey, but he discovered where she lived. He could always find her, if he had the time.

8

NO TRACE OF Philip Winter had been found.

Lesley tried to carry on as usual, but each day she expected to hear that his body had been discovered. Jackie, too, could not stop thinking about her father, at one minute blaming herself for driving him away from home, the next furious with him for what she saw as his betrayal. In that angry mood, she shared her mother's belief that he must have done something to the woman, even if it wasn't total rape.

But Jackie knew that people sometimes made up stories, often only just for fun, though often to shock or impress their listeners. At school, a girl had alleged that a master had put his hand on her leg in class. It hadn't happened; she'd done it for a joke, telling her parents who had instantly complained. The incident soon spiralled out of control; the master was suspended, and the girl, frightened now, stuck to her story. None of her friends wanted to get her into trouble by exposing the lie, yet it seemed unfair to the master, who taught history and was not particularly unpopular; he wore pebble glasses and rode a bicycle to school, and, had he been one of the children, might have been a target for bullying. The girl had picked him rather than one of his less vulnerable colleagues. In the end, she had, in tears, retracted her allegations, but only after some other pupils had threatened her with dire consequences if she did not. It could so easily have ended the master's career; as it was, he lost his enthusiasm for teaching and some months later he left the school. No one knew what he was doing now.

If something like that had happened to her father, he was to be pitied, not punished. But had it? Why had he visited that flat? Had the woman really left her purse behind deliberately? Couldn't she find herself a man, if she wanted one? Round and round in Jackie's confused head churned the various possibilities, the doubts and fears.

And now, what if he were dead?

She ran through various scenarios, including his funeral with herself in black, down to the ground, weeping into a lace-edged handkerchief. People would pity the poor orphan. To lose a father's reputation and then, after his name had been cleared, the father himself, was surely tragic.

But had his name been truly cleared? Always, it came back to that, and how would she ever know the truth? People were vile and disgusting; she knew some awful things that would have shocked her mother if she had mentioned them. Jackie was beginning to find the world a frightening place, and you were alone in it. Who could help her now? Andrew was away, and since the trial had been home only briefly. He was afraid his girlfriend would dump him on account of his father's disgrace. He rang up sometimes, and Mum had told him about Dad going off. When he heard about the discovery of the car, he came home for a night, but Mum had sent him back to college. He couldn't help, she said; they must all carry on, and when some journalists wanted her to tell them how she felt, she said she didn't know.

'What if he's committed suicide?' they asked, and she refused to answer.

Lesley could not face the possibility that his despair had been so great that he could no longer face life, yet wouldn't he have left a note, if that was so? Most suicides did, didn't they, sowing guilt behind them as they did it, the sort of guilt that she felt now, the sense that she should have given him the benefit of the doubt.

But why should she do that? Why put the blame on her? It was Philip who had seen the woman and crossed swords with her.

When no body was found, the papers' interest soon died down. The car had been examined, and eventually the police said that Lesley could fetch it; the radio had gone, but as it had been left unlocked, thieves could have taken that with little effort.

Lesley could not face the trip. She said her son would go over for it when he next came home. They'd keep it for her, wouldn't they, meanwhile? Perhaps one of them would like to buy it.

This suggestion, thrown away, was taken seriously. It seemed that a new owner from the force might be found, after an appropriate interval.

The police officer who came to see her described how the river, now in flood, might yet yield up a body as the water fell. He spoke of tides, but not of gases which might bring it to the surface.

'Don't give up hope,' he added. 'Sometimes people go missing just to get away, when things get too difficult. Then they come back.'

'But with no money? No clothes?'

'He'll have had some money on him,' said the officer.

'Not much. He's been unemployed for months.'

He might still use his bank card. Lesley would not put a stop on it; there wasn't a great deal in the account, but he was entitled to some of it. The bank would let them know if money was withdrawn.

But he didn't use his card and first days, then weeks went by with no news. If he was found, the police would come and tell her personally; such information was not given in a telephone call. Lesley went to the office as usual, worrying about Jackie who wasn't eating properly and whose school work was suffering. How could he do this to them, after what he'd done already, Lesley thought, in anger. She went to see Jackie's teacher to explain the situation, though everyone must know all the details from the press.

If he were to walk in now, Lesley was not sure how she would react, nor could she predict Jackie's response.

At least we'd know, she thought: the uncertainty would end.

Mrs Sandra White had also read that Philip had disappeared.

How feeble, was her first reflection. The fact that she had wrecked his life and reputation did not worry her. Though she sought sexual satisfaction from men, she despised most of them, living comfortably on generous alimony. Her husband had had to make it worth her while to let him go.

Sandra had planned to find another husband, but if she did, she stood to lose her handsome income. So far, she had failed to attract a man as rich; those who might be detachable from existing spouses wanted young, fresh flesh; one had told her so. Sandra White was forty-six.

In her mail, one morning a few days after Philip's car had been found, she received a letter in a plain manila envelope. It contained a newspaper cutting reporting her victim's disappearance and hinting at the possibility of his suicide. Across the cutting, printed in the same bold black felt pen as the address, were the words: YOU ARE RESPONSIBLE FOR THIS.

Sandra stared at it, bewildered. Then her anger rose as she understood that whoever had sent her the cutting believed she had provoked the stupid man to kill himself.

What nonsense! He'd been let off, which he didn't deserve because he had insulted her and a term in prison would have done him good. Why should she now be blamed for what he chose to do afterwards?

But who could have sent this to her? Not Philip, if he was dead. Some friends of his? That woman from Lavery's who had spoken up for him?

It had a South London postmark.

Next day she received another, reporting the same tale but in more sensational terms, cut from a different paper. After that there was a brief lull.

Philip's former colleagues at Lavery's had been concerned when they learned about his disappearance and the discovery of his abandoned car. Betty, the defence witness, went to see Lesley, taking flowers from several of the staff, offering sympathy and wanting to know if there was any further news. She lived in quite another district and had made a special journey after work.

Lesley had to ask her in, accept the flowers and thank her for them. How kind she was. Lesley's eyes filled with tears and Betty misinterpreted the reason. She put an arm round Lesley's shoulders, in a sympathetic gesture.

'It's awful that that woman could get away with it,' she said. 'In spite of what the papers said, I know you believed him, but so many people didn't. And everyone knows who Philip is but no one's been told about Mrs Sandra White. She'd tried it on before, I'm pretty certain,' Betty added. 'No one was going to admit it, though, because of wives and so on. Families could break up, if any of the men had come forward.' Mrs White had been through most departments, Betty had heard, from hardware to men's outfitting. 'Are you going to make an appeal to him on television?'

'What's the good, if he's dead?' said Lesley.

'But he may not be. He may simply have run away,' said Betty. It would be in character. After all, according to Philip himself, he'd run away from the allegedly rapacious Mrs White.

'Well, if he just wants some time to himself, he'll run back again, no doubt,' said Lesley. Her tone was very bitter. Betty looked at her pale, unhappy face and felt her own heart harden. No wonder Philip had had to escape from home, one way or another.

'How's Jackie?' she asked. 'And Andrew?'

'All right. Jackie's upset,' said Lesley.

And you're not helping, Betty thought.

'I'm very sorry,' she said. 'We all liked Phil. Most of us think it's a terrible business. Cases like this make a mockery of the law – and all the time there are men out there really raping women, and getting away with it, who do it again and again and don't get put away because they make out the woman's a slut. No one asks about their sex lives.' Even Philip's sexual history had been left unexamined by the court.

She turned to go, refusing the cup of coffee which, belatedly, Lesley was offering. She'd be late getting home, but she'd warned her husband, who was older than she was and who had already retired. He'd have a hot meal waiting for her. She looked forward to it, and to the warm welcome she would receive.

She was one of the lucky ones.

It was your work which gave you your identity, thought Philip, on the road again. He'd bought himself a thick donkey jacket at a charity shop; it was only five pounds. Some dead person's garment, he supposed. Buying it made a big hole in his shrinking exchequer but the nights were getting cold and his trench-coat wasn't warm enough. It would do as a groundsheet, though, for sleeping out.

He'd been head of a department in a large branch of a well-known store. That had given him status – not as much as if he were a professional man – a doctor, say, or a solicitor – but you could command a high salary if you rose to manage a whole store. He wasn't capable of that; he'd reached his limit; but he had more rank than when he was a mere salesman. A road sweeper, even a refuse collector, had his role in life. Now, Philip had none. He was a bum, almost a beggar. He wasn't dead, however, and without a body, Lesley could not have a funeral.

He'd got a lift in a car with two young lads.

'Nice of you to pick me up,' he said, getting into

the back of their very shabby Allegro.

'We know what it's like, trying to get a ride,' said the driver. 'We're going to Plymouth to see our Mum. Want to come with us?'

'Thanks,' said Philip. Plymouth: why not? In another age he could have joined a ship there, no questions asked, and sailed the world as crew. Perhaps you could still do that.

The boys were brothers; they had been working as labourers on a building site, raising funds to go abroad. They were about Andrew's age, thought Philip, and, though not identical, were, they told him, twins. The one who drove pushed the old car on, and Philip thought it was making a rather nasty noise; a knocking sound was coming from the engine. Sure enough, after a while it began to falter, and the young man just managed to get it off the motorway at the next slip road and away from the roundabout at the top. All three of them then pushed it to a safer place, the driver leaning in to steer it through the window.

'I hoped it'd get us there,' said one twin.

'We had a bet on it, and I won,' said his brother, but he looked quite glum.

'It may not be anything much,' said Philip, though it had sounded bad. 'Look, I'll walk on and send you help. I'm sure to come to a telephone box or a place where I can use the phone before long.'

He left them, and after walking for a mile or more, he came to a small group of houses. He chose a bungalow, and rang its bell.

Footsteps approached the door. He sensed an eye was being applied to a peephole. He couldn't be a reassuring sight, dressed in his heavy jacket, with his new beard, not very clean. The door was opened, very cautiously, on a chain, and a pale blue eye looked round.

'I'm sorry to bother you,' he said.

'I never buy anything at the door,' said the owner of the eye, and banged the door before he could speak.

Philip tried the next house, where there was no answer, but at the third he found a woman working in the garden. She was digging the border over, and she held her fork protectively before her as he approached. However, she let him state the reason for his visit.

The young men had written down the number of their car, and the road reference. The woman said that she would telephone a local garage and get them rescued.

'They're nice young lads,' he told her. 'Not yobs. They were giving me a lift.'

'I see.' The woman looked him up and down. His anxious eyes peered at her above a pale face adorned by a moth-eaten moustache and beard. He wasn't your usual roadie, she thought. 'Would you like a cup of tea?' she asked.

'Please,' said Philip.

'I'll telephone, and then I'll bring you out one,' she volunteered, going off towards the house.

He watched her go. She wore jeans and a light

padded jacket that had seen better days, and boots, which she took off before entering the house. Philip picked up the fork and went on turning the soil over. It didn't do his shoes much good, but the ground was still quite dry. He'd always enjoyed gardening and last year had bought a greenhouse, quite a small one, big enough to grow tomatoes in and a few plants for the house.

The woman, bringing back his tea, was quite surprised.

'Would you like to finish it off?' she said. 'Then I can tidy up the roses and put in the wallflowers. I'll give you five pounds and something to eat. Oh, and I can find you a pair of boots to borrow.'

She brought him out a pair of wellingtons, a size too large and with a hole in the sole, and told him they'd been intended for a jumble sale.

Philip put the boots on, and continued digging. He asked her for some secateurs and cut down the withered herbaceous plants, carrying the dead cuttings to her bonfire spot.

'It's a lovely garden,' he said. 'Have you lived here long?'

'Ten years,' she answered.

She brought him some ham sandwiches for lunch, and another cup of tea. He enjoyed his meal sitting in the thin autumn sunlight.

He worked on after lunch, cutting dead wood out of an apple tree and neatening up the edges of the lawn. Then she said she had to fetch her children from school.

'Where were you going?' she asked him.

'To Plymouth, but I might as well go anywhere,' he said.

She frowned.

'Have you been in prison?' she asked.

'No.' He'd spent a night in a police station after he was charged, but the next day the police had allowed him bail.

'One has to be so careful,' she declared.

'I understand,' said Philip. 'I've got a wife and daughter,' he told her. 'And a son. We're separated,' he added, for good measure. After all, it was the truth.

The woman resolved she would take a chance.

'I'll take you to Darsingford,' she said. 'You can decide where to go from there. There are buses and trains.'

She dropped him at the edge of the town, then turned off for the school. She gave him ten pounds, too, and said he'd earned it.

So he had. He could afford a bed tonight.

9

WHEN DARKNESS FELL, Denis knew he wasn't going home – if you could call it home – that night. So what? He'd go when he felt like it. He might lose his corner in the hut, and the blanket he had hoarded since it was given to him by charity workers, but he could always find Biff and the other guys whom Biff counted as his mates; he knew where they hung out and which pubs they used. Denis wasn't so keen on pubs. They cost, because you had to pay for other people's drinks, and he had a weak head so that a couple of pints made him lose his bottle. He knew himself to be a coward, though he'd once tried to join the army, thinking that then he'd get clothes and food, and have a roof over his head, and be told what to do so that he didn't have to make his own decisions. He'd failed the medical. He had flat feet and a rattle in his chest which he'd been told to take to his own doctor. Denis had no doctor, but he had had asthma as a child. It seldom bothered him, these days.

He was hungry. He had a couple of pounds on him, enough to buy some chips and have plenty left for tomorrow. Surely there'd be a chippie in the place where the hunt had met? The minibus had dropped them outside the village; he walked on towards the cluster of houses.

But there was no chip shop, nor a café, only a pub which wasn't yet open. The short November day was ending; lights were on in windows and cars buzzed along the main road. As it was a Saturday, families were at home, but he saw two boys sparring in a friendly way near a telephone kiosk. Probably there were rough kids, even here, he thought, and, streetwise, he wondered if there were houses with unlatched windows, asking to be entered.

He wandered up a branching lane. It was narrow; cars must find it difficult to pass, he thought. He passed a block of cottages fronting the footpath and went round the back of them, looking for his opportunity, but a security light came on instantly and he shot back to the lane. On he went, now leaving the village, and he caught the smell of woodsmoke in the air. At first he didn't realise what it was, but then he saw, over a hedge, the sudden flare of a bonfire as it received a new forkful of dry withered stalks. In the light of the flames he made out a figure stoking the fire. Man or woman, he could not distinguish which, but he gave that no great thought. While this person was busy out of doors, the house might be unlocked.

He must be quick, but he knew this game.

Denis found the entrance gate, opened it carefully – it worked on a latch and did not squeak – and padded up the path towards the house. He was shielded by its bulk from the busy gardener's view. A dim light from within the house showed through the window panes, but no halogen glare sprang into action as he tested the front door, which was firmly locked. He moved round the building, hugging the wall, and came to another door, half glass, and this one was not locked. He slipped inside, closing the door behind him. It was warm in the house, and he breathed in deeply, unaware until then of how cold he had become.

He moved towards the lighted room. It was the kitchen, and what a snug, cosy place it was! There was a stove against one wall; he hadn't seen one like that before: it wasn't gas or electric. It had two silver circular slabs on top and he touched one. It was hot. There was a large table made of wood in the centre of the room, with chairs tucked round it. He must hurry: the person from the garden might come in at any minute and block his line of retreat. He'd grab some food and run.

But there was a purse on the table.

Denis opened it, took the bank notes from it, leaving the small change, and fled.

Frances Dixon, who had not realised quite how dark it had become while she was working in the garden, came in a little later. She put on the hall light, and noticed a trail of earth on the carpet leading from the side door to the kitchen, but attributed it to her own careless progress from the garden on the several journeys she had made to supervise her bonfire.

Denis had closed the gate carefully behind him, then he went back the way he had come. The darkness wasn't yet complete: the sky was grey against the blackness of the buildings and the trees, and he could see some stars. He ran for a bit, then slowed again to a walk. He had money now. There had been a wad of it in the purse.

By good luck, a bus came along as he reached the centre of the village. He couldn't read where it was going, but he simply said 'One single, please' to the driver who also gave out the tickets, and pulled out his own two pounds from his breast pocket.

'To town?' asked the driver.

'That's right,' said Denis.

The driver gave him back some change, and Denis settled down to enjoy the ride. His legs felt tired. He'd been on them, walking round, for hours.

There were very few other passengers, and they took no notice of him. Their journey carried them to another village, where a woman got off and two girls joined them. Denis gazed out of the window at the dark shapes of hedges, trees, and occasional buildings. There were no street lights, except by the clusters of houses, and not always then. When they reached the outskirts of the town, the bus did not stop until a woman who had been sitting at the back rang the bell, and it halted near a crossing to let her off. Denis decided to remain where he was, and the bus went on towards the town centre, where it stopped again and the driver said, 'All change,' getting out himself.

Denis alighted. There were some shops around him, mostly shut now, and a lot of traffic as people drove home or went out for the evening. He sauntered along the pavement looking at the goods displayed in the windows, and eventually came to a chip shop where he bought a large portion of chips and a sausage. Eating his meal from the wrappings, standing in the road, he saw a group of lads some fifty yards away; they were larking about together. He moved off the other way. He wasn't one of their gang and they might beat him up and take his money. A police patrol car drove past, not slowing down. No one took any notice of him.

He was tired. It had been a long, eventful day. He walked away from the centre of Darsingford, not realising that he had visited this town before, with Tessa and Orlando. He recognised no landmarks, and he was not in the area where Guy Frost and his family lived, but soon he was in a different residential neighbourhood. Here, it was quieter. Hardly a car went by, and the houses were dark, their curtains drawn against the night, with just a sliver of light showing here and there. In this part of town, most people had space to park inside their boundaries, even where they lacked garages, and very few cars were left beside the kerb.

Modern cars had effective alarm systems. Denis didn't try to risk opening any of those among the few left in the street. He looked for something older, where he could spend the night, and he found a Maestro parked well away from a street lamp, outside a semi-detached house where there was a glimmer of light at several windows.

It wasn't late. The owner might come out, he thought, to go to a club or pub.

Denis decided to take a chance. If he was found, he'd simply tell the truth – that his friends had dumped him and he'd nowhere to go. That was no crime. He wouldn't be taking the car; he'd simply be using it as a shelter.

It had a steering lock to deter thieves, but as he wasn't stealing it, that didn't matter. Denis opened the door fairly easily, as his pockets contained several useful bits and pieces. Then he lay down on the rear seat, pulling his anorak hood up round his head so that his face wouldn't show if anyone looked in. His feet, inside his trainers, felt quite dry; he didn't take his shoes off in case he had to run for it, but no one came to disturb him. Well fed, and only slightly chilly, Denis soon fell asleep.

Denis woke the next morning because he was cold in the back of the car. This saved him from discovery. At first, when he opened his eyes, he could not remember where he was; he was stiff and uncomfortable, and the only break in the darkness came from the street light along the road, for it was not yet dawn.

Slowly he recalled the events of the previous day, and now he did feel a sense of panic because he was so far from any familiar landmark. The spirit of adventure which had filled him earlier had departed, but he knew there were houses all around him. He could find his way back to London as soon as it got light. Someone would tell him the way to the main road where he could hitch a lift. Then he'd find Biff and resume his normal life. That was, if he wanted to.

He extracted himself from the car, unfolding his thin legs, and standing outside it, looked about. It must be very early. As he stood there, the headlights of an approaching car shone on him, so he turned to walk in the direction in which it was travelling, to hide his face. The car went past without stopping. Denis walked slowly on down the road. No one seemed to be stirring. Wouldn't people soon be setting off for work? Few of his acquaintances had ever had a steady job but those who were employed often left home early. It took him some time to realise that this was Sunday. By then he had reached the centre of the town, where all the shops were shut and everything seemed to be completely dead.

Buses would run, wouldn't they? And weren't there corner shops which opened at all hours? He could buy anything he liked, he thought happily, now he'd got all that money. That had been a bit of luck. He felt no guilt: it was a good snatch: the chance came and he took it. Biff would have approved, but Biff needn't know about it, for he'd want half the pickings.

Though Denis had grown used to having Biff around, thinking of things to do for both of them and generally taking charge, he was also accustomed to being uprooted, plucked away from people he knew and dumped amid strangers. When he left the final home for good, officially a school-leaver but usually a truant, and now responsible for himself with no one to control him, he had felt quite pleased. Free, he could do as he liked. It was later that the fear crept in, the sense of isolation though the streets were full of people. He had never had a constant figure in his life. Soon, though, he made friends with other youngsters without families or homes. You saw a guy for a few days, a few weeks, and then he went away. Someone else would always come along. Denis thought it would be nice if there was a person to come back to, someone who would notice if you went missing. No one would, if he did. Even Biff would think he'd just moved on.

Maybe he had, anyway, for now.

Squaring his shoulders, Denis walked towards whatever the new day had to offer. He wouldn't mind another look at those woods and fields. He might even explore the idea he'd had of building a den in a wild spot. If you did that on waste ground in town, you were flushed out, but here, no one would care, for who would find you, unless it was that pack of dogs? They might, of course. That wouldn't be too nice.

He could find his way back to that place where the hunt had met, couldn't he? But what had it been called? Could he locate the spot where he'd got off the bus, and catch one travelling the other way? This wasn't much of a town; if he returned to the chip shop, he'd see where the bus had dropped him last evening.

He could find that house again, where he'd got the money. It had been an easy place to do, and there'd be more stuff there, like radios and such. On the other hand, he'd need to find somewhere to sell it on: before, he'd known which pubs to go to and where there were shops who'd deal. There'd be buyers in this place, too, but he'd have to track them down.

Normally, the days of the week made little difference to Denis, but on Sundays things were quieter. In one of the foster homes where he'd been briefly, sometimes at weekends rows had broken out between the adults; and the various children, not at school, had scrapped and quarrelled and got into mischief. He hadn't liked the rows, because during the week his foster mother had been nice. The foster father had had a job; he worked on the railway.

Lights were on in a newsagent's shop and it was busy. Denis saw some youngsters and a few older people coming out with heavy bags of papers. One boy wheeled a bike away. He could pick up one of those bikes, thought Denis; you could bet the kid wouldn't chain it up outside every house, nor wheel it in where there was a driveway. He'd remember that, in case he needed wheels. It would be better to nick a car, though, to get back to London. He'd never done that himself, but he'd been with Biff when he fancied a run around and he knew how to hotwire a car. Hadn't he got into that Maestro last night? He could have driven it off this morning, just like that, if he'd broken the lock.

But as it was, he'd done no harm. He hadn't even broken the door, just undone it with a piece of wire. Biff said you should always carry wire, a small screwdriver, and a good penknife with various gadgets on it; you could use it to defend yourself, if you had to, though a knife was described as an offensive weapon and you could be charged for carrying one.

He'd do things right today, though; then he needn't be looking out for cops. He'd got money, so he had no need to steal. He'd have a look around, see what was on offer here. There might be an amusement arcade. That, in Denis's experience, was the place to go to while away the day.

But Darsingford did not run to such delights. It had a population of twenty thousand, a weekly market on Wednesdays, eight pubs, and one two-star hotel, five churches of differing denominations, two primary schools and a mixed comprehensive school which catered for a wide area around the town. There were industrial outcrops on the perimeter: furniture emporia, a do-it-yourself superstore, packing depots for health foods and cosmetics, and the scientific research complex where Guy Frost worked.

Denis did not get as far as these working outposts on that Sunday morning, though he had passed some of them on his bus ride into town. He found it hard to take in that the place was so small. Until his trips with Biff, his whole experience had been urban. He had never lived where the buildings ran out into empty landscape. If he kept going long enough on foot, he'd see fields and trees again. It was weird!

He could pick up a car and go driving down those little roads until it ran out of petrol. Even then, he had enough money to put more in the tank. He might do it for a laugh.

He wasn't bored yet. He went on and eventually he reached a river. Once again it was a lovely day, and Denis walked along the towpath till he reached a bench seat. There, he sat down to count his money. He could do that, well enough.

There was, he calculated, nearly two hundred pounds. Frances Dixon had just collected two weeks' pension from the post office, and she already had some money in her purse. Such an enormous sum spelled bliss to Denis. It would last him for a long time, though he'd rather like to buy a new pair of trainers. Maybe he could steal some.

Quite a lot was happening on the river. A skiff with two men rowing went past. They'd got up early, Denis thought: so had he, much earlier than was usual for him. Then two bigger boats slid by, with four oarsmen in each, and a cox. A jogger came along the path, panting and intent on his solitary progress. To look at him made Denis feel quite tired. He got up, and walked slowly on towards a bridge. He was very hungry, but he hadn't seen a single snack bar or café, though near the bridge there was one shuttered building which looked as though it might sell food. He could read the word SHUT on a sign on the door. Certain words, by usage, were familiar to him, and he could sign his name.

Reaching the bridge, he went up some steps and made his way back into the town. The main street was a little busier by this time; he found a supermarket which was open, and went in to buy something to eat.

It was a lovely shop, he thought: huge. At home he bought food from corner shops; though he sometimes walked round large stores, even nicking stuff from some of them, he was never an official customer. Now, he picked up a basket and went round the loaded shelves. What you could do with money! It would be good to have a regular supply but because Denis had no fixed address at present, he did not qualify for state aid.

He could get a fixed address here but he'd have to be in it for six months before he'd receive any money. At least, that was what he thought was the regulation. It'd be easy to find places for sleeping here, however, with all this space. Maybe there was a hostel, but he couldn't read any notice there might be which would tell him.

He bought a can of Coca-Cola, a Bounty Bar and some crisps, paying for them very circumspectly at the checkout. Then he went back to the river bank to eat his feast. He was sitting there when Philip Winter came along the towpath. He, too, had been shopping in the supermarket, and he had bought a date-expired pack of cheese sandwiches and a small bunch of bananas. He sat down at the other end of Denis's bench, and started on his meal, washing it down with water from his bottle.

Because the weather was good, Philip had decided not to spend his gardening money on a bed; he'd need that when the rain came, and the frost. He'd spent the night wrapped in his trench-coat, over his new warm jacket, on the towpath underneath the bridge. He'd looked around the town, after he arrived there, and passed the evening in a pub, choosing one which looked as though it might be quiet. Darsingford was still a country town, though the night life could include rowdiness and there had been the arson attack on the scientist, but on that Saturday night, Philip was able to avoid all fracas, and after midnight the river bank was quiet. Even the traffic crossing the bridge was minimal.

The shabby, grubby youth already on the bench looked up when Philip sat beside him. From his largesse, Denis offered the man, who he could see at a glance was down on his luck, a packet of crisps. Philip hesitated; then he accepted it.

'Thanks,' he said, and added, 'Have a sandwich.'

'You've only got the two,' said Denis. 'I've got plenty,' and he displayed the contents of his supermarket bag.

In his former life, Philip would no more have dreamed of speaking to a scruffy lad like this than he would have thought of flying to the moon. He was the sort of person to avoid for fear of being mugged. At best, he looked like one of the beggars in the London streets. Philip sometimes tossed coins into their caps or bowls; more often he walked past, deciding they had wished themselves into this condition. He'd done that: he'd run off, of his own free will, and now he was a destitute person. Here was, presumably, another.

'I've got some bananas, too,' said Philip. 'Have one of those, if you'd prefer it.'

'Ta,' said Denis.

They sat there munching in companionable silence. Two cabin cruisers chugged past, their occupants enjoying a last autumn weekend on the river.

'Must be great on one of them boats,' said Denis.

'Yes,' agreed Philip, who had once spent a holiday on the Norfolk Broads in such a vessel when the children were quite young.

'Come far?' asked Denis.

'Yes. A long way,' Philip said. He had come a great distance, not only in miles but in perceptions and experience. 'And you?'

'Yeah. From London,' Denis said. 'I don't know if

I'll stay, though. What's this place called? D'you know?'

'Darsingford,' said Philip.

'Oh.' Denis frowned. He'd heard that name before.

'How did you get here?' Philip asked, genuinely interested. Then he thought perhaps he should not have asked: there might well be some code among tramps and down-and-outs, a moratorium on curiosity.

But the lad did not seem to mind. He must be around Andrew's age, or somewhat younger, Philip thought, as Denis answered.

'I came with some mates. They went back and I didn't,' Denis told him.

'Oh.'

'We were in this wood,' said Denis, suddenly confidential. 'It was great.'

What was? The wood, or what went on there? Was he part of some cult?

'There were these dogs, see. They was going to catch a fox if they could find one. I suppose it's cruel, really,' he added, thoughtfully. 'But it didn't seem like that.'

He'd come with hunt saboteurs, Philip realised. He had no opinion in this dispute; an urban man, he lacked knowledge of country ways, but if hunting was banned, what about shooting and fishing? And what about all the associated jobs and businesses?

'Where did you spend the night?' he asked.

Denis told him about the car.

Two weeks ago, Philip would have been deeply shocked and disapproving. Now, he felt admiration for the boy's nerve.

'I've got some money, though,' Denis could not avoid boasting. 'I had a bit of luck,' he added.

Philip was not going to enquire into the nature of this piece of good fortune.

'That's good,' he said. 'Are you going back to London?'

'Not yet,' said Denis. 'I'd thought of camping in the wood, just for a bit. It's not far away. I came in on a bus.' He couldn't remember what the place was called, where he'd picked up the purse. CH something, it was, like chips. He could recognise that word.

'Got a tent?' asked Philip.

'No. I could make a hut, with branches,' Denis said.

'Be a bit chilly. The nights are cold now.'

'I could make a fire. Cook sausages and stuff.'

'People would see the smoke and come and shift you,' Philip said.

'People always mess things,' said Denis. 'Where did you spend the night, then?'

Philip told him.

'I had a wash in the public toilet,' he said. It hadn't been too wonderful. Some drunken citizens had left their marks there, all too noticeably.

'What are you going to do today, then?' Denis asked.

'I don't know,' said Philip. 'Everything's shut, or nearly everything. I want to get a job. I was going to look for advertisements in shop windows. Newsagents usually have them.' He'd seen some in the supermarket, too, but hadn't stopped to study them. 'I got some gardening yesterday,' he added proudly. 'Made ten pounds.'

Perhaps he shouldn't have said that. The lad might try to take it from him.

But Denis said, 'Great. That must be quite good. Gardening. It's in the space.'

What an odd remark, thought Philip.

'That's true,' he said. 'There's not a lot of it to do in winter, though. We're lucky that the weather's good at present.'

'Yeah. It is nice, isn't it?' said Denis. 'You don't see it in the city. The weather.'

'I suppose not.' Philip stood up. 'I'm moving on,' he said.

'Mind if I come with you to look at them adverts?' Denis asked. 'I might try for something, too.' This guy would read them out to him.

'Good idea,' said Philip. Then he smiled and held out his hand. 'I'm Phil,' he added. 'What's your name?'

Denis told him, as they both shook hands.

10

'NOT MUCH GOING on, is there?' Denis said, as they walked back into the town.

'Well, it's just a country town,' said Philip. 'It must have been built here because of a shallow place where you could cross the river easily. A ford. That's how it got it's name. There are other towns named like that – Oxford, for instance. Cross on foot, I mean,' he added, seeing Denis looking puzzled.

'Oh.'

There were more people about now and the traffic was increasing. The river was busier; a few boats were still available for hire and were being rowed downstream past them as they approached the bridge. There was a family group, the father, and the son, aged about twelve, manful at the oars, the mother steering and a small girl in the bow trailing her hands in water that must, Philip thought, be rather cold. Denis watched them, amazed. Lucky sods.

'Nice way to spend a fine Sunday,' said Philip.

'Suppose it costs a lot,' said Denis.

'I've no idea how much it is,' said Philip.

They went on, at length reaching the super-market where a notice in the window said that shelf packers were required. Philip took a pencil and diary out of his pocket and wrote down the details, with the telephone number. Denis was staring at the notice, trying to make out the words that Philip had just read.

'Let's try the newsagent,' Philip said. 'There might be more to chose from, there.' There might be rooms to let, as well. He wondered if there was a Darsingford local paper; probably there was, and it would have details both of jobs and lodgings.

They made their way along the pavement where by now there were enough pedestrians to force them sometimes into single file. Philip caught sight of their reflection in the large plate-glass window of a shop selling furniture. He could barely recognise himself: the thick donkey jacket made him look almost sturdy. His hair seemed to have grown a lot and developed strong curls, and his beard was quite respectable. It needed neatening up, he thought: or should he let it flow, become like Edward Lear's? The disguise would be complete, but would a prospective employer be put off? Beside him was the scraggy figure of the youth: Denis's legs were spindle-thin in the tattered, faded jeans. His train-ers were cracked and splitting; they must let in the wet. His anorak must once have been a warm beige colour but now it was stained and faded. He loped along, his face thin and pointed, fair wispy hair on end, his feeble stubble gleaming in the sun. How different he would look cleaned up and given fresh clothes, thought Philip, so used to inspecting junior staff.

The newsagent's was closed now. Its door was full of cards and the two stood looking at them, Denis baffled, Philip scanning them swiftly. One sounded dubious: French lessons given by genuine Frenchwoman, ring after 5 p.m. Then he remembered that this was Darsingford; she might really be a teacher, not a prostitute. He pointed to a postcard.

'That looks possible, for me. Or for you,' Philip added generously. 'I expect you can drive.'

'Yeah,' said Denis, and added, 'But I haven't got a licence. Which one d'you mean?'

'That one.' Philip gestured at a card. It said that a van driver was required, clean licence. Otherwise, apart from a telephone number, there were no details.

Denis stared at where his finger pointed. He tried to spell the words out, then turned away quickly, lest Philip realise his inability to make it out.

'Yeah,' he said.

'There's one for you, if you'd got a car or motorbike,' Philip said. 'Look.'

Once again, Denis concentrated on the card he indicated.

'I can't work out the writing,' he prevaricated.

'Pizza deliverer required. Own transport needed,'

Philip read aloud. The message was not typed, that was true; it was, however, very clearly printed. 'Good pay and mileage allowance,' he added. Denis watched the words as he read them, trying to take them in. Phil went too fast for him. He could pick out the D – his own name began with that. He looked for E, and the other letters in it and found them all. That made him smile.

Philip was watching him. The boy couldn't read, or not properly. You heard about adult illiteracy; here it was, right in front of him. Poor kid. He read out several other advertisements, slowly, a finger on each word as he repeated it. Cleaners were wanted; items were for sale. Philip wrote down the telephone number where the van driver was required.

'I'll try it in the morning,' he told Denis.

'Try it now,' said Denis.

'But it's Sunday. There'll be no one there.'

'You can't know that till you try,' said Denis, quoting a favourite phrase of Biff's.

'That's true. All right. I'll do it,' Philip said.

They walked on until they found a public telephone. It needed a phone card, but Philip had one in his wallet. He had always kept one for emergencies.

To his astonishment, the number answered, and he came away having arranged to be interviewed later in the day.

'The man needs a driver as he's lost his licence.' Philip was almost chuckling. 'He's desperate! I must clean myself up a bit, Denis. I need somewhere better than those public toilets near the bridge.'

'Try a pub,' said Denis. 'Best buy a drink, of course.'

'Good idea,' said Philip. 'You coming?'

'Sure,' said Denis.

Philip bought them each a lager from his tenner of the previous day. He drank half his, then went to the cloakroom, which wasn't wonderful but at least had hot and cold water, and some paper towels. He'd chosen, in the end, the public bar of the two-star hotel, adopting a bold demeanour as he entered, since they were a pair of down-market customers. They attracted some curious glances but the Sunday drinkers soon lost interest. Philip returned with slicked-down hair and a shining face, and wearing his clean underclothes and socks: amazing what it did for you.

'You could do with a wash too, Denis,' he told his companion.

Denis went meekly off. He needed the toilet, but hadn't thought of washing. He did, though, since it seemed to mean a lot to Phil.

While he was gone, Philip had thought of walking out and leaving him. How else was he to shed the youth? Then he remembered that Denis had offered him the crisps. He stayed.

The pub was warm and full of noise, the customers mostly couples in their thirties and forties, but some men on their own. Philip watched them while he waited. What about their Sunday lunch? Had they given up the habit, as so many people had? He and Lesley had maintained it; she was a good cook and it was a time when all of them met round the table and could talk. But had they communicated? These people in the pub were talking, but were they getting through to one another? If he and Lesley had really been in touch, would she have lost faith in him?

Denis was not gone long. He reappeared with a clean face and still grubby hands. The dirt in them seemed to be ingrained; his nails were bitten and he had a crooked finger on his left hand. He looked so pale, his pallor pocked with small outcrops of acne. The country air down here would do him good, thought Philip, as they left the hotel.

Philip's interview was at an address to the south of the town. He had tried to take in the directions he had been given on the telephone but was none too clear about where he had to go after he had crossed the river.

'I'll ask someone when I get near,' he told Denis. 'Right, then. Goodbye, Denis. Good luck.'

'Hope you get the job, mate,' Denis said.

Watching the older man walk away, he felt suddenly bereft. It had been good, the last few hours, going round with Phil. For an old bloke, he was all right. If he hung about, they might meet again later; Phil could do with a bit of help over finding a place to doss down in, if he didn't get the job.

After a while, Denis decided to follow him.

* * *

Crossing the bridge, Philip wondered if he should have changed into his trench-coat, then decided that a potential van driver should project a rugged image; his new beard and longer hair fitted in with this type-casting. For over twenty years he'd been a suited citizen; perhaps it was time for a change.

What would Denis do now? Would he stay in Darsingford, where there couldn't be much going on that would appeal to him, or would he decide to head back to London? He'd get a lift eventually: you did, if you waited long enough; Philip had learned that. What chance had the boy got? He had probably never had a job. He seemed taken with the great outdoors: in other circumstances and in an earlier generation he could have found employment on the land. Civilisation, with its so-called blessings and its labour-saving devices, had not contributed all that much to human happiness, Philip decided, marching stoutly onwards on the main road, which he had been told to follow until he met a rounda-bout where he must turn left. He followed these instructions, continuing along this lesser, resi-dential road until he came to a park, and here he had to turn right. Fortunately, he remembered what he had been told about the route and soon he found himself in Wilton Road, where the advertiser lived in Number Twenty-Three.

He found the house, a thirties semi-detached set well back from the road behind a privet hedge.

Philip took a deep breath, walked up the path and rang the bell.

* * *

Denis kept Philip's tall, thin form in view. The bulky jacket gave him breadth, but he was not a powerful man. Denis did not wonder why he was on his own and sleeping rough; you met all sorts on the streets and it was better not to be too curious. Bad luck could hit anyone. He might have been inside; that was the most likely reason for him to be wandering about, without work. An educated man like Phil ought to be able to get a job if he really tried.

When he turned off the main road something struck Denis as familiar, but he couldn't have been here before, could he? He walked on, and saw the park, and Philip far ahead of him. Denis had been to so few places in his life that it wasn't difficult to eliminate possibilities as he ran them through his mind. Was this the town where he had come with Biff and Tessa, and Orlando? He hadn't recognised it yesterday, but then they had only driven to the house Tessa hit, and away again.

He saw Philip cross the road and turn right. Denis, hanging back, did the same. It was the place where Tessa had fired the shots. They'd waited for her here, by this junction, looking out towards the park. He was sure of it: it was weird.

Well, so what? Philip wasn't going into the same house; he'd already walked past the one where Tessa had carried out her mission.

Denis didn't, though. He walked right up to the front door and rang the bell. He'd say that it was

135

Sunday and had they been to church? Had they been saved? He had. Biff had tried this ruse several times, he'd told Denis, and had been rudely told to go away on two occasions, but once, it had worked well. He'd got into the house, asked for a glass of water, and while it was fetched, lifted some useful stuff. All you needed was a story to get you to the door. Another trick was to have a few bits and pieces for sale: tat picked up in a market. Proper pedlars had licences; a householder might ask to see one, but that didn't matter because the trick had served its purpose and you'd discovered that some-one was at home. Those who asked were capable of ringing the police, so it was best to move on if that was your reception. If the house was empty, you could look for a way to enter.

When Denis rang the bell, he had his story ready. He adopted a meek expression, glad now that he had washed earlier, though you didn't have to be clean to be religious. There was some noise behind the door, and he heard a man's voice. It was too late to flee; he stood ready to brazen it out.

On the chain, the door was opened, and he faced Guy Frost, who had had a peephole fitted and unless the person on the step was recognised, insisted that the chain be used.

Denis saw a thickset, balding man. He wore spectacles with metal rims, and had very strongly marked eyebrows. Guy, in his turn, saw a grubby spindly youth who looked nervous.

Denis went immediately into his spiel about

Sunday but Guy cut him short.

'Go away at once or I'll telephone the police,' he said curtly, and banged the door shut.

Biff would have been angry at such a hostile response, and on his way out might have uprooted a plant or done some other minor damage, but Denis, made of frailer stuff, merely shrugged and went away.

Guy telephoned the police, however. The slightest suspicious incident must be reported. The young man had been alone, when most proselytisers came in twos and threes; he'd held no book nor pack of texts, and though he'd fastened an ingenuous gaze on Guy, he hadn't looked quite honest.

Denis didn't hang about; he knew when he'd been sussed. He hurried back the way he'd come, and went into the park. He was sitting on a bench there when a police car drove past. He hoped the fuzz wouldn't stop Philip and ask him questions; Denis didn't think he'd be very pleased.

He waited quite a while before returning to the centre of the town. He'd blown it, and he'd never know, now, if Phil had got the job.

11

ORLANDO WAS VERY worried by Tessa's action against the scientist, and he was afraid the police might trace them. That would be so dreadful. Quite apart from being arrested, tried, and even sent to prison, the disgrace would be a nightmare. He'd lose his job, and wouldn't Tessa be struck off, or whatever happened to law-breaking lawyers? And what about her father, an enlightened judge who tried, when not tied up by coils of legal string, to fit the sentence to the crime? How would he survive the notoriety of his daughter's trial?

Tessa was sure they wouldn't be caught. When they met, she refused to talk about it. They'd been on no more raids since then, not even demonstrations organised by recognised protestors. Orlando was thankful. It was wise to lie low for a while. This meant, however, that he saw much less of her because she didn't need him or the recruits he drummed up to add muscle to their exploits. Why did she want them, though? Biff, it was true, had gone with her to reconnoitre on that trip to Darsingford, but the two of them could have done it on their own: why Biff? Perhaps she knew that he, Orlando, would have tried to talk her out of the domestic part of the escapade, and it was true that several people spraying walls were more effective than only one or two. Tessa hadn't done any actual spraying and Biff had lobbed the petrol bombs over the wall. Maybe she was hedging her bets. None of the other four had any idea who Tessa really was; they knew only her first name. They had, however, seen her car.

He fretted about her. To take his mind off this preoccupation, Orlando had begun to persecute Mrs Sandra White, the unnamed false accuser of the unfortunate Philip Winter who had gone missing. The man's disappearance had sparked off this plan. Poor guy, it could have been the fate of any man who misread the signals. He wouldn't put it past Tessa, if she found her private space threatened, to do the same. But no; she would scorn such conduct. Tessa would never let such a situation develop. It would be a reckless man who tried anything on with Tessa without making sure his attentions were welcome. Orlando could never understand why she sometimes favoured him; maybe it was pity, because she knew he loved her so desperately. In her kinder moods, no one could be sweeter; she was much respected in her firm, and popular.

Though they'd met Biff together, on a demonstration at the docks, she'd never asked how
Orlando had acquired the rest of the team. He'd
discovered Jet one day when killing time in a bar in
Covent Garden. He was going, on his own, to a
concert. Orlando had a wide casual acquaintance
among patrons of various bars in the area, but he
was not part of any close, involved group. Standing
alone, he saw a thin, dark girl, also alone, who was
approached by a big blond man, a broker Orlando
knew by sight. The man had begun talking to her,
pinning her against a pillar. Jet had replied brus-
quely, turning her head away, but the man had been
persistent, moving nearer, closing her line of
retreat. Orlando had stepped forward. Physically, he
was no match for the broker, who could have floored
him with one blow, but in his own way, Orlando
was a smooth operator.

'Ah – there you are, Jet,' he said, coming round
behind the broker to Jet's side. He beamed at her.
'Sorry – I couldn't see you in this crowd. You must
have wondered if I'd stood you up – as if I would!
Have you got a drink?' She had. She was holding a
glass which turned out to contain apple juice.
'Excuse me,' he addressed the broker. 'Do you
mind?' and he elbowed the man aside.

The broker, scowling, moved away, and Orlando,
pleased at his success, was also embarrassed, ready
for tough talk from Jet, because some girls – like
Tessa – wouldn't thank you for a rescue, saying they
could handle the situation themselves. This one,

though, had looked apprehensive, and she was so small.

And she was grateful.

'Thanks very much,' she said, and smiled. 'Why did you call me Jet?'

'Well, I was pretending we had a date, and I thought saying darling might seem presumptuous,' he said. 'Your hair's so gorgeous, just like jet,' he added, to explain. 'The name came to me in a flash.'

'Felicitous,' she suggested, and he agreed.

'I don't suppose it is your name,' he said.

'No, it's not,' she said. 'But you can use it.' She didn't tell him what her real name was. 'I am waiting for someone,' she went on. 'And he's late.'

'I'll stay with you until he arrives, then,' said Orlando. 'If that's all right?'

'I'd be glad,' she said.

He thought that she was pretty, and her thick, shining hair, cut to just below her ears, was beautiful. He hoped her expected date would fail to arrive. At that moment, Orlando was prepared to abandon his concert and risk inviting her to dinner, but then Steven appeared, a pale, thin lad looking just like many others you saw around. It seemed that they were students.

After that, returning to the bar once or twice a week, Orlando ran into them again and several times bought them dinner. Most students were hard-up, and these two displayed endearingly hearty appetites. When Tessa required extra recruits, he asked them what they felt about

imperilled wildlife, and had no difficulty in trans-
forming their vague views into firm belief in the
justice of the cause. The chance of spending a day
together at no cost, and, in fact, being paid,
completed their conversion. Soon Jet developed real
enthusiasm, shouting slogans and brandishing banners; Steven caught fire from her, yelling loudly and
waving his fist. Orlando thought that these two had
developed into the most dedicated of them all, not
excepting Tessa, and they went on other demonstrations, ones not patronised by either Tessa or
Orlando. He began to wonder if they were becoming excited by the event as much as by the cause.
Reasons could be blurred. He, for instance, used any
excuse to pursue Tessa.

Pestering Mrs Sandra White made an excellent
diversion, and he was grateful that he had learned
her identity so easily. He would have tracked her
down, even if it meant telephoning every S. White
in London – quite a task – but Tessa had simply
handed him the information. He wrote her several
letters, and delivered one in person to the block of
flats. It was a good address; she must be comfortably
off.

He'd asked Tessa what she thought about the
case.

'The man couldn't have scored. She wouldn't
have waited before complaining,' Tessa said.
'There'd have been definite evidence. She could have
scratched his face when he turned her down, as he
said had happened.'

'Doesn't a man also have the right to say no?' asked Orlando, and at that Tessa had laughed and, to his delighted astonishment, had kissed him.

'Do you want to say no now?' she'd asked.

'My God, no! I mean, no, I don't want to,' he'd replied, but even as he banished all his caution, he recognised that Tessa was capable of turning this situation around in a sudden change of mood and making it seem quite different. She was hardly a tranquil companion. Wherever had she got this wild side of her nature from?

He ordered a pizza for Mrs White, saying she would pay on delivery. He used a public call box, and watched the delivery arrive. In the end she paid, to get rid of the unpleasantness, coming down to the main front door to do so. He saw her then. He would recognise her now.

Sandra herself did not connect the false order with the newspaper cuttings and some anonymous letters she had received. It was only when further incidents occurred that she began to take the matter seriously.

Seeing her, putting a face to the woman who had been vicious enough to bring down a harmless, if ingenuous man, spurred Orlando on to further efforts. Devising them stopped him brooding about Tessa, or growing bored. The woman, seen in the lighting from a street lamp, was quite tall; she had dark hair, and was slim, in a black skirt and high-heeled shoes, and a black sweater. Orlando had waited not too far away, standing near a bus stop; he pretended to be looking at his evening paper.

He sent her some old, stale cod, wrapped in layers of clingfilm inside a padded bag. He posted it from a post office in the country, where he had gone to spend a weekend with a couple he had known since university. By the time it reached her, it was stinking, but she had to unwrap the outer covering to find that out. His next gambit was to telephone the electricity board, reporting a fault with the cooker, arranging for someone to come and mend it. He simply hoped she would be in when the fitter arrived; if not, at least she'd have the bother of his card to deal with, and his follow-up, assuming there would be one. He spent long periods of time trying to arrange new torments. He filled in advertisement coupons with her name and address so that brochures on every conceivable subject would arrive for her. Some of the products covered were of a nature to embarrass her. He chuckled, completing those.

His most ambitious scheme was sending her tickets to a city dinner which he was attending and at which, miraculously, Tessa had agreed to be his partner. He photocopied the invitation, deleting his own name, traced it on to a piece of heavy gilt-edged card which he bought at an art shop, then painstakingly inked it over. It was not embossed, but it might deceive her. He wrote her name on it – Mrs Sandra White and partner – in italic script.

He couldn't loiter at the entrance to the city hall where the dinner was taking place, though he would have liked to witness her reception, if she turned up, but he did hear later that a couple had arrived who were not on the guest list. Orlando did not know that Sandra White had hired her partner from an escort agency, and had had to pay him as well as suffer the embarrassment of being denied admittance.

After this, Sandra realised that she was the subject of a vendetta. Who could be doing this to her? Who was playing all these tricks? The fish wrappings had been thrown away – the smell seemed to cling to her hands for hours, no matter how often and how thoroughly she washed them – but she kept the letters.

Orlando had started to follow her – not frequently, for he had very little opportunity in the working week – but he began on a Saturday when he had nothing planned. He decided to wait outside her block of flats for half an hour or so, to see if she emerged. If she did, he'd pursue her.

He could hardly believe it when the big door opened and she came out. Now, in daylight, he could see her much more clearly. She wore a suede coat and had on high-heeled boots. He followed her as she stepped aboard a bus.

She left after only a few stops, and went into Lavery's, the very store where Philip Winter had worked. There, she sauntered through various sections, and, in the glass and china department, examined several bowls and vases. Orlando started looking at them too, and when she took a cut-glass bowl to the pay desk, he selected a small pottery vase that was not expensive, and lined up behind her. He'd use cash. He didn't want to leave a trail. The vase was nice enough to give someone for Christmas, which was not far off now; the store was very busy with people buying presents.

An assistant who knew nothing about her story served Mrs White. The next customer seemed to be chafing with impatience while his purchase was wrapped, but the salesman scarcely noticed his appearance.

Orlando caught up with Sandra as she wandered through soft furnishings; she eyed curtain fabric, studied bedspreads, and moved on to towels and bath accessories. He tried to think of a way to humiliate her in the store without discovery, but there would be surveillance cameras watching everyone, and the two of them were doubtless already captured on tape. Annoying someone anonymously was challenging. It was just as well, for the sake of the innocent. But she wasn't innocent; he was sure of it. Here was a woman who was in charge of her own life, confident and assured.

What if he got to know her? Suppose he somehow contrived to talk to her – pick her up – get friendly? Could he lead her on to make an approach to him and catch her out? That was entrapment, wasn't it? Sometimes it was a questionable ploy, but it could be justified. What could he do with the evidence, if he obtained it? He couldn't sue her; that would be too costly, but he'd have a defence if she accused him of rape.

He thought about it, following her out of the shop. She walked down the street, turned a corner, and went into a small new restaurant which was popular among the women with whom Sandra played bridge two afternoons a week. At weekends they were often busy with their families, and she had time to fill. She would go to the cinema, or to a theatre matinée, and occasionally to a gallery or on excursions to stately homes or gardens, always seeking company, but, too intense, she ran through so-called friends fast. They dropped her. Only the bridge club remained constant because she played well, and when it was her turn to be hostess, the refreshments she supplied were excellent.

These women knew nothing about her appearance in court. They wondered why she had no career. They were older than Sandra, with husbands near retirement, and all had interests outside their homes. If she did not need a salary, she had energy and time to work in some constructive way, maybe for a charity, they thought.

Apart from their bridge games, Sandra never met them, though she knew they saw each other. She had been drawn into the group when one member moved to Norfolk. Sandra had met another on a bridge weekend at a country hotel, and thus was asked to join.

She hoped she might run into an acquaintance at the restaurant. Sandra was very lonely.

She was bitter, too: her husband's abandonment of her in favour of a typist from his office had humiliated her. He had two children now and lived in Sussex. She'd made him pay in terms of cash, and as long as she was single and not earning, he would have to go on supporting her in considerable style. Such were the terms of her settlement.

Orlando knew none of this as he followed her into the restaurant, which was run by an Italian family but provided an eclectic menu. He wondered if she was meeting someone, but when he was shown to a table in a dark corner, he looked across the room and saw her sitting at another set for one. A half bottle of white wine appeared before her very swiftly, and he decided she was a regular customer; she was treated with some deference and he thought she must be a good tipper, but changed this opinion when she called the head waiter over and made some point about her first course. It looked like Parma ham; how could that be faulty? He decided she was an imperious person who could cause trouble if her every whim was not gratified.

Halfway through the main course she glanced at him, and, when he did not immediately look away, she held his gaze. Orlando felt a frisson, not of sexual excitement but of something more like his emotions when going on a raid with Tessa: half fear, half thrill. He let himself meet her glance a second time and then, with an insouciance he could never summon when he was with Tessa, he raised his glass in silent toast, expecting her to frown and turn away. To his astonishment, she responded, raising her glass and tossing her head almost flirtatiously.

Because he knew her history, he felt disgust: but wasn't this evidence that, like a spider, she was capable of luring the unfortunate Philip Winter into her web, ready for the kill?

She did not know that he, Orlando, was responsible for the recent irritations which had come her way. The knowledge gave him pleasure.

He finished his meal before she did, and left, not wanting her to think he would be easily ensnared. Next time, she would be the victim.

Orlando had not seen any of his team since the episode in Darsingford. He missed Jet and Steven. His means of communicating with them was imprecise; after each encounter they had either arranged to meet at a pub, or Jet had telephoned him. He knew their full names now, however, and their addresses in term-time. In return, he'd told them his, and truthfully, though this was contrary to Tessa's rules.

'If they don't know who we are, they can't cause us any future trouble,' she had said, but Orlando thought the young people risked more than he and Tessa; Biff and the new recruit, Denis, were likely to be known to the police, though probably Jet and Steven had blameless pasts.

Having fixed, with a different pizza company, for Mrs Sandra White to receive another order, Orlando sent a note to Jet, saying that in two days' time he would be in the bar where they had originally met at six o'clock, and hoped that she and Steve might be there too.

On the way, he met Biff who was begging in a subway. Orlando stopped. He couldn't walk right past.

'Hi there, Biff,' he said. 'How's everything?'

Biff, who was sitting cross-legged on the ground, looked up and shrugged. He indicated an upturned cap in which there were a few small coins.

'Not good, squire,' he said. He'd started calling Orlando 'squire' as a joke and the habit had stuck.

Orlando fumbled in his wallet and found a ten-pound note. Silently, he dropped it in the cap and, also silently, Biff palmed it and transferred it to his pocket.

'How's Denis?' asked Orlando.

'All right,' said Biff, lying, for he did not know.

He'd worried a bit about Denis, when he wasn't in the minibus after the hunt saboteurs' expedition. Still, he'd thumb a ride back. After such a day, begging was dull, but as a rule he did quite well. His cheerful, if grubby, round face and large brown eyes appealed to passers by. Biff never intimidated them; that wasn't his tactic.

He'd been thinking of looking for Orlando. He knew his mobile phone telephone number, for Orlando had had to open up some line of communication and he could not rely on finding Biff.

Now, Biff got to his feet.

'Seen Tessa lately?' he asked. 'She got any plans for the weekend?'

'Not that I know of,' said Orlando.

'She's great,' said Biff, and his face took on a knowing expression. A smile curved his mouth under his scruffy unshaven upper lip, and the word lascivious came, unbidden, into Orlando's mind.

She wouldn't, he thought, genuinely shocked.

He remembered how he and the three others had been sent on a long walk while she and Biff went off alone. She could have, and she might: anything for a buzz.

'Yes, she is,' he agreed, in despair.

'We might do one of them farms,' said Biff. 'Where they take those little calves from, scarcely dry from their mother's innards. Cruel, it is.'

'I'll tell her you suggested it, when I see her,' said Orlando. 'Cheers,' and he walked on. Tessa carried out her wilder deeds for kicks; he went with her because he was in love with her. Biff came for the ride and the money pay-off; probably only Jet and Steve came from conviction, he reflected.

Why did he bother with Tessa, Orlando asked himself, standing on the escalator. There was no future in it; she'd toss him aside as easily as she had shot those rabbits. Yet she fascinated him, as a snake is fascinating. She was wonderful in bed and that was part of it; she even made him feel that he was special then, when he knew that he was a very ordinary man, competent at his job but no more, nothing much to write home about. If they were to marry, he would never know a moment's peace for fear of what she might be up to, but think of the delights that there would be!

Sitting in the train, he pictured children, dim figures flitting across the lawn of the judicial garden, with James and Millicent fond presences in the background, but where was his place in this idyllic scene? And where was Tessa?

She'd have no children; not his, not anyone's. He had a sudden intense feeling of impending doom, but dismissed it as caused by jealousy because he knew that Biff and Tessa had had it off together. His mind raced on. Did Biff do drugs? Orlando knew that he mixed with criminals. Needles, he thought: shared ones. Aids.

He shut his mind down on that possibility, stepping from the Tube. He'd think about Sandra White instead.

If he caught Aids from Tessa, could he pass it on to Sandra White? That would be a fine revenge, he thought. Perhaps he should try to pick her up, become overtly friendly with her, prepare the ground. She'd almost given him a signal in the restaurant, and if Philip Winter's story was true, she wouldn't need much wooing; she was a nymphomaniac.

Meanwhile, he'd made out an interesting advertisement for her, a business card he'd had done at one of those machines where they could be printed instantly.

Madame Sandra, it said, in Gothic script, and ran on to offer:

Interesting massage. All tastes, followed by her telephone number.

That was all: it was enigmatic. She'd get enough calls to be a serious nuisance. He'd stuck the cards in telephone booths and in various public lavatories, always taking care that no one saw him. He was not going to risk shop windows or newspapers, where they might question his identity. He sent them, also, to a number of men who advertised in Lonely Hearts columns. A few might bite.

Neither Steve nor Jet turned up at the bar. Disappointed, and lonely himself, Orlando went to the cinema, then home to bed. He dreamed, surprisingly, of Jet. She was screaming, pleading to be saved from some black horror that was threatening her. He woke without discovering what it was.

12

SANDRA WHITE WAS a very angry woman. Several unordered pizza deliveries had been made to her flat, and now she was receiving junk mail by the bundle. Brochures she had never sent for arrived daily; they advertised all sorts of goods from holidays to incontinence pads and contraception. She had written to the Mailing Preferences address, demanding that her name be withdrawn from any data base that could be providing it to companies, but still the brochures came, for Orlando filled in a new coupon almost daily.

Sandra tried to divert her mind from this nuisance by remembering the man she had seen in the restaurant. He had been quite nice-looking in an ordinary, mousey-haired, blue-eyed way, reasonably tall, and his casual dress was good. She knew that he had noticed her. Sandra wanted a lover, one she could control. She'd even thought of replying to some of the dating advertisements in a glossy paper, but so far an innate caution had prevented her. Besides, it would mean admitting that she had been unable to find a man another way. But how did you, these days? People did not ask her to parties, where she might meet an unattached male, and she shrank from going on holidays aimed at singles. She went to aerobics classes – all women – and had aroma-therapy, which was soothing, and there was her bridge. When nothing else offered, she read block-buster novels and wished that she was one of their successful women characters. She wanted power, and she had very little, except that she could make waiters, shop assistants and other inferior persons squirm.

Like that Philip Winter man. She had made him pay for his rejection of her. Now, it seemed, he'd drowned himself. Well, he was no great loss. She'd bought one of the tabloids when the story broke, and had read a sensationalised re-run of the trial. There were pictures of him and of the discontented-looking wife who had failed, it was implied, to offer him support. His family life was wrecked. So what, thought Sandra; he deserved it. She did not care if he were alive or dead: good riddance, for he had beaten her in court.

At first she hadn't meant to let it go so far, intending merely to get him into trouble at Lavery's, perhaps lose his job, because she did not want to see him there when she went shopping and she would not give up going to the store. Once started, however, the process had grown and grown, until she became elated at the lengths to which the man could be hounded down and, in the end, destroyed. The exhilaration of it had kept her going through the months before the case came to court.

They'd tried to dissuade her, of course: first the police and then her solicitor. They'd told her she'd be crucified. Well, they were wrong; it had not happened. It was Philip Winter who was pilloried, not her. She'd stood up to their questioning, implacable and cold. By paying Philip Winter out, she had avenged herself on other men who had failed her in her life, particularly her former husband.

It was some time before she began to wonder if Philip were still alive, and whether it was he who was subjecting her to all this harassment, and then she didn't think of this herself. She had notified the police after she had received more than thirty telephone calls which implied that she was a prostitute. The callers had even used her name.

'Have you any enemies?' she was asked. 'Someone with a grudge against you?'

But the police knew she had. They were the same officers who had investigated her rape charge. The problem was that it seemed her alleged attacker was now dead.

There were no clues to who was behind this present campaign. Sandra was able to name the last pizza firm, and the police said they would try to discover who had given the order, but were not optimistic. They'd be in touch, they said. Meanwhile, she should consider, if the trouble did not cease, changing her telephone number and going ex-directory.

Detective Sergeant Sykes, who had all along believed Philip Winter's story and had hoped the Crown Prosecution Service would decide not to pursue the case, was not too concerned about this new complaint. There was no proof that the woman was not orchestrating this herself in a plea for attention. She could have sent for the brochures, and she could be inventing her story about the telephone calls from punters. If her account were true, something would turn up; there would be further incidents, or more letters. She could have constructed those herself, and any future ones she might produce. With a suspect in mind, saliva on stamps could be tested. Philip Winter's DNA profile had not been needed, but it seemed unlikely that he had staged a disappearance simply in order to harass his accuser.

It could be the woman's former husband, of course, but why now, so long after they separated?

An officer went to see him in his large house in Sussex. When he heard the story, he laughed uproariously, even slapping his thigh with delight.

'Serve her right,' he said. He hadn't believed the rape allegation for a minute. Some poor guy had got across her and it was her revenge.

Orlando, ignorant of what she might be doing about his campaign, was sure that she would change her telephone number. He tried calling the old one and found it was not operating. That trick was one he wouldn't be able to repeat; he hoped it had caused her a great deal of irritation. No clients would have turned up on her doorstep; he hadn't given her address.

He went again to the restaurant where he had seen her eating on her own. Twice in the evening he failed to see her there, but the third time, on a Saturday at lunch-time, there she was. Perhaps she went there every week. She looked just as smart, and seemed just as poised, as on the previous occasion. He wasn't hurting her enough, he thought. She needed a more public humiliation. She'd utterly destroyed that unfortunate man, who was now lying dead somewhere, and what about his family? They'd lost their major earner. The daughter was still a schoolgirl and she'd been deprived of a father and of the father's good name.

Hunting Sandra White was more worthwhile than pursuing scientists and farmers, Orlando decided. How could he start talking to her?

But he didn't have to find a way, for she took the initiative, apparently recognising him when he was shown to a table near hers. For a wild moment, as she smiled at him, he wondered if she really was a tart, but surely that would have come out at the trial? Defence lawyers always tried to shred the rape victim's reputation. She might, he supposed, be a high-class hooker with a private clientele; she certainly seemed to have plenty of money.

She left the restaurant before he did, and, passing

near his table, dropped her purse.

Her purse! Wasn't that what she had left in the shop, for Philip Winter to retrieve? Had she done it on purpose then? He was sure it was intentional this time, for as he stopped to pick it up, though she was now by the door where the waiter was ready with her coat, she half turned, expectantly.

Orlando was already on his feet, bearing the purse before him, on his way to hand it back. It was an expensive one, made of tooled leather with her initials on it.

'Excuse me. I think this is yours,' he said.

'Oh – did I drop it? How very careless of me,' she said. 'Thank you so much,' and she smiled at him.

Close to, she looked older than he had first thought her. She wore a lot of eye make-up, and there was a small scar on one cheekbone. Did she get it in a fight? Orlando pulled himself together. This was his chance.

'Lucky it was here, not in the street,' he said, and tentatively smiled. He was, whilst pleased and excited, rather frightened. This was a terrifying woman who could eat your balls for breakfast, the sort he would never choose to tangle with in a thousand years. But he wasn't going to tangle with her: not like that, not intimately; only indirectly.

By now she was doing up her coat – a long black one with a velvet collar. He had none to collect, but he had to pay his bill. He paid cash, as he had done the last time; he did not want to leave a credit-card trail.

'No coat?' she asked, as the waiter, who had produced the check at a gesture, took his money.

'It's in my car,' he said.

'Oh? And where's that?'

'Just round the corner,' said Orlando. Then, riskily, he plunged. 'Are you going far? Can I help you on your way with a lift?'

'Oh, you are kind,' she said. 'I live about a mile away.'

He drove her, at her directions, to her door. Because it was a Saturday, there was space outside to park.

'Won't you come in?' she asked him, but he didn't dare. He might find himself in court before Tessa's father, on a charge of rape. Cravenly, he said he was going down to the country and must get on.

'Let me give you my card, then,' she said, and dipped into her handbag.

Sitting beside her, Orlando saw that its interior was extremely orderly. He thought of the handbags of other women he knew; most were too full and caused problems when they hunted for their keys. Hers was not the handbag of a woman who was careless with her purse. She withdrew a card from some section and gave it to him; then, confidently, she waited for him to get out of the driver's seat and open the passenger door for her. He did, of course.

He saw her long, slim legs emerge. She was quite sexy, he supposed, but she was frightening. Would he have thought that if he had not known her history?

She gave him a little wave before walking up the steps to the main door of her block and opening it. Orlando got back behind the wheel and glanced at the card. She'd crossed out her old telephone number and substituted the new one.

He couldn't use it to annoy her, though: she'd remember whom she'd told about the change. But she had given him some information on their short journey together. She'd said that she played bridge on Tuesday and Thursday afternoons, sometimes at home, sometimes with friends. If he followed her on one of these occasions, he would learn more of her habits and that could help him find a new way to inconvenience her.

He'd take time off to do it; he'd say he had to see his dentist.

Jet rang Orlando that evening.

She said she was sorry about not meeting him, but she and Steve had been to a rally and they were going on another demonstration the next day. Buses would take them to a port where lambs were loaded, live, for export. Would he like to join them?

He had nothing else to do. Tessa wouldn't ring him now, wanting to make a plan. He wondered how she was spending her weekend, and with whom. He agreed.

'What about Biff and Denis?' she asked him. 'Will they come? There's no money in it,' she added.

'If I can find them, I'll ask them,' Orlando said.

He'd take a turn around the streets where Biff often begged.

'Its awful, you know,' Jet said earnestly. 'They go for hours cooped up, with no food or water.'

'Yes, I know, Jet,' he agreed. 'I'll be there. I'll try and find the others.'

Looking for Biff would give him something to do. He'd go first to the subway where they'd met a few nights earlier, but he didn't know where Biff was living; he had a base somewhere, in a squat, Orlando thought, but no proper address. He might be hanging about hoping to touch the sympathies and pockets of club and theatre-goers. Orlando could ask other street characters if they'd seen him; many of them knew one another. He could suggest that if anyone saw Biff, they should ask him to call Orlando.

He saw no Biff, but he met a girl who knew him. She said she'd pass the message on. Orlando went back to his flat alone, opened a bottle of red wine and turned on the television while he drank it. There was nothing special on; he channel-hopped, and thought about the people in the streets. What a way to live! It was shameful that they had to; he understood that some of the young ones were trapped, with no means of support because they could not get either a job or state aid without an address. Some of them must have parents who were desperate to find them. Was it pride that stopped them going home? He knew there were charities which succeeded in helping many of them, but others fell through the net and took to prostitution, thieving, drugs. How did you subsist with absolutely no income whatsoever?

You begged, of course, and took what ever else came along.

On his fourth glass of wine, Orlando's thoughts turned towards himself. What was his aim? To be chairman of his or another firm? Not really. To marry Tessa? Not really that, either, because he knew it was impossible and would not work – yet if she were to suggest it, he would ecstatically agree. How could it be that in your head you could clearly know a certain course was the path to disaster, yet still follow it? Was it a sort of death wish?

His thoughts had reached this gloomy point when the telephone rang. It was Biff.

He agreed to come along the following day. He didn't know where Denis was just now, he added, so he'd bring a different friend, a girl, if she was free.

Well, now there was a plan for the next day.

Orlando, when the wine was finished, took himself off to bed.

What a pity I'm not power-mad at work, he thought; what a pity I lack drive and ambition, and, he feared, ability.

He might lose his job, because there were colleagues much abler than he was, and no one's post was safe. He might end up on the streets, like Biff.

Biff, unaccompanied despite his optimistic

declaration, had joined Jet at the meeting-place the next day by the time Orlando, in his drab demonstration garb, had arrived. Steven wasn't coming, Jet reported, giving no reason. They piled into the waiting coach and all sat together at the back, Jet in the corner by the window, Orlando next to her with Biff beside him. Orlando was missing Tessa. He had never been on a protest without her. Soon the bus filled up. There were a few students but some of the passengers were pale, angry-looking men and women, not particularly young, and they brought with them an atmosphere of hostility and almost, Orlando thought, aggression. He was sensitive to atmosphere and, in the office, caught mood swings by instinct. He felt uncomfortable in confrontational situations, favoured underdogs, but was no cavalier.

'How did you hear about this trip?' he asked Jet.

'At that rally I told you about,' she said. She glanced at him almost pleadingly. 'I thought it would be good,' she said.

'Well, it will be and it's a fine day,' he reassured her. 'We'll be at the seaside.'

'We won't see much of the sea,' said Jet. 'They're going to block the roads. Listen.'

The bus had moved off now, and a woman was explaining the plan. The battle plan, she called it. They would form a chain across the road to stop the lorries; several chosen operators would slash the lorry tyres, while others would crack windscreens. Local support would be out in force.

'But we're the commandos,' cried the leader.

Orlando knew that he should not be here. This wasn't his sort of scene at all, but nor could it be Jet's. He saw now that tears were rolling slowly down her cheeks.

'Why didn't Steve come?' he asked her.

'He decided not to,' she said. 'He didn't like that thing we did – you know, with Tessa.' She'd been unhappy about the attack at the house too, but, stubbornly, she had told Steve that sometimes harsh actions were necessary to get results.

'Oh dear,' Orlando said, inadequately. Obviously they'd quarrelled.

Jet went on crying for another mile or two, and Orlando produced a large and spotless handkerchief, which he passed to her. Jet, who had only a few crumpled tissues in her pocket, accepted it, wiped her eyes, and laughed.

'Just like in an old film,' she said, 'Thanks.'

She grew calmer then, while round them the other demonstrators got noisier.

'Don't worry, Jet,' said Orlando. 'We can always run away.'

He was becoming increasingly uneasy because of the mood developing inside the coach. A few individuals were, quite clearly, spoiling for a fight. This wouldn't be lawful protest; it was potential disaster. Biff was enjoying it, however. He'd brought some cans of beer; he'd had beer on the raid in Darsingford, Orlando remembered. Maybe including him wasn't such a brilliant idea after all.

Near the coast the weather deteriorated, and a fine rain began to fall. They left the coach in a side street in the town and were marshalled into a group to be addressed, through a loud hailer, by the woman who was so obviously their leader. Who had elected her, Orlando wondered: what organisation did she represent? She told them they would meet others in a few minutes. Lying down in the road to block the passage of the livestock was a passive way to protest. More active methods were up to the individual. They were to move off now, and join the rest of the protestors.

As they did so, carried along by the surge of those around them, Orlando saw that sticks and cudgels had appeared in various hands. His heart sank. Jet, however, had thrown off her earlier despair and was looking animated. She fell in beside a punk-like woman and a man with ringlets. They had begun shouting, and Jet joined in. Orlando heard cries of what sounded like 'Free God's creatures' but surely that couldn't be what they were yelling? He thought the mob was like the revolutionaries who shouted round the guillotine. The different contingents had now converged and there was a noisy crowd pressing towards the street leading to the docks. He saw Jet's woollen cap ahead of him and then she vanished. She was so small. Though height was not a common factor among the protestors, the human mass was great and Orlando felt alarm as the noise increased. He'd lost sight of Biff. With one of them on either side of her, Jet might have been protected, but it was too late for that. He pressed forward, elbowing people aside, trying to reach her bobbing dark green hat.

Suddenly the crowd halted and fanned across the street in a solid phalanx. Ahead, the first lorries were in sight and there was a rush towards them, but the police were there too, walking along beside the vehicles.

They did not stop the most determined demonstrators. Sticks and stones were thrown at windscreens; there were shouts, and more police appeared. They began dragging people away, and some protestors, triumphant at the chaos they had created, started lying down in the road. Others copied them as bleating sounds came from the trucks; through the sides of some of them, lambs could be seen, by now terrified.

Orlando, too, was afraid. The movement of the crowd was impossible to resist; unless you were on the fringe of it, you were carried along in a tide of bodies. Local residents had joined in; he saw elderly men and women lining the pavements. Soon they were swept along by the current of the crowd.

The lorries could no longer move. Resigned, the drivers switched off their engines as the police tried to clear a passage for them. More officers appeared and began bundling people off. Making themselves limp and heavy, the experienced protestors put on martyred looks and hoped their pictures would be in the papers.

No demonstration Orlando had gone to with

Tessa had ended in violence of this order. Sheer hate was manifest and it was not merely in defence of the livestock; this was hate for hatred's sake, hate for authority, defiance of the rule of law. Orlando did not approve of the sheep being transported, comfortless, for hours, and to a fate which ended in their death, but after all, they were bred for fodder; it was sentimental to think that but for this undertaking, they would have spent their lives gambolling about in verdant fields.

Then he saw Jet. Two policemen were carrying her away, and, impotent, Orlando saw her shut into a van.

Now, like the lambs, she was a prisoner, and he would have to rescue her.

But how? Should he get himself arrested, too? No, that was ridiculous. He'd go to the police station. Which one, though? She'd be entitled to a solicitor. He'd make sure she had one.

Tessa was a solicitor, but she wouldn't touch this.

Orlando turned aside from the sea of people. Once he'd managed to break through the barrier they formed, there was space and air, and the police did not pursue him because there were plenty of militant resisters to be dealt with.

A grey-haired woman was sitting on a doorstep nursing a cut knee. Orlando stopped beside her.

'Can I help?' he asked, solicitous, but Jet still had his once clean handkerchief. 'Shall I get an ambulance?'

'No – no. It's just a graze, and I'm a little shaken,' said the woman. 'Thank you, though.' She looked up at Orlando. 'What a dreadful day this is,' she said. 'I thought I was going to walk peaceably along, protesting at live exports, and it turned into a riot.'

'I thought much the same,' Orlando said. 'And the friend I came with has been arrested.'

'Oh dear!' The woman looked dismayed. 'Was he violent?'

'It's a girl,' Orlando said. 'And no, she couldn't have been. She's very small. I thought she might be trampled on. We got separated in the crowd. Were you alone?'

'No,' said the woman. 'My daughter's in there somewhere.'

'Perhaps she's been arrested too,' Orlando said. 'It's a bit indiscriminate. I suppose they're just dragging off whoever they can grab.' He looked at his new friend, who was now struggling to her feet. 'You ought to get that knee seen to,' he said.

'I'll wash it when I get home,' the woman answered. 'There's no need to bother a busy doctor with a trifle like this. You'd better go to the police station, if you want to find your friend.'

'But how will you get home?' Orlando asked.

'I came in my daughter's car,' the woman said. 'She left it in a multi-storey car park. Even if I could find it, I haven't got a key.'

'Is it far to where you live?'

'Two miles or so.'

'Maybe I could find a taxi for you,' said Orlando. 'Could you walk a little way, out of this area, to a place where we could phone for one?'

'But what about my daughter? She'll wonder where I am,' the woman said.

'Well, you'll be at home. She'll think of looking there eventually,' Orlando said. He was impatient to be rid of her, freed to go in search of Jet, but he couldn't just abandon her.

'I suppose you're right,' the woman said. 'Yes, I can walk, but not two miles. If you'd give me your arm.'

Limping, leaning on him, she guided him along the streets until they reached a wide square with a large church at one end and a hotel facing it.

'Let's go in there,' Orlando said. 'They'll ring for a cab.'

She looked at him.

'Have you any idea what you look like?' she said. 'They won't let you in. You're filthy.'

'Surely not?' Orlando had been clean and tidy when he started out, though it was true he had on what Tessa called his combat gear.

'They'll let you in,' he said. 'You're respectable, if wounded.' And she was; she wore a tweed coat, thick, though torn, ribbed tights, and sensible shoes with rubber soles.

'I'd rather try phoning for a taxi,' the woman said. 'There's a call box over there,' and she pointed.

Orlando's supply of phone cards, needed for the

harassment of Sandra White, was at home, with his wallet; he carried nothing on him which could reveal who he was, just some money in a pocket. This wasn't going to help Jet, if it came to bail, he realised. Then he saw a taxi, coming slowly up the road. He flagged it down. It had a passenger, but the driver stopped, and, on his radio, summoned another cab.

Orlando waited with her till it came, and she gave him a lift to the police station.

It was a long time before he was able to get Jet released. Because she was docile, weepy, and so small, they let her off without a charge, but she was cautioned.

They went back by train. Luckily Orlando had enough cash on him for their fare.

Jet told him that she thought she and Steve were finished now.

'But he was right,' she said. 'He said getting violent was wrong, and it is. Like today. And what Tessa did was awful.'

'No one got hurt then, though,' Orlando said, forgivingly.

'But they might have done. The rabbits died,' she said. 'They were shot.'

'I know. It was bad.' Orlando had to agree with her. He reminded himself that Jet knew nothing about Tessa apart from her first name, and he mustn't let slip any more information, in case Jet got an attack of conscience and went to the police.

Apart from Tessa herself, what about the judge? The tabloids would just love it.

'The animals suffered today, you know,' Jet said. 'The police were talking about it – I hadn't realised – they were going to be delayed so long, they'd be without food and water for an even longer time than if they'd gone straight through. I thought we were campaigning to ban cruelty to animals.'

'I think we were. You and I were,' said Orlando. 'And an old woman I met who'd got hurt in the scrimmage. But some other people weren't.'

What were they campaigning for, those others? Mob rule, or simply for the thrill of violent action?

When they returned to London, he put her in a taxi which would take her back to the flat she shared with other students.

'I hope you make it up with Steve,' he said. 'You must mind, or you wouldn't have cried.'

'I do mind,' Jet replied.

Things ended, though, he knew. Maybe they'd each reached the moment to let go.

He would with Tessa, one day; but he couldn't bear to think of it.

13

FRANCES DID NOT discover that she had been robbed until Monday morning. After clearing up Denis's muddy trail, and stoking her bonfire for the night, she had put her purse in her bag without opening it. He'd left the coins, and, never thinking, she did not notice it was slimmer than before. It still contained her credit cards and driving licence.

She had to go to Darsingford that morning, to the dentist. As she drove in, she thought about her daughter Arabella's various children, some of whom had stayed with her during the summer. They liked the order in her house. Meals were taken at set times, and the very few rules Frances imposed must be obeyed. She had bought two old bicycles which, if used, had to be maintained by their riders, who were obliged to say roughly where they were going, and approximately when they would be home. Games, such as Cheat, Rummy, Scrabble and Monopoly were played. At home, things ran to no particular schedule; everyone still at school could get there on foot or by local bus, and those who were hungry helped themselves to food. At weekends there were often brunch parties with other academic families, and some of the youngsters thrived on this, but Charlotte, Arabella's second daughter, who was rather shy, preferred routine. She had not visited her grandmother during this vacation, which was unusual, but she had been staying with a family in France.

After her session at the dentist's, Frances went into the supermarket, though Monday was not her normal day for shopping. It would save a trip later in the week. Chingbury no longer had a village shop; competition from the supermarkets, with their Sunday trading, had forced it to close, which was a sadness and a nuisance. The post office still clung on, selling minor items such as sweets and postcards, and hand-knitted goods made locally.

She wheeled her trolley round the shelves, stocking up today with cleaning items and other things she bought on a monthly basis. Then, when it was time to pay, she found there were no banknotes in her purse.

After her first instant's panic, she concluded that she must have left the money she had just cashed in a drawer, but she knew there had been other notes still in her purse; she wasn't down to nothing when she collected her two weeks' pension.

She hid her dismay. She had her bank card and her cheque book, so she could pay her bill, but as she left the shop, her mind squirrelled round the possibilities of what could have happened to her money. Sitting in the car, she checked her purse again. No, there was not a single note.

She'd have to go to the bank to get some more. Trying to keep calm, Frances put away her groceries, made sure her car was locked, then returned to the centre of the town. In the bank, she wrote a cheque and cashed it; luckily she had funds. Frances had a tight budget but she kept within it and had a nest-egg to fall back on in an emergency. After that, feeling slightly shaky, and with the injection the dentist had given her while he filled a tooth now wearing off, she went to Pandora's Box for a cup of coffee.

Drinking it, she ran over in her mind what her movements had been after visiting the post office. She'd come home and put her purse down on the table, then gone out to work in the garden. Normally, she cashed her pension on a Tuesday, but this week she had been to a lecture in Bristol and had left it, intending to postpone collecting it till the next week, but had run low in cash. As it happened, she had not needed any over the weekend. The travelling fishmonger had called on Friday night; that was before she'd got the money and anyway he was above suspicion; he had been coming regularly for years. She'd had no children in, washing the car; she'd had no one to the house at all. The purse, though, had lain on the kitchen table throughout Saturday and she had been in the garden for much of the day. The hunt had met in the village; someone following it might have walked in and helped himself. Or a saboteur. They'd been out in force, she'd heard from the Wares, whom she saw on Sunday. By then her purse was back inside her handbag.

She'd better report the theft to the police; other people might have been burgled, too.

She went to do it, before going home. They took down her statement, but were pessimistic about catching whoever was responsible, agreeing that it might have been a saboteur.

'Won't you come and test for fingerprints?' she asked.

They thought they could send someone round tomorrow or the next day, but there were other crimes to investigate: more important ones, was the inference.

'If he was a saboteur, he's miles away by now,' the desk sergeant told her, when she left.

She had to agree.

On Sunday afternoon she had been round to the Wares with some Michaelmas daisy roots she had divided the day before. She had promised to give them some varieties they had admired. When she arrived, she found Guy Frost's wife, Amanda, there. She had obviously been crying. Hugo bore Frances off, with the plants, to the garden, ostensibly to decide where to put them.

'Sorry – I've come at a bad time,' Frances said.

'You've rescued me,' said Hugo. 'I can't bear to

see a woman cry. Dorothy will calm her down.'

'What's the trouble?'

'It's that attack they had on Guy's workshed in the garden. Seems the children keep having nightmares imagining the new rabbits have been shot, and Amanda can't bear to look at the post in case there's a letter bomb.'

'Poor girl. It must be very difficult,' said Frances.

'Yes, I suppose it is,' the general allowed. 'The children, in particular, I can understand.'

'You're thinking she should pull herself together,' Frances deduced. 'People can't always manage it, Hugo. We're not all as brave as you.'

'I'm not brave,' the general said, but the decorations he had received proved otherwise. Courage, however, came in various forms and physical valour was his proven area. 'I'm a coward when it comes to problems,' he declared.

'What about Guy? They haven't come to grief over this, have they?' Frances asked.

'I don't think so, but a rough-looking lad came to the house this afternoon and Amanda took fright. Thought he was a vandal,' Hugo said. 'But he said he was some sort of evangelist. Guy didn't think he was genuine – he rang the police, but they couldn't find the fellow.'

'Oh dear!' said Frances.

'If he really was an evangelist, he'd have been calling at other doors,' said Hugo.

'You're right, of course, and Amanda knows that.'

'Yes. She's taken the children to her parents for a few days, but looking after them for more than a short time is too much for her mother, with her father failing.'

'Perhaps she'll bring them back after a little while on her own with Guy,' said Frances. 'They don't get much chance to be alone together.'

'I think she's more likely to move in with the parents too, from how the conversation was going,' Hugo said. 'I don't understand these things, but Dorothy does.'

'Leave it to her, then,' suggested Frances. 'How's the book coming on?'

'I'm stuck in Korea,' said the general, who had been there literally.

'Are you writing much about your brother?'

The general's brother had been taken prisoner after the fall of Singapore. He had survived, and rebuilt his health amazingly, but in his last years of life his war experiences had returned to haunt him with nightmares and he had wept over the fate of his lost comrades. Dorothy had told Frances that Hugo had recently had bad dreams about his battle campaigns. In those days there was no counselling; people just got on with it, without complaining.

'Yes, I am,' said the general. 'I'm amazed he made such a good physical recovery, but it was sad to see him experience it all again at the end.' He made no reference to his own reawakened memories.

Frances decided to keep him walking round the garden for as long as possible while Dorothy comforted Amanda, who was a friend of the Wares' daughter. Frances had grown very fond of the Wares, and, in turn, her self-sufficiency had impressed them. She was no clinger. The general had even said she would have made a good army wife, the highest form of praise he could bestow. Frances found him vulnerable and soft beneath his stern carapace. He had seen and experienced suffering. He knew the score.

'Guy can't give up,' she said. 'He mustn't let these people frighten him away.'

'They're cowards,' said the general fiercely, his thick grey eyebrows twitching. 'Attacking women and children.'

'They didn't fire the house, did they?' Frances pointed out. 'Just his workshop. Does – did he do much important work there?'

'I think he kept many of his records in the shed,' said the general. 'It meant he could do calculations and write reports at home. Of course the main tests, particularly those involving animals, have to be done at the centre. And it's heavily restricted. Nowadays no reputable scientist tests animals without good reason. It's all licensed and inspectors come around.'

'Life has become so precious, hasn't it?' said Frances. She bent to pick up a fallen chestnut leaf and inspected its faded tracery of veins. 'Death's the last enemy, which can't be defeated and must often be a welcome friend, seen from the patient's point of view.'

Hugo Ware did not want to accompany her down this avenue. Frances was a great one for dissection, but he thought some things were best left undisturbed.

'Guy built that workshop and worked there so that he could spend more time with Amanda and the children,' he said. 'Now it's rebounded on him.'

'Amanda can't want him to give up his post,' said Frances. 'That would mean surrendering to intimidation.'

'To be fair to them, some of the more reputable protest groups have denounced what happened,' Hugo said. 'This was some splinter movement, it seems. No one knows – or is saying – who they were. The youth who called on them today is probably up to no good, but not a terrorist. Guy was right to be suspicious, though. I suppose it was the last straw for Amanda.'

Now, a day later, discovering her burglary, Frances knew that it was illogical to connect the Frosts' visitor with either the hunt saboteurs or the theft at Badger's End, but someone had walked into her house and stolen from her. It could have happened at any time while she was busy in the garden.

It gave her a very nasty feeling. Here, in the country, she had felt safe, though it was true that a car had once been stolen from outside the only pub; vandalism and theft were rare in Chingbury.

She'd meant to have security lights fitted to the house; the Wares had got them and said that apart from the deterrent aspect, it was handy when you went out at night to have them come on automatically, though they were set off by passing cats.

After her coffee, she called at the electrical shop in the centre of the town to ask about them. She'd ring the electrician when she understood the choices available.

This research concluded, she went into the library. Though funding had been cut, it was still open every weekday.

A man sat at a table. He was going through advertisements in a newspaper. Frances noticed him only because he seemed so intent, and he was a stranger. She often ran into acquaintances here, and was always ready for a few minutes' conversation. It did not occur to her that she was lonely; she knew she was content and who could, or should, ask for more? The man had dark hair, greying round the edges; he'd taken off a donkey jacket which he had draped over the back of his chair, and the sweater he wore was a good, expensive one. Somehow it didn't go with the donkey jacket, although Frances wasn't really aware that this bothered her; it simply made her look at him more closely. As if he felt her stare, Philip looked up at her and she saw the short, new beard and soft moustache, but it was his haggard, exhausted face which really registered. She turned away, quite shaken. Whatever had gone wrong for him?

Reluctant to go home because her house had been invaded by a stranger, at last Frances could put it off no longer. Randomly choosing two biographies, she checked them out and left.

Philip had not got the driving job.

When he reached the advertiser's address, he discovered that there were two other applicants whom the man was already interviewing. One of them was known to him; Philip was not, and he could not offer a reference.

Walking away, he felt total despair. How was he going to earn money? He'd wasted the afternoon. He had lost Denis, though, and that was an advantage; alone, he might not be so good at surviving, but he stood more chance of getting a job than if he was followed by the shadow of the boy; after all, they were competing in the same narrow market, though Philip had the advantage of a clean driving licence.

He had nothing to do and nowhere to go, nothing even to read. No wonder layabout lads in cities got into trouble; he would be in trouble soon himself. As he had no address, he could not advertise his services. He'd been very lucky to earn that ten pounds, working in the woman's garden; Lesley would never employ a casual passer-by in that manner, or he hoped she would not do so.

He contemplated looking for a room for the night. It was still dry, but cooler; he had not heard a weather forecast and had no idea what to expect as darkness fell. The thought of a warm, dry bed, like the one in the Lake District, was as a dream of paradise, but he would not use money on that until he had a chance of earning more. He'd spend the evening in a pub, as he had done before; a beer would be nutritious, and he might run to a sandwich or some crisps. Something might turn up in the morning.

When the pub closed, Philip, who had exchanged no chat with other drinkers, staying in a corner reading a paper someone had left on a seat, remembered what Denis had done: spent the night in a car.

Philip wouldn't have the nerve to do it, even if he found a car that had been left unlocked. He was afraid of falling foul of the law. He knew what it could do to you although you had done nothing wrong. If he were to lie down in the entrance to a shop, the police might move him on, arrest him for vagrancy; wasn't that an offence? But he wasn't begging; he hadn't been reduced to that: not yet. He remembered what Denis had said about building a hut and living rough. It might be possible, but what about food, and washing? Philip had never been so much as a boy scout, let alone a commando: he would make a poor show at living off the land.

If he didn't find work tomorrow, he'd hitch to some much bigger town, where there would be cheap rooms and perhaps better opportunities. This place was too small.

Eventually he went back to the bridge where he had spent the previous night. It began to rain as he walked there, and at least he had some shelter, though the water trickled down the towpath in a rivulet towards him. His trench-coat, wrapped around him, soon grew sodden.

In the morning he drank some water from his plastic bottle and ate a banana. Then he went to the nearest public toilet, where, in cold water, he washed after a fashion and brushed his teeth.

When Frances saw him in the library, he had been there for some time. It was warm and dry in the large room with its chairs and tables. He even dozed a bit, before he scanned the job advertisements.

There were some possibilities. He left at last, to pursue them.

14

DENIS TRIED TO believe that he was glad to be rid of Phil. The guy had no idea of how to look after himself, and Denis had enough to do without taking him on, too, he told himself. He'd most likely got the job, so he'd be OK.

Though he had money now, Denis thought about looking for one himself, but with not being able to read the adverts, it was difficult. He could try asking, of course: he could ask if pubs wanted washing up done, or offer garden help. That mightn't be too bad. If he hadn't already blown it at the place where Tessa set the fire, he could have tried there. That garden was a mess, full of bushes. It wouldn't be too hard to sort it out, he thought; you'd need a chopper, a spade and a broom. The weather wasn't so nice today, however, and the idea he'd been playing with of building a hut in the woods had retreated from the forefront of his mind.

It was quite lonely without anyone to talk to.

Even old Phil had been better than nothing. Before, there'd always been someone else around, other folk his own age, and lately Biff, who'd taken charge. Not knowing what to do next was unsettling.

This was a terrible town for getting food. Nowhere was open, early in the morning. The chip shop hadn't opened the night before, and Darsingford didn't have the sort of cheap cafés he was used to; it was a place for toffs, he thought, though some of the passers-by weren't all that smart. A garage shop could have food; he remembered that from the expedition with Tessa and Orlando. He fancied a nice strong cup of tea, with lots of sugar, but he might not get that at a filling station. He was not only hungry; he was bored. There was nothing to do here. All the people he had seen so far this morning in the street were walking purposefully along. They were not even looking in shop windows. It was still early. He had spent the night in the same Maestro, reckoning that no one would have realised it had been unlocked. It was parked in the same spot; he waited until it was quite late before entering it. He'd had a meal in a Chinese restaurant he'd noticed earlier. Debonair, he'd enjoyed every course, paying for it in a lordly way. He'd learned from Biff how to put on an air of affluence, but it sat less comfortably on Denis. He didn't look the part, exactly; he knew that; but he'd been ready, if challenged, to produce his money, showing he could pay.

It was a great meal, and it went on for a long

time. He couldn't read the menu, so he'd said he'd lost his glasses and could the waiter recommend the best value choice; he'd had the cheapest all-in meal but there was a lot of it. He liked the fried rice. He hadn't had that before. Afterwards, he walked round the streets, avoiding the few groups of young people who were clustered here and there, though he was tempted to talk to some of them. Experienced in the ways of gangs, he did not risk it.

In the morning, it was not like Sunday. A milk float came along the road quite early, while it was still dark. Denis cowered in the Maestro, rolling on to the floor in case the milkman looked inside and saw him, but he didn't. When he had gone, Denis left the car. People would be going to work today and might soon be stirring in the street. He helped himself to a milk bottle from a step, pulled off the top and walked along drinking it; then he pitched the empty bottle across a hedge as he walked by. Soon the first cars set off, just a few passing down the streets; then he met the paper boys and girls out on their rounds. Again, the thought of snatching a bike occurred to him but it was too risky, with so few people about. He slouched on into the town and saw early buses in the streets. The traffic was increasing, and he watched it for a while, standing outside the chip shop, hoping it would open, but it didn't. Soon, though, a sweet warm smell wafted across to greet him; it came from a bakery. A small independent baker still flourished here and he went in. He bought three jam doughnuts, pointing to them because they looked so good and he had had one once.

Later that morning, leaving the library, Philip, too, found the bakery. It sold filled rolls, and he bought one before telephoning round for work. By then Denis had given up on Darsingford and was heading back to Chingbury. He'd got that money easily; the gardening person might need help and wouldn't know that he'd already been there, thieving. And if they wouldn't find him something to do, he might try the idea of sleeping in the wood. He'd light a fire, which would be cosy. He bought some matches and firelighters before setting out, not by bus but hitch-hiking: why waste the fare?

It took him quite a time to get a lift. Most cars, including, eventually, Frances in her Viva, drove straight past him.

After several abortive calls, Philip went directly to one of the factories on the outskirts of Darsingford, which had advertised for a driver. He might as well; walking there was cheaper than buying a new phone card. His was finished. There had been no more about him in the papers; interest in his disappearance had evaporated and now, with his beard, he looked so different; if there were any comment, he could say that it was an ordinary name, a coincidence.

The van driver's position had been filled, but, he was told, a temporary security guard was required as the regular man had had an accident over the weekend and was in hospital. They wanted references, but Philip had thought of this. He had gone into a large stationer's, which now housed the post office, and had bought a pad of Basildon Bond on which, in a neat italic hand, he had written out a reference signing it in the name of Robert Bruce: a total fiction, with an invented address. For this sort of job, it might just be enough; not everyone checked up on things. Denis's cheek in sleeping in the car had inspired Philip; he realised that he might need similar nerve.

Because the guard was urgently required, and because Philip's manner and speech were good, he got the job. Now he had only to last out the day and he would have shelter for the night.

The factory packed cosmetics; they had had a watchman only since the recent raid on a research laboratory nearby. The management feared further raids, and their products were not guaranteed as never tested on animals. The human guard could summon help more rapidly than alarms, and could activate sirens to scare off intruders. This was a short-term plan, he was told; more sophisticated measures were being contemplated.

Philip walked away on air. As soon as he was paid, he could rent a room. He'd need to sleep by day; he must not falter at his post. The short nap he'd had in the library had set him up enough for this expedition, but he had been wakeful for much of the night, cold and wet and wretched. Now he'd have a meal, a good hot one, in the bar at The Swan

Hotel, and if he could find a corner seat, perhaps they would leave him there to doze afterwards. The Swan was where he and Denis had washed and had a drink on Sunday. Philip went into the cloakroom where, again, he washed as thoroughly as he could. He took off his donkey jacket and, carrying it, his trench-coat and the plastic bag which contained his spare clothing and his bottle of water, he went into the bar where he ordered steak and kidney pudding and half a pint of bitter. In his good sweater, he did not look like the tramp he was.

The place was busy; it did a brisk lunch-time trade. Philip found a wing armchair in a corner, and a waitress brought his meal. Never had food tasted so good! He began to feel better as he ate the first mouthfuls and sipped his beer. You took so much for granted, he realised: home, food, warmth. That boy Denis had never really known the sort of security which Philip, though he worked hard for it, had never questioned. If he hadn't got this job, what would he have done? How much longer could he have held out without help? Eventually he would have had to go to the social services and plead for emergency aid; they might have shipped him to a hostel and perhaps provided funds. He wasn't sure what he would be entitled to if he used a false name or, at best, a false address. They might want proof of identity.

He wouldn't look too far ahead. He'd settle into the job, perform it well and conscientiously, and maybe by the time he was no longer needed in that capacity, another opening would appear. There were more factories around; he could try calling on their personnel managers. He'd have a reference from the packing firm by then. Life seemed a great deal brighter, now.

He'd got a paper, which he opened when his plate had been cleared away. It gave him an excuse to linger in the bar, which, with the new freedom in the licensing laws, stayed open all the afternoon. When the waitress saw him sleeping, tidy in his sweater, though she noticed, frowning, that his collar and shoes were not too clean, she left him undisturbed. He'd tipped her, after all. She went off duty soon. Philip slumbered undisturbed for nearly two hours. As no one wanted his seat, even the manager left him alone. Eventually, though, he started moving chairs and tables round noisily, to wake him up. He'd used their space quite long enough.

Philip went drowsily out into the street. Then he did some shopping. He'd been shown the small office where he would monitor the closed circuit television screens which had been installed. It had an electric kettle. The injured guard's mug and spoon were there in a cupboard. Philip bought packet soup, bread, cheese, and more bananas. He loved them, and Lesley had said they were full of potassium which was good for you.

He set out early for the factory, and, with enthusiasm, took up his post.

* * *

When Frances arrived home, she felt a moment's fear as she unlocked the back door to let herself in. She used that entrance because it was near the garage if her car was full of shopping which had to be unloaded – groceries, as now, and sometimes garden requirements, such as fertilizer; she grew most plants herself, in her greenhouse.

The thief had entered here, probably on Saturday afternoon while she was busy outside.

She did not touch the door frame, in case he had left a print. She hadn't dusted the hall since then, though she had vacuumed up the mud he had left. Would the police bother to come? They hadn't been too interested, but as she had been burgled, others might, too, and she decided to warn the Wares. Hugo and Dorothy left their back door unlocked when they were in the garden – of course they did: everybody did, even in towns. You went in and out.

She put her shopping away, then, locking up meticulously, walked down to Friar's Court, where she was easily persuaded to have a restorative glass of sherry and stay on for a bread and cheese lunch in the kitchen.

She and the Wares all shared a mild depression. She and Dorothy had tentatively touched on it, as summer wound down and the days shortened. It was something to do, Frances thought, with the much criticised plans for marking the passage of fifty years since the end of the Second World War. As a young officer, Hugo had taken part in the D-Day landings and he had not wanted to go back to the beaches to celebrate the event, but he had felt it his duty to be there. He had returned in low spirits. Dorothy had been in the ATS, and Frances was in the WAAF. Her husband had been a bomber pilot. All old now, the two women felt that their youthful sacrifices had been thrown away. Neither had been physically wounded, nor lost those close to them, so they were luckier than many, but they had often been in danger; this was worthwhile in the cause of freedom, but now one wasn't safe even in such spots as Darsingford, where Guy had come under siege, and here in Chingbury, Frances had been burgled. Only a few years ago, such a thing would have been impossible.

'It probably was one of the hunt saboteurs, or rather, one of the rag, tag and bobtail that attaches itself to the genuine protestors,' said Dorothy, who could not understand why drag hunting was not substituted for the live quarry. Surely that would end the argument, retain the sport, and protect those landowners who did not want the hunt running over their property?

'If you're right, that means he's long gone,' said Frances. 'I suppose he could have got in without my noticing. I was busy in the garden until it got dark.'

Badger's End was isolated, on the fringe of the village, offering more of an invitation to an opportunist thief than the grander Friar's Court, which sat amid its satellite buildings like a castle sheltered by walls and towers. Neither Ware mentioned this to their guest, who they could see had lost her usual calm.

'I'm sure it was a one-off,' said Dorothy reassuringly.

'I went into Brown's to look at security lights,' Frances said. The Wares had been urging her to instal them for more than a year. 'I've seen the varieties you can have. I'll ring up Jack when I get home and ask him to fix me up.' Jack was the local electrician who was employed by most people in the village to do their wiring and repairs.

Hugo was relieved to know she would have this in hand before the days got even shorter.

They went on to discuss the Frosts. Amanda's parents lived only ten miles away. Hugo, though sympathetic to her fears, thought she should back Guy up in his important work and return. Dorothy was more tolerant. When children are at risk, nothing else counts, she told her husband.

'She'll probably calm down quite soon,' said Frances. 'It's shock. The rough young man calling wouldn't be enough on its own.'

'She wanted to go to her parents straight away,' said Dorothy. 'They did, in fact, while the police examined the damage. All of them went. But they came back as soon as the house was cleared.'

Belatedly, Frances remembered that the police fingerprint man might come that afternoon, and so she went home. Meanwhile, Denis, who had decided not to seek employment, was on his way through the village once more, aiming for the woods. The sky had cleared, and again he felt the freedom in the air, the sense of space. In the wood, if he lit a fire, he wouldn't be too cold, and he'd see the stars.

Finding his way to a clearing in the wood at dusk was not quite the same as walking through it in daylight on a path marked by other feet. Denis tripped over undergrowth and caught his face on a bramble. It was wet, too; the rain that had fallen in the night had made the ground muddy, and water still dripped from boughs and the remaining leaves. As he left the village, lights had been coming on in houses, but his eyes had soon adjusted and he had not realised that it would seem darker among the trees. He began to repent of this enterprise, but he wasn't done for yet. He lit a firelighter, which flared and spurted, then he sought twigs and small branches to build his fire, but by now they were much too damp to catch. Some smoked a little, but he lacked the skill to build them into an ignitable shape and by the time he had used several fire-lighters, all he had achieved was a smouldering heap which would not catch alight.

This wasn't what he'd hoped for. He stayed there, nursing his smoking pyre, searching around him for drier material and bits of wood, but when he burrowed down, the buried leaves were damper still. He shivered. If he stayed here, he'd be frozen stiff. Briefly he thought fondly of a warm grating near a café where he had slept comfortably for several weeks last winter. The wood would be all right with the proper equipment, he decided; a little stove, for instance, and a tent and sleeping bag. Now, though, he'd go back to the village and look around; there might be a shed open. But, as Denis decided on this action, it began to rain quite hard. He'd get soaked if he left the wood in this. He moved in deeper, finding a thick bush and trying to crouch under it for shelter. There he stayed until, after more than an hour, the rain eased off, but by then it was pitch dark. He would never find his way out and over the fields. Faced with the limits imposed on him by the elements, Denis had to remain where he was. Though he felt very cold, the night was relatively mild for the time of year; however, fright and discomfort contributed to his sufferings. The rain, pattering through the trees, made an eerie sound, but after a while it stopped, though water still dripped around him. He hugged his parcel of food and crisps, and through the night ate much of what was in it. One after another, he lit the remaining firelighters, simply to break the darkness. He heard strange rustling sounds and squeaks; animals, he thought: rabbits and such, perhaps. Then a dog fox barked and startled Denis almost out of his wits. He had no idea what it was and imagined wolves. If only Biff were here; Biff would laugh off his fears, and he'd be able to get a fire going, too. Denis could look after himself in a town; there was always some corner where you could go. Out here was different.

He whimpered, clutching his bundle, legs drawn up against his body, a sad, lost boy, very frightened, weeping, but eventually, as children will, Denis cried himself to sleep.

When he woke, the air felt different, fresher somehow. It was still dark, and he still felt miserable, but it wasn't raining. It was much colder, though. He got up, and as the first streaks of the new day appeared, he began to struggle back the way he had come the previous evening. By the time he reached the edge of the wood, the sun was rising and, for the first time in his life, Denis watched it as day broke. A brilliant red globe appeared at the end of the field, above a ridge of trees. It was huge. He thought it must be a monster fireball as the sky around it became tinged with fiery red. Denis was spellbound, puzzled by what he was seeing, even frightened, but not in the terrified state he had known during the night. He was awed.

The sky changed all the time as he watched, and at last becoming capable of movement, he walked slowly over the field towards the gate. As it rose, the sun's vivid colour faded but the sky stayed red around it, growing paler only gradually. It was now much colder than the day before. A bright, fine day lay ahead.

Denis reached the road and started back towards the village. He had passed the house he had robbed and seen lights on, on his outward journey; now it was in darkness. Whoever lived there was still in bed, he thought, misjudging Frances who had also seen the brilliant sunrise, watching it from the conservatory at the back of the house.

She had had a shock, the previous day. When she returned from visiting the Wares, her grand-daughter, Charlotte, was sitting on the doorstep, with a rucksack, looking like a ghost.

'Why didn't you let yourself in, my dear?' asked Frances, when she'd kissed her warmly. 'You know where the spare key is. You must be frozen.'

'I didn't like to. You weren't expecting me,' said Charlotte.

'Silly girl,' said Frances. 'You know I'm always pleased to see you.'

This was true, but Charlotte was in trouble: Frances knew it, by the girl's expression.

15

ORLANDO HAD TELEPHONED Sandra White
on Sunday afternoon.

He was feeling depressed. The previous day's
demonstration had been a scary affair; he'd felt
endangered, and Jet had been at risk. There had
been a command from Tessa on his answerphone;
she sounded cross and had told him to ring her
when he got in, saying that it was important, but
when he obeyed she wasn't there. He left her an
affectionate message and said he would call the next
morning.

Who was she with, he wondered jealously; some
suave barrister, probably. Into his mind, unbidden,
came the image of Jet. What a sweet girl she was,
he thought, and probably she was as upset about
ending her affair with Steve as he was over his
unsatisfactory relationship with Tessa. You could
scarcely even give it that name: it was a coming
together in bed in a rapturous manner, very

infrequently, when for once he felt himself her equal, with between those occasions a rare summons to aid her in her crusade, and rarer invitations to partner her to some function. He was her fall-back man, no more. He would do better to pick up Jet's fragmented pieces and help her repair herself, he thought, sombrely drinking strong coffee. He had a lot going for him, after all: a lucrative career in which he was adequate, if not brilliant, with a salary that provided him with a good car – his BMW – and paid the mortgage on his flat, which was a spacious one in Pimlico. If he married Tessa, together they could buy a nice house in, possibly, Highgate. But he couldn't see himself coming back to a calm, married Tessa, though she might return to an insecure Orlando, busy preparing the dinner. He'd be the house-husband, but he wouldn't mind that, if Tessa were the wife.

Why couldn't he rid himself of this longing for her? It would bring him no enduring joy; he knew that, intellectually. Was he confusing lust with love? It had happened before, and to better men. She makes hungry where she most satisfies, he thought, like Cleopatra. What was it about some women, that they had this power? Could it ever work the other way?

Orlando rang up a friend to see if he felt like a game of squash, and persuaded the friend, who was reluctant, to consent. Afterwards, sweating and invigorated, he felt less gloomy, but the friend went home to his partner and Orlando was once more on his own. Tessa's answerphone again intercepted his call.

He decided to go and see Jet. She might still be shaken up by her arrest and he suspected her principles had taken a knock. He'd decided that he had none, himself. Even Biff professed an interest in animal welfare. We're a rootless generation, Orlando decided. Young men in earlier decades had fought wars, built empires, expanded overseas trade, explored tracts of land where no foot had fallen. You could still excavate unrevealed archaeological ruins and you could, perhaps, explore space, but there were few worlds left for the average man to conquer. Perhaps he should learn to fly, or buy a small boat and sail. Orlando sighed, parking his car outside Jet's flat. She might like to go for a drive.

But she was out. One girl was there, and Orlando asked her to say that he had called. He hoped she'd remember.

It was rotten, being alone at the weekend. He wondered if Biff was all right, and, by association, Denis. What hope was there for either of them, long term? They'd drift into petty crime, as Biff had done already. The demonstrations gave them an interest and some action. They ought to be apprenticed to some useful trade, as, a generation ago, might have been the case. What could be done about all these ill-educated young men, few of whom had hopes of a job and whose fathers might not have had one, either? No wonder they turned to crime, for a bit of excitement as well as for gain.

Thinking like this, Orlando's gloom returned, and so he had decided to take further steps to annoy Mrs White.

He rang her up and invited her to have dinner with him that night. She prevaricated a bit, but in the end she accepted. Now it was Orlando who was in a flutter of excitement, because he was taking a gamble and wondered if he could see it through.

He met her at the restaurant he had chosen, one where he had never been before. It was not far for her, in a taxi. He had not offered to pick her up; he was not going to risk physical proximity in his car, going home. She arrived five minutes late, and he was waiting for her, wearing a dark green velvet jacket which he thought she would like.

She did, commenting on it at once.

To Orlando's surprise, she was an easy guest and the evening went well. She chose expensive dishes, but he didn't mind that; avenging Philip Winter was a worthwhile investment. He asked her about her life and if she had done much travelling; he had found that most people, these days, had been somewhere abroad and often enjoyed recounting the ordeals of delayed flights, gales weathered on cruises, and half-built holiday hotels. She had been on a garden tour in Provence when it had rained every day and the hotel was indifferent. She had had to buy some weatherproof boots and had caught a cold.

'Did you go with a friend?' he asked, and she said no, but the other travellers were, on the whole, agreeable. She said there was usually someone who needed a helping hand, which she, Sandra, ever ready to aid a lonely soul, was always prepared to offer.

'There was this one elderly woman,' she said. 'She was so discourteous – refused to dine with me when I asked her. I thought it only polite, seeing her going off by herself. She said she liked speaking French.'

'And did she? Speak French, I mean?'

'Oh, she did,' Sandra allowed. 'She spoke excellent French.' And Sandra did not, and would have welcomed her own personal interpreter. 'I shan't go on a garden holiday again,' she said. 'It was an experiment. I prefer bridge vacations.'

She'd opened the subject herself. Orlando had been wondering how to work round to it. A few subtle questions here and there and he had managed to discover where she would be playing next week, and at what time.

He put her in a taxi and paid the driver more than enough to take her home.

'Thank you, Bobby,' she said. He had told her that was his name. 'It was a delightful evening. We'll do it again, shall we?' and her eyes held his.

He returned her gaze steadily, but he did not touch her, evading her outstretched hand and ignoring her expectant cheek.

The following day he ordered a male kissogram, in the guise of a police officer, to call on her at her bridge game. He had no trouble arranging it

203

anonymously, paying in cash after telephoning to enquire the cost, posting instructions with the money through the agent's door. That should upset the apple cart, or rather the card table, very nicely, he thought.

It had to be Philip Winter. Who else would sink to such depths and seek to mortify her?

Sandra, after the arrival of the kissogram, was more than mortified; she was distraught. The resting actor who had arrived, garbed in police uniform, was used to provoking embarrassment, and the recipient of his attentions was not always gratified enough to be won round. Humiliation was often partly the object of his mission. This time, though, he had had his face soundly slapped and was shown the door quite smartly, once the assembled bridge players understood it was a set-up.

They let him in, of course: a policeman's disguise was the easiest way to gain admittance to a target's presence: gorilla-grams and such were harder, even where he was expected by the prankster, and much more uncomfortable to deliver, all hot and hairy in a synthetic fur suit.

'Sandra, the officer wants to speak to you,' the smart woman who had admitted him had said. Her Portuguese maid had whispered something to her first. He'd waved his driving licence under the maid's nose, making out it was his warrant card. People were so easy to con, and after all, as an actor, his job was to pretend to be other than what he was.

This was good practice. He hadn't reckoned on the swipe, however; it hurt, and she was aiming to follow it with another blow but the hostess intervened. She was dignified and calm, and older, and the unhappy actor did not persist. He'd done his job, though with no kiss, and none of those present confessed to having arranged his visit. Not everyone responded well when tricks like this were played.

The hostess, lips grimly pursed, showed him to the door.

'I believe impersonating a policeman is an offence,' she said. 'But I realise that this is someone's tasteless idea of a joke. The less said the better, in my view.'

She let him go while Sandra was submitting to the ministrations of the two other players and the hovering maid. Brandy was produced, and after a while the game resumed, with Sandra sighing heavily at intervals. That day, they finished early, and she left first.

The others, free to discuss the incident, were amazed that she should be the target for some prank. They all found her austere, with little conversation beyond the game. In the end they decided it must have been an act of spite by her ex-husband.

But Sandra knew it wasn't. It was not his style. Only one other person could harbour such malice towards her, and he, allegedly, was dead.

Of course he wasn't. He had gone into hiding to carry out his plan of vengeance, and he was following her. How else did he know where she would be this afternoon? He must have tapped her telephone or bugged her flat. Everyone knew you could buy tiny devices to carry out surveillance; he'd had plenty of time to find out about them and acquire whatever he needed. He'd had to fake his disappearance, so as to avoid suspicion, but she knew.

When she reached home, she called the police, and later that day a detective constable came round. She had expected at least Detective Sergeant Sykes himself, if not the Detective Inspector, and was affronted, but DC Proctor was a conscientious officer, aware of the ramifications of the case, and, being a woman, should be safe if Mrs White attempted any contact beyond what was formal.

After interviewing her, DC Proctor went to the house where the incident had taken place, and took a statement from the hostess. No one had thought to enquire where the kissogram messenger had come from, but there were not too many such concerns in operation now; their novelty had worn off, to some extent. It shouldn't be difficult to track down the source.

'But if it's the same person as ordered her the pizzas, he'll have managed it anonymously,' said Sykes, when DC Proctor reported back. 'Still, try to trace it,' he commanded. 'If Philip Winter is behind it all, we need to know. It'll mean he's not missing and we'll have to pick him up.'

As no sign of him had turned up, and no body

had been found, Winter was now on the missing persons list. If he was responsible for all this, he was doing rather well at upsetting Mrs White; still, such harassment was against the law and must be stopped, when the culprit could be traced.

Someone had better go and see the wife: make sure she'd had no news.

Lesley had received a lot of sympathy at first, but now her friends were finding other claims upon their time and their compassion; there was always someone needing attention and it wasn't as though anything could be done for her or the family; there was no corpse, no funeral.

'I wish we knew what had happened,' Jackie said one night. She was feeling guilty and inside her chest there was a great lump of pain. She did not recognise the agony of grief. 'Why didn't he leave a note? Even if— ' She meant, even if he had killed himself: it was not knowing that was so terrible.

Lesley had decided that he had wanted them to suffer. They hadn't fully believed his story, hadn't stood by him. All of them, Andrew included, had felt there must be some basis for the woman's allegations, that he'd tried something on, otherwise public money wouldn't have been wasted on prosecuting him. Andrew said it was to warn other people. On the other hand, girls blew hot and cold and you couldn't always gauge their moods correctly; he'd found that out. There could be some truth in his father's protestations of innocence, but a man of his age ought to have more sense than to get himself into such a situation.

Philip was having the male menopause, Lesley decided. He went sniffing after some rich female customer and lost his head. You read about such things in the tabloid press. Stupid fool. Now what was going to happen to her and to Jackie and Andrew? They were disgraced, and were left without his support. Her salary wasn't enough to pay the mortgage and maintain their style of living. And they couldn't claim on his insurance unless his body was discovered; not for seven years.

She wouldn't let herself think back as far as their first years together, their early happiness, the joy when Andrew was born. There had been good times; Philip was kind and took part in their family life, not disappearing off to golf or cricket or the pub, leaving her alone with the children, as some other husbands did. He'd worked hard and done well, if in an unspectacular fashion; he would never have made the board of Lavery's, but he had been, she would have sworn, reliable. Then this. Her illusions had been shattered, and she had realised how little they had really communicated in recent years. Everything had been at a superficial level because life was so busy, and she was very much tied up with the children. Even with Andrew away, she had got into a routine of work and chores which left scant time for talk. Philip had begun collecting old prints of London; he went round market stalls and boot sales looking for them, and he kept them in a drawer in the dining-room.

Were they really only prints of London? She'd never looked at them, shown no interest in them. She'd been much too busy.

Maybe they weren't prints at all, but porno-graphic pictures. She'd better check. If they were obscene, that would be proof of Philip's guilt.

The police had suggested he might simply want to disappear. People did, especially after some traumatic experience, and the trial had been that. Sometimes they had a loss of memory, in which case they could turn up again years later. Lesley had wanted to know how such people managed, without any money and no documents to prove identity.

'They do,' she was told. 'Sometimes they get new ones. The state is wonderful at looking after people.' And some of them soon learned to work the system. Philip Winter, if alive, would find a means of survival, or if he couldn't, he would reappear.

He'd done this to punish them, she decided, or to punish her, and he was succeeding. The uncertainty was wearing in the extreme. She could not mourn, nor could she embrace freedom. Did she want him to be dead? Going into the dining-room, deter-mined to inspect his prints, she recalled, unbidden, their first meeting at a party which she'd gone to with another man, one she'd been seeing for some time. Philip had been there on his own. He'd seemed quiet and steady, ready to settle down, and he'd chased her, not hard but with persistence, giving her flowers and trying to find out the things that interested her. He'd been gentle in his court-ship, and that had been the tenor of their marriage: unexciting, but secure. Until now.

Someone had said, 'It's always the quiet ones,' as though he were a serial killer or some other deviant. But he'd been a good father and a reliable, if dull, companion. She'd wondered, rather often, if there could be more to life than this, but there was no discord, no quarrelling of any consequence. She'd never been unfaithful to him, nor had she cause to suppose that he had ever been anything but true to her. How stupid can you be, she thought, her hand on the drawer knob. He could have been sleeping around for years. But if he had, why try it on with a customer?

If he were dead, was she free to look around? To find someone else, someone more exciting, before it was too late?

She had just pulled out the prints, wrapped carefully in tissue, in a folder, and had seen one of St Paul's in the eighteenth century, when the doorbell rang.

She put the folder back. The top prints could be camouflage. She'd have to look more thoroughly some other time.

A police officer was at the door, a detective she had seen before. She let him in.

Later, when Lesley checked the prints again, all were as innocent as he had alleged: old prints of London.

16

LESLEY WINTER COULD not believe what Detective Sergeant Sykes had come to tell her.

Someone had been harassing Philip's accuser by sending her anonymous letters, and he was thought to be the only person bearing her a grudge. Sykes did not mention the other tricks that had been played on Sandra.

'He wouldn't do that,' said Lesley straight away. 'He wouldn't even think of it.' And anyway, wasn't he dead?

'Why not?' asked Detective Sergeant Sykes.

'He just wouldn't,' Lesley said. 'It's not in him.'

'Yet you thought attempted rape was?' he asked her.

She shrugged. How could she really know the truth?

'It wasn't proved,' she said.

'But you believed he'd at least done something stupid,' Sykes persisted.

'Why do you say that?'

'Because you didn't stand by him in public.'

'I don't know what to believe,' said Lesley. 'Anyway, if he's dead, he can't be writing letters to that woman.'

'If,' emphasised Sykes. 'You haven't heard from him? Not a word? Nor your son or daughter?'

Lesley shook her head.

'Who else has she accused?' she asked. 'Has she alleged rape before?'

'No,' said Sykes. 'Or not officially.'

'If Phil is alive, he'd better come forward,' Lesley said. 'At least he could clear his name over this.'

'I wish he would,' said Sykes, sighing. There were thieves and muggers out there, really dangerous criminals who ought to be locked up, and he was wasting his time over some poor stupid sod who'd got the wrong side of a vain woman with nothing to do but cause trouble.

He left, sure that Lesley herself was not responsible for the harassment; her hostility, and, he was sadly certain, her children's too, was reserved for Philip. She'd promised, however, to get in touch if she heard from him, even though it could mean his arrest. After the last prosecution, a mere hate campaign would be a minor matter.

Lesley said nothing to Andrew or Jackie about the police enquiry. Someone else could have it in for Sandra White if she made a habit of such accusations.

But why had Philip gone to see her? Lesley could

not accept that the purse had been left in Lavery's as bait. Could he still be alive? Did she want him to be?

She did not really know, shedding tears after Sykes left. It was lucky Jackie was out when the sergeant called. By the time Lesley had collected her from her friend Rachel's house, where she had spent the evening, her anger had returned.

How could Philip destroy them all in this manner?

After his first night's work, Philip walked back into Chingbury. He was very tired, but he had been able to wash himself all over in the cloakroom, and he had washed one set of underclothes and dried them on the radiator. The thought that he could do this every night was very comforting; it was strange how being grubby undermined your spirits. He'd had his bread and cheese, and packet soup, and he'd managed to stay awake and watch his screens, and to telephone in at the required intervals. He'd walked round the premises three times, as instructed, and he had been alert, eating a banana when the works manager called unexpectedly to make sure that he was not sleeping at his post.

It was only after this visit that he dared to spend time in the washroom. He'd have to vary it, he realised; these inspections might come nightly, and at staggered intervals. It was what he'd do, were he the man in charge.

Where could he go now? What he really needed

was a warm bed, but he would not be paid until the end of the week – he hoped he'd get his wages then – and after that he'd find a room. He'd stay in the job until another opportunity arose, or until, by demanding papers from him, his employers pushed him out. He was sure that giving his home address would mean a computer check revealing his detailed history. Why should this be so difficult for him when all the time one read of frauds successfully contrived against the social services?

It was a fine, cold day. He must sleep somewhere. He couldn't go back to The Swan, not unless he hired a room, and there would be cheaper places.

He felt good. He'd worked, at last, and he was clean. Six hours sleep and he'd be better still. Life had been reduced to basics now.

When he left, the works had been sliding into gear, with early shifts clocking on and the regular door-keeper taking over. There had been smiles and nods, and 'Hi, there,' from one or two. Philip felt that life was possible. He needed food, however. By the time he reached the town centre, the supermarket had opened and he went there, on the lookout again for sell-by-date reductions. The store was not yet busy; he bought some more bananas and a pack of sandwiches. Nearing the checkout, he heard shrieks and yells, and saw two small children among the cardboard boxes piled in a pen for customers to use. The children were screaming with delight, trampling on them, causing them to fall about and crushing some. Sharply, Philip remembered his mother cutting flaps for doors and windows in large boxes in which Andrew and Jackie had played happily for hours, when very young, using them as houses. Where was the children's mother? Practised at keeping an eye on customers in Lavery's, Philip glanced around and saw no woman who was obviously responsible for them. He frowned. Surely she'd come forward soon? The store should take some action, lift the children out of their enclosure and take them safely to an office, then broadcast for their mother. The bigger child was old enough to know his name. At the Five-Items-or-Fewer check-out, Philip, waiting for his turn to pay, glanced along the row of tills and saw the children suddenly submerged beneath a pile of boxes. One of them began to scream hysterically. Surely the mother would now appear? The shop, so early, was sparsely staffed: it did not pay to have it manned at full strength until later, Philip understood. Then he saw a scruffy young man approach the children. As Philip paid, the man lifted both of them out and set them on their feet beside the pen, bending to talk to them.

It was Denis, and in seconds Philip had taken him by the arm and led him forcibly away.

'Leave them,' he hissed, and Denis, bewildered, allowed himself to be removed.

The children had stopped yelling and were climbing back again among the cartons; meanwhile their mother was in Pandora's Box, having coffee with her lover who worked in a nearby office. They had so little time to meet and the kids were safe in the supermarket; she'd done this before. Then she took them on to nursery school before going to her own job in a dress shop which did not open until later.

'What's the panic?' Denis asked. Philip had dragged him out before he'd had a chance to buy anything. He'd entered the store and seen the kids enjoying themselves, and then the avalanche of boxes. The little girl had been buried underneath them. Denis didn't think about the mother; he was used to seeing kids running round on their own.

Philip bundled Denis away from the shop. If the surveillance cameras were working, the details would have been recorded – Denis had set both children on their feet; he'd not walked off with one of them. All the same, if the mother had approached, she – guilty because she had dumped them with the boxes while she shopped, presumably – could have made all sorts of accusations against the boy, and he could have had a very awkward time explaining himself. He'd probably already been in trouble; all his finesse with cars pointed to the likelihood. He was none too articulate, and even if you were, the law, once it had made up its mind that you were in the wrong, could make supposition look like the truth.

'It doesn't do to touch kids, even if they're lost,' said Philip. 'You could be accused of molesting them.'

'I never!' Denis was indignant. 'I'd not do that –

them as does is animals,' he said.

'Animals don't do that sort of thing,' said Philip. 'Animals behave, within their species.'

Phil did talk grand, thought Denis. Whatever did he mean? He didn't ask, however; the subject, now, had changed. Denis was extremely glad to see the older man: someone he knew; and, in an odd, resigned fashion, Philip, too, was pleased.

'I've had a sodding awful night,' said Denis.

'Have you? What happened?' Philip asked. By this time they were walking down the street.

Denis began describing his nocturnal adventures in the wood.

'If it hadn't rained, it'd have been brilliant,' he declared.

Denis had liked the wood when he went there with the hunt saboteurs. Philip remembered his description of it and he'd thought the boy had been excited by the action; now it seemed that the surroundings had impressed him. But it couldn't have been much fun overnight, with no protective clothing and no cover. It hadn't rained for long; Philip knew that from his own night's observation; but it had been cold. After all, it was November.

'You must be tired and hungry,' he suggested, suddenly reluctant to part from his companion but moved, too, by sympathy. Ahead, he saw the sign advertising Pandora's Box, which was open now and serving breakfast, a new venture in its weekly programme since coffee, light lunches and after-noon teas did not make enough profit. He could run to treating Denis to breakfast. Afterwards, the boy might be able to find them somewhere to sleep. He must be in as much need of that as Philip. 'Let's go in here and have some food,' he said.

Pandora's Box was not the sort of place Denis would have patronised alone, but he could see that old Phil had known better days. You met toffs on the streets, men who'd been in the army or in business, big earners whose marriages had ended and who had nowhere to live because they'd got no jobs. Their evident failure had disheartened Denis; what chance had he of finding work if educated guys like them could not? Some of them drank, which didn't help their chances, but they'd come off the booze if they could get a break. Or so they said.

Never one to pass up an opportunity, Denis fell in with Philip's plan. There was a vacant table in a corner and Philip, who wanted to be inconspicuous, made for it, with Denis following. The café was furnished with cane chairs and pale tables, and there were climbing plants adorning the walls. Its ambience was light and airy and most of the customers were female, though there were a few men in sharp suits here and there. Philip picked up the menu. Whatever hole it made in his budget, he'd have a good meal and see that Denis did, too. With the sandwiches he'd bought, that would do him for the day. He'd still got some packet soup to have at work.

Pandora offered an all-in cooked breakfast for two pounds forty-nine, including bacon, eggs, sausage and baked beans, with toast, roll and butter. Tea or coffee was included.

'How do you like that?' said Philip, showing Denis the menu and pointing to the small square of attached paper announcing this repast; at lunch-time, the dish for the day would be substituted. This system had begun to work quite well, the management was finding; at lunch-time they did salads and a vegetarian dish, and a three-course set menu. Shoppers liked it, and on market days they were very busy; though they were competing with the pubs and with The Swan, their clientele was different.

Denis stared at the small black symbols which had such significance if only you understood them.

'All right,' he said. 'Yeah. Same as you.'

Philip remembered, then, what he had suspected earlier. Denis was illiterate. He pointed with his finger and read out, quite slowly, every word. Denis went on gazing at the page and nodding wisely.

'Can you read at all, Denis?' he asked finally. 'Can you show me where it says "egg" for instance?' Surely that was easy enough.

Denis couldn't. Guessing wildly, his finger pointed to 'beans'.

Patiently, Philip read it out again, pointing to each syllable. The waitress arrived during this exercise and took their order, frowning slightly as she glanced at Denis, who let down the general tone because he was so grubby, but perhaps the father, as she designated Philip, had problems with the boy.

At least the older man was clean and nicely spoken.

'It don't matter,' Denis answered. 'I'm not bothered.'

'But you ought to be,' said Philip. 'How do you manage?'

Not well, was the obvious reply, but Denis did not give it.

'It's OK. I read books,' he said, and pulled a tattered comic from his pocket.

Philip glanced at it. There were pictures, but no words except for the occasional balloon coming out of someone's mouth and saying 'POW!' or 'ZAP!' or with only exclamation marks and stars enclosed. So that was reading.

'Put it away,' he said, as if to a child; this poor boy, as far as literary comprehension was concerned, was about equivalent to four or five, though he was capable enough of looking after himself in street conditions.

Philip had a ballpoint in his pocket, but this was not the place to give Denis a reading lesson. He'd try later, if they stayed together.

Their meal came quickly, and Denis fell upon his greedily, shovelling it into his mouth so that Philip felt constrained to say, 'No one's going to steal your food, Denis. You're in a nice place now. Watch it, can't you?'

Denis did not react with anger to this criticism, as many other youngsters might have done. Instead, he meekly watched how Philip ate and slowed down the process. Both drank several cups of tea.

'What are you going to do next?' Philip asked, pouring out the last few drops.

'Don't know. Get a bit of kip, maybe,' said Denis, who had been thinking of hitching back to town. He might try a bit of random thieving first, if he saw the chance, but not if old Phil was around. He'd not like it.

'Me too,' said Philip.

He wouldn't tell Denis about his job. Wary now, Philip thought the boy might demand to be taken on to the premises, to gain a roof over his head, if Philip had the run of the place. When it was time to go to work, he could lose Denis, even if they spent the day together.

'I passed some sheds, like,' Denis said. 'In gardens, you know. No one was around.'

'Where were they? Can you find them again?' Philip asked.

'Yeah. Course I can,' said Denis.

And he could. When Philip had paid the bill, Denis led him unerringly through the streets into a residential area where there were two acres of allotments with attendant sheds. A man was working on one plot; otherwise, the place was deserted.

'What's he doing?' Denis asked, seeing the lone man planting something.

Philip did not know what he could be putting in at this time of year. It might be broad beans, hoping they would germinate early in the spring. He suggested this as an answer and Denis did not query it. Cultivation of the soil was a mystery to him.

Now, he loped across the ground beyond the single working figure, testing shed doors and at the same time keeping a sharp eye on the bent man.

'Get behind them sheds, Phil,' he ordered, and Philip, obedient here to Denis's superior skills, took care to keep a shed's bulk between him and the potential for discovery.

Denis soon found a shed whose door he was able to force open causing minimal damage. It was well away from the man. Other gardeners might come out later, Philip knew, but you had to take a chance if you were out of luck. Maybe Denis had an instinct for choosing the shed least likely to be used that day. He slipped inside. It was empty, except for some paper sacks in a corner. They made good groundsheets, though they smelled of fertiliser. One at either side of the quite spacious shed, the two companions stretched out. Denis was very soon asleep. Philip spent a while pondering how short a time it had taken him to sink from comfort to this level. He'd rise above it. He'd improve his status. He'd show Lesley a thing or two, and as for Sandra White – well, one day he might find a way to avenge himself on her. She was the one who'd brought about his downfall. She was the one who needed to be brought down herself. But how?

Wondering if there was a way, he fell asleep.

The sound of hammering woke Philip, and he sat up abruptly, stiff and chilly, unable for some seconds to remember where he was. The noise was coming from somewhere close at hand, and he glanced across at Denis who was still asleep.

Grey chinks of light came filtering through gaps in the shed walls, though it was a fairly sturdy building. Denis had chosen well. Philip stood up and went to the door, opening it fractionally to peer out. He could not see anyone; the hammering came from somewhere behind the shed.

He could slip away now, leaving Denis. Perhaps that would be the best thing to do. Neither had an obligation to the other, but, left on his own, Philip would not have found so good a place to spend the day. He felt reluctant to abandon the boy, who might sleep for hours, but if he were to leave without waking him, no explanations would be needed. He would do so.

Philip slipped silently out of the shed and closed the door, then walked resolutely away. Once he'd put some distance between him and it, he felt safer. The hammering went on and, in the late afternoon light, he saw a man mending another shed not far from his recent shelter.

Denis did not follow Philip. He slept on.

17

THE POLICE CAME to see Frances at four o'clock on Tuesday afternoon. She and Charlotte were in the kitchen. The girl had gone out for a walk after breakfast, saying she had to think things through, and she still had not given any clue as to why she had so suddenly appeared.

She'd had a bath, and supper, and Frances had tucked her up in bed much as when she was still a child. Frances found her daughter Arabella, Charlotte's mother, easier than Hazel; she was vague and not unkind, but she was unheeding. Perhaps, if you had a flock of children to look after, some not your own, it was wise not to delve too deeply into what was worrying them. Problems unaired could resolve themselves without everyone concerned becoming upset.

The day was bright after the brilliant sunrise, belying the adage about the shepherd's warning. Frances spent the morning in the garden, trimming shrubs and tidying up the greenhouse where her cuttings were all potted up. Charlotte would tell her what was on her mind, in time, or else would leave, having sorted out her thoughts.

'We might go down to the pottery after lunch,' she suggested, when Charlotte returned, and, to Frances's relief, did justice to a plate of ham and salad. 'At least, I mean to,' she amended. 'I always get some Christmas presents there. You stay here, if you'd rather.'

'No, I'd like to come,' said Charlotte, who had witnessed, over the years, the Wares' transformation of their stables into the workshops now installed there. She had tried her hand at the potter's wheel, more than once. 'There's no future in it, is there?' she remarked, as they walked down the road.

'In what?'

'In rural crafts. In pottery,' said Charlotte.

'There may not be great riches in pottery, unless you become fashionable,' said Frances. 'But Jonathan makes a living and he's happy. He sells at shows and craft fairs and so on. I think he's doing quite well. The rent's not high, out here, and the surroundings are peaceful.'

'I suppose that's right,' said Charlotte, frowning. 'It's so difficult to know what is.'

'You mean what's right? Or what's right for you?'

'Both, I think,' said Charlotte.

'Truth and justice, law and order – those are right things,' said Frances. 'But we hear much too much about individual rights, these days. The rights of various groups who consider themselves down-trodden and persecuted, and who, in making a fuss about what they consider are the wrongs they suffer, harm other people. We don't hear enough about the duties we have to one another.' Parents to children, for example. Frances thought; too much was said about parents' rights concerning children. In her opinion, parents had no such rights, nor the right even to have children. They were a consequence, a privilege, an expense, often a worry, as well as making sense of life, after a fashion. She said none of this, in case consequences of some grim kind were Charlotte's present problem.

'What do you think about testing drugs on animals?' asked Charlotte.

'Where necessary, it must be done before experimenting on people,' said her grandmother. 'It's very strictly controlled now.'

'Is it? How can you be sure?' asked Charlotte.

'It happens that I'm very sure,' said Frances. 'Recently some protestors carried out an attack on a scientist who lives in Darsingford. I've met him. His home workshop was burnt out and valuable computer files were destroyed. His children's pet rabbits were shot. If he'd been at home, or his family, any one of them could have been wounded, if not killed.'

'Oh,' said Charlotte, adding, 'I'd heard about that. I suppose something went wrong.'

'Wrong? The whole thing was wrong,' said

Frances firmly. 'I saw his wife yesterday at the Wares', as a matter of fact. She's been so unnerved that she's taken the children to stay with her parents.'

'I can't understand why the rabbits had to be shot,' Charlotte said, as they reached the pottery, where Jonathan was busy decorating some tulip-shaped vases, ready for the kiln. Charlotte had been coming here for years, and now he let her throw a pot, watching as she struggled with it, then found control and brought it up between her fingers, sending it outwards in a curve and elongating it again.

'You haven't lost your skills,' he said. 'Maybe you should take it up professionally.'

'I've thought about it,' Charlotte said. 'How's Brian?'

'Pretty good. He's had a cold,' said Jonathan. 'He's out earning the real money now.'

Jonathan's partner was an accountant. They had been together for a long time, Brian rescuing Jonathan from a failed career in advertising. They lived in an old stone house in Darsingford whence Brian set off to Swindon every day. Their garden, near the river, was, in June, a bower of roses.

'You're not doing so badly, Jonathan,' said Frances. She knew he had some orders from big stores for some of his figures and bowls. His designs and glazes were striking, improved after a holiday the two men had spent recently in Spain. Jonathan had come back with sketches and fresh ideas.

'Things have looked up lately,' he admitted. 'How long are you staying, Charlotte? What about coming to supper tomorrow night? Brian would hate to miss you.'

'I – er, I don't know how long I'll be here,' Charlotte said, with a sideways glance at her grandmother. 'But if gran will keep me that long, it sounds lovely.'

Frances, who liked to have her days planned well ahead, nodded.

'Thank you, Jonathan, we'd like that very much. Now, let me decide what I'm going to buy from you for Christmas.'

She liked to patronise him, but posting pottery was not a good idea. She chose a bowl for Hazel; if it could not be delivered until after Christmas, that was just too bad. She thought Hazel would be sure to like it, and she might mention Jonathan's work to some of her contacts, but asking her to do it would not be wise; she would have to seem to think of it herself.

Frances would be invited to one of her daughters' homes for Christmas. This happened every year, after they had worked it out between them – tossing for who lost, she sometimes thought. She'd gone in previous years because she wanted to maintain contact and to see her grandchildren; maybe she wouldn't, this time. Why not simply stay at home? She could ask Jonathan and Brian to dinner.

Walking back with Charlotte, they discussed

Jonathan's work and the peaceful atmosphere in his pottery. Even if he was working at full stretch, there was a calm ambience.

'He's happy, isn't he?' said Charlotte.

'Yes, I think he is,' Frances agreed. 'He and Brian are a very solid pair. Much more so than many heterosexual couples.'

'I suppose they aren't so often being tempted away, are they?' Charlotte said.

'Are married couples constantly tempted away from one another?' Frances asked her. 'And unmarried pairs? Surely not.'

'Sometimes. Sometimes they just get tired of one another,' Charlotte said. She wondered if that could possibly have happened to her grandmother and grandfather, had he not died so young, but she did not like to ask. However, Frances answered her unspoken question.

'I don't know if that would have happened to Dick and me,' she said. 'We were often apart and I had to make a life for myself and your mother and aunt. But we were always very happy when we met again.' Their reunions had been like honeymoons. There had never been anyone else she would consider marrying, though for years she had had a lover, a geologist, and married, whom she met in secret when it could be managed. She did not know his wife. Eventually he died, but their affair had petered out long before that, though occasionally they had met as friends. She might tell Charlotte about this one day, if the information could either interest her or help her with problems of her own.

They let themselves into the house and had just taken off their coats when the doorbell rang. Frances, on her way to put the kettle on, called out to Charlotte, asking her to see who was there.

A man stood on the step. He announced himself to be from the police and held out a card which Charlotte took to be some form of identification. He was not in uniform, but a white van stood outside.

'Oh!' gasped Charlotte, and banged the door in his face, then ran in to the kitchen.

'It's the police!' she cried, sat down at the kitchen table and laid her hands on it, then, bursting into tears, hid her face on her folded arms.

'Gracious me!' Frances was stunned. 'What is the matter, Charlotte? It's only about my stolen purse. They said they might come today, if they weren't too busy. What have you done with them?'

Not waiting for an answer, she went into the hall and opened the door, where the fingerprint officer was waiting patiently.

'I'm so sorry,' Frances said. 'My granddaughter should have let you in.'

'She looked as if she'd seen a ghost,' said the man. 'Perhaps I reminded her of someone she'd rather forget.'

'Perhaps,' said Frances, distractedly.

Or something, thought both of them.

Had she been in trouble with the police?

Charlotte had pulled herself together and found a teapot and some cups and saucers. She concentrated on making the tea, standing by the kettle while it came up to the boil, while Frances detained the fingerprint officer in the hall, explaining where there had been mud from the intruder's feet, and suggesting where he might have touched the door.

'But of course I've touched it since, and so has Charlotte,' she declared.

'I'll have to take your prints, and hers, for elimination,' said the officer.

'Yes, of course,' said Frances. 'I'm grateful that you've come. I haven't heard of any more break-ins in the village,' she added. 'Not that this was a break-in. I'm afraid it was all too easy for the thief to walk in while I was in the garden with the door unlocked.'

'Was your granddaughter here at the time?' asked the officer.

'No. No, she came yesterday afternoon, after I'd reported the theft,' said Frances, and walked through into the kitchen. 'I haven't told you, Charlotte. Someone got in here on Saturday and helped himself out of my purse, which was on the table.'

'Oh dear,' said Charlotte. 'That's awful. Did you lose a lot of money?'

'Enough,' said Frances. 'But he left my credit cards. Wasn't that strange? I believe you can sell them.'

'Perhaps he was an amateur,' said the fingerprint man, who had now unpacked his kit. 'Well, ladies, let's do you first and then I'll recognise a strange set.

Though I expect you've had other visitors.'

'Probably, but I may have dusted round,' said Frances, who did all her own housework. 'I could have dusted them off.'

'Shall we have some tea?' suggested Charlotte, whose colour had now come back. She ran a hand through her short dark hair. What it was to have a guilty conscience! 'I'm so sorry you've been burgled, gran.'

'I should have put the purse away,' said Frances.

'Or locked the door,' said the fingerprint man.

'Out here, in the wilds? When I was in and out all afternoon, working in the garden?' said Frances. 'I'm not going to start doing that.'

'The hunt sabs were out on Saturday. They were in Chingbury,' said the man, confirming that he shared her suspicions. 'They don't really go in for thieving, not the genuine protestors, but they bring all sorts of riff-raff with them. That may explain your visitor.'

'I hope it does,' said Frances. 'That'll mean he's gone again, even though he took my money.'

'They weren't too bad this time,' said the man. 'Though a horse was hurt and had to have its leg stitched.'

'Why hurt horses when you say your aim is saving foxes?' Frances asked.

'Why indeed?' said the man, proceeding with his task.

18

PHILIP WAS LOOKING forward to his next work session. He had his carrier bag, containing his packet soup and his date-expired sandwiches, with two bananas, and a book he had bought for ten pence at the charity shop; it was a tattered copy of, appropriately, *Hard Times*, the thickest volume on display and one he had never read. Somehow he'd never got into Dickens, though he'd enjoyed film adaptations on television. Reading on duty wasn't forbidden, as long as he remembered to watch his screens and carry out his inspections.

He wondered if they'd check his references. If he took on a security guard, he'd certainly check. Weren't ex-convicts sometimes employed as patrols? Who better, in a way, to know how to catch a thief?

Tonight, he'd wash and shave as the hour for release drew near. On his first duty spell, he couldn't wait to get cleaned up in comfort. Philip understood, now, how people ended up in hostels for the homeless – and they were the lucky ones. He'd be in another one himself if he lost this job, and if he could find one which would take him in, for sleeping out in winter would be too much for him. Though the one where he had stayed was not unduly squalid, he imagined stinking blankets, soiled pallet mattresses, and other horrors. He was too fastidious, he thought; years of comfort taken for granted by most citizens of the western world had made him soft. Maybe he'd always been weak; if he'd been a bolder, tougher man, would he have got himself into such a situation with the evil Sandra White? For she was evil: she had set him up in a manner which a more sophisticated man would have seen coming.

And Lesley had doubted him. What did that say about their years together, their whole marriage, the trust supposed to exist between them? He'd trusted her: he'd never questioned her fidelity, any more than he questioned her ability as a mother and as organiser of the household. He did his share of chores and was a fair cook, but she was the domestic boss, just as he took charge of their finances. He considered his prime duty was to be the provider but he wasn't providing for his family now; he couldn't even provide for himself.

It was time to do his rounds. He rose, took his torch, and set off.

The building, two storeys high and surrounded by a high wire fence, was made of concrete blocks, plastered over. It was not custom built for its purpose, having been adapted from its former use. Philip walked through the silent areas where, by day, the mostly female staff packed cosmetics first into jars and then into cartons. Everything was clinically very clean. He saw the different pots and bottles, into which were ladled cream and lotions for which the customer paid according to the package. The contents did no harm to anyone, and probably even benefited users, he supposed, though miracles were fables. Dream emulsions, he decided: those were what were being processed here.

He had dreams no longer. Even the aspirations he had had for Andrew and Jackie were in limbo now as he had no power to help them; they would have to achieve their own successes.

He went from section to section, shining his torch here and there, putting on lights and turning them off again. Then he returned to his surveillance screens and surveyed them all. There was nothing out of place. It was time for some refreshment. He went to boil his kettle: tonight his first soup packet was beef and tomato; he'd have the cream of asparagus and his sandwiches later, punctuating these meals with strong black instant coffee which helped to keep him awake.

At intervals during the night, Philip did exercises. Hands on hips, he swung his torso round, did press-ups and ran on the spot. He'd be stiff next day, he thought, but this was a way to pass the time and would make him fitter. He was so feeble, so flabby;

he needed to build up muscle. The hours wore on, and again he was subject to a sudden unheralded inspection. All was in order, however, and he had made the correct recorded notes about his inspection drills.

No one would really want to hit this place, surely: there was no money here except on Friday, pay day, and the cosmetics were of limited value to sell on: only packed jars would find a market and thieves would do much better going after goods in transit – lorry loads of cigarettes, designer clothes or spirits. Still, there had been that incident at the depot down the road and the arson attack on the far side of Darsingford, across the river; that had been a nasty business.

People grew obsessed, became fanatical, saw no other viewpoint as of merit but their own.

He'd never been fanatical about anything, not even the sales figures at Lavery's, nor his print collection. There wasn't much time for hobbies when you were married, with a garden to keep tidy, and the necessary household repairs and decoration to be done. He was a skilled paper-hanger and painter and could put up shelves and lay patio stones in competition with anyone, just as Lesley could make curtains and clothes for herself and Jackie – though Jackie, now, elected to buy her own and wore drab skirts or jeans when not in school uniform.

He wondered how Jackie was. He loved her, he admitted, and he minded bitterly that he had lost her respect. What if he returned to London and sought out Sandra White, loomed over her, bearded and gaunt as he now was, demanding that she retract her allegations? She'd simply call the police and have him arrested for threatening behaviour, if not assault, and he'd be in still more trouble, for, again, she would be believed, this time with some justification.

He could write to her, though: for the price of a stamp, he could frighten her with an intimidating letter. He could do it here, compose it on the typewriter in the front office. There'd be some paper in one of the cupboards.

There was, but it was headed with the company's name. He cut that off, and typed his message out.

YOU LIED, he wrote. It was enough.

He found a plain manila envelope and addressed the letter, then put it in his pocket. Leaving work early in the morning, now washed again and with his clean laundry in the plastic carrier, he set off to walk back into town. On the way, he saw a dry dog turd on the footpath. He'd send her a bit of that, next time: just that, no message. The turd would keep until tomorrow, or he would find another one; there was no shortage.

He felt happier, with this decided and the letter posted. He forgot about the postmark, and the fingerprints he had left on the sheet of paper, but when it arrived some days later, by second-class post, and was followed by the piece of hard dry excrement, the police officer who took the evidence from Sandra's flat did not. The matter, however, was not urgent.

When he had posted his letter, buying a book of stamps from a machine, Philip went to Pandora's Box for some good hot coffee and toast. He'd bought a paper, too, and scanned it briefly before settling down to do the crossword. He still had some cash in hand but he was afraid an emergency would force him to use it for his own subsistence. On Friday, he'd be paid; two hundred pounds would be put into his hand and he would be able to pay out forty for a week's rent for a room.

He could do it now. He had forty-five pounds left, and his watch, but he had to eat. If he had a room, he'd go back to it, get into bed and sleep like the dead. But he was managing. Once he'd got the room, he'd look for another job, maybe stacking shelves in the supermarket, if they had a vacancy. It was coming up to Christmas; they must be taking on extra staff and he wouldn't mind anti-social hours. But he'd need an address: he couldn't apply without one.

He'd given a false address to the cosmetic company, choosing the number of the Public Library, or what he assumed it to be – fifty-four, Church Road – as he'd seen number fifty-five to one side of it, a large pebble-dashed house behind a privet hedge and railings. Would they check him out? Not yet, he thought. He'd had to take a chance.

It was so easy to slip into lies and deceit; here he was, involved in both, though not a criminal, and Sandra White had set him on that course.

By the time he'd drunk his coffee and eaten every scrap of toast, the library would have opened. He went along there. He'd pretend to read and attempt to doze; if that didn't work, and he was expelled by one of the librarians, he'd seek the allotment shed again. Soon, with a periodical on his knee and his chair turned away from the librarians' working area with its computer terminal and shelves of reserved books and videos, he slept.

One of the two librarians on duty noticed him snoozing, but she did not disturb him. She did not recognise him as a regular reader, but he looked quite respectable. Perhaps he had a troubled life at home and needed to escape. You saw all sorts in libraries, and redundancies had produced more customers.

When Denis came in some time later, she noticed he was dirty and unkempt. He was entitled, as a member of the public, to be in there, but she'd keep an eye on him. He did not look to be a keen reader. She was quite surprised when, after being busy at the desk, she remembered to look out for him and saw him seated at a table with the older man, both their heads intently bent over whatever they were reading.

She was curious enough, when her duties permitted, to glance over their shoulders, and saw that it was a book about Little Bear. The older man seemed to be teaching the younger, grubby man to read.

Well, that was admirable. She left them undisturbed.

Denis, waking the day before to find Philip gone, had been quite hurt. Weren't they mates now? He'd thought so. Although Phil wasn't streetwise, knew nothing about finding a good spot to kip and wouldn't wear a simple bit of easy theft, he was a good bloke.

He'd been really scared, out all night in that wood, yet in a way he'd like to do it again. With Phil, it'd be OK. He'd probably know how to make a fire and build a shelter; old guys like him sometimes did. One of Denis's foster fathers had been good at outdoor things: he'd been a big man, much bigger than Phil, and he'd got the children playing games and making model aeroplanes. They'd respected him. After Denis was moved on, he'd never seen the man again. That was what happened; you were never settled. He'd once tried to explain that to his social worker but she hadn't seemed to understand. Funny how many of them were women; you'd expect them to be scared of some of the folk they had to deal with. Maybe they were. More guys should take it up, he thought: the kids might respect them more; most of them were dead scared of their fathers – those who had a father. He wondered if Phil had any kids.

He'd gone into the town and bought some chips.

There was nothing to do in this place; it was dead. Maybe he'd move on. He drifted into one of the pubs, where there were some fruit machines, and he played one for a bit, ending up by losing over four pounds. He'd bought a Coke, and stayed there for a while joshing with two lads who'd come in together and saw him lose his money. One of them took his place and soon cleaned up.

'Lucky bugger,' said his friend, and Denis agreed, moving on. He felt uneasy with them; if he upset them, there were two of them. If Biff were here, it'd be different. Biff always knew what to do or say to keep out of trouble, unless it was the sort of trouble he had asked for and could handle. Denis had seen plenty of fights and didn't want to get mixed up in one.

He'd drifted off, and had found a van to sleep in, a delivery van parked in a quiet road – someone's old jalopy with a strong lock on the steering wheel but an undefended door at the back. Denis opened it with ease, was able to shut himself inside, and was hidden from any passer-by. There were some old sacks in it. He wrapped them round him. They made good insulation and he slept well, only waking when the van's engine suddenly started and it was driven off.

He lay where he was, quiet as a mouse, not yet seen by the driver, who, in the dawn light, Denis saw had long hair in a pony-tail and wore a denim jacket. The van stopped at a petrol station and the man filled the tank. When he went into the shop to pay, Denis nipped out smartly and fled down the street. The driver, on his way to work on a building site, never saw him.

Denis, once he was sure he'd got away with it, chortled in triumph. What a breeze! He'd have liked Biff to see him handle that one. He strode on up the road in the direction from which he'd just come, returning to the safety of known territory.

It was chance that took him into the library. He recognised it when he looked through the windows. He'd been in libraries before; they were warm and dry, and there were books with pictures in, which he could look at. If he was quiet, no one would turn him out. They were for the public, weren't they? He went up the steps and through the door, and there, to his astonishment, sat Phil, dozing in a chair. He woke when Denis laid a hand on his knee, starting up, amazed to see him in these surroundings.

'Would you like a reading lesson?' were the first words spoken by Philip as means of diverting questions and accusations before they could be uttered, and Denis accepted eagerly.

As they pored over the Little Bear book, it was clear that Denis had a lot to learn if he were to be declared a competent reader. It was a task worth tackling, though, thought Philip, trying to bestir his drowsy brain. The boy might get a decent job if he could be rendered even slightly literate. After the lesson, he'd take him out and make him try to find one, even if it was only washing up or moving rubbish.

But who would employ such a hopeless-looking applicant, dirty and unshaven, and malodorous? And how could Philip get him cleaned up, with no spare clothing or facilities?

Denis wanted to keep the book when they left the library, and Philip gave him a stern lecture on theft.

'But it's public. It's for everyone, and free,' said Denis.

'You have to join,' said Philip. 'They wouldn't take us on as registered readers, not without someone to vouch for us or a proper address.' He couldn't invent another: the library would soon find out, if he tried. 'We can come back,' he said, rashly.

'Why don't we get a room?' said Denis. 'Then we'd have an address.'

'I haven't got enough money,' Philip said.

'I have,' said Denis, and he showed Philip what remained of Frances Dixon's pension.

Two hours later they were sitting in a small single room in a cheap lodging house in a down-market part of the town. While Denis kept out of the way, Philip had rented the room for a week, paying in advance.

As Denis had produced the funds, Philip had felt obliged to tell the boy about his job, which meant, said Denis, that they could take turns to use the bed, thus saving money as a double room cost more. Now, Philip declared that he must get some sleep before he went to work.

'I'll find us some food,' said Denis. He was

beaming. He was doing things to help old Phil, who was going to make a scholar of him.

Philip crashed out as soon as Denis left, too tired even to worry whether the boy meant to shop legitimately. He set the alarm on his watch for five o'clock. Then, warm and comfortable at last, though the bed was hard and the coarse sheets scratchy, he was soon sound asleep. Denis was not back when it was time for him to leave. Mistrustfully, and from habit, Philip took all his possessions with him. There was a bathroom on another landing at the lodgings, but it was not as clean and shining as the cloakroom at the works.

When Denis returned, he was as happy as a sandboy. He'd bought sandwiches and crisps at a newsagent's which sold snacks and sweets, and he'd stolen a Little Bear book which he saw on a stall in the market. He'd got there just as it was packing up and had bought some apples for ten pence from a trader wanting to clear his stock. He'd need more money soon. He'd get that while Phil was out. There'd be an unlocked door or window simply waiting for him, if he went seeking one.

Phil had let him take the keys. He could come and go as he chose, but he'd better be there to let the old guy in, next morning.

Phil said he'd refund the rent as soon as he was paid. He meant it, Denis guessed: he was a good old boy.

On his own, Denis felt restless. The room was on the top floor of a tall house high above the town, looking across to where Tessa had done her damage. He wondered if Biff had seen her again. Biff thought she was quite something. Denis briefly felt a pang; he missed Biff. Still, Phil would see him right now, for a bit, and Denis knew better than to think further ahead than the next few hours. He lay on his bed trying to puzzle out the words describing Little Bear's adventure. He could recognise *Bear* now; it was repeated often and there were drawings of Little Bear and either his mother or his father on almost every page.

Painstakingly, Denis tried to spell out each short word, but he could not concentrate for more than a few minutes. After a while he sat up, opened a packet of crisps, and ate them. Then he decided to go out. He walked down the steep stairs, which were uncarpeted. You'd make a noise, entering late, he thought, testing for sound as he tried to move quietly in his trainers. He'd look for a house to enter. He could always go back to that one in Chingbury. He'd already thought of that. There'd be money because the person he'd seen in the garden would soon get more. Who else lived there, wondered Denis: it was a huge place, by his standards. Maybe he'd just been lucky to find someone there alone. He might go over tomorrow; he'd have to find something to do while Phil was sleeping.

From a room on the ground floor came the sound of pop music, played quite softly, but otherwise there was silence. He thought about trying some of the doors in search of pickings but decided that was too chancy. Thieving was better done away from your own patch.

Denis, who had always been only an opportunist thief, had never broken into a house in darkness, though Biff had. His pickings had mostly come from shoplifting. He might try those houses in the area where he'd found the car to sleep in, Denis thought, setting out on a fine, dry night. He felt better when he was in the street. The quiet in the room, so different from the silence in the fields, had been unsettling. He was used to the noise of traffic, but what he heard now was much reduced in volume from the roar he was accustomed to hearing. Darsingford was not a very busy place at night.

The street lights lit his route as he walked through the town. Cars swished past and a bus was collecting passengers. He contemplated catching it, going off to wherever it would take him, which might be livelier than here. He tried to read the signboard above the windscreen and was just beginning to pick out and mouth S – W when it moved off. Good old Phil would teach him more tomorrow; maybe they'd have breakfast first, in that café, which was a really cool place. Denis had liked Pandora's Box with its cane seating and pretty decor, but he'd be scared to go in there alone; they might not want to serve him, and as he couldn't read the menu, ordering could be a problem, though he could always ask for sausage and chips. But the money was running low now. He wouldn't be able to afford too many more meals of that sort.

Once in the main street, he set off towards the road where he had slept in the car, but on the way, passing the bridge, he had a better idea. The area on the further side might offer more scope for his planned activities; the houses were much bigger and with larger gardens. There would be more cover where he could hide while assessing his prospects. If he had no luck, he could always move on to other streets.

He walked over the bridge and up the hill. He wouldn't go near the house Tessa'd done over and where he'd called on Sunday. Instead, he turned to the left by the park and went along a narrow road where the street lights seemed set further apart than in the busier part of the town. The road wound round, taking him back towards the river, and here the houses were older and, some of them, more cottage-like than those built when the town expanded. Here, in two renovated cottages transformed into a long, low house, lived Jonathan and Brian who were, this evening, entertaining Frances Dixon and her granddaughter.

Denis progressed methodically down the road, testing every parked car in case it had been left unlocked. He peered inside, for opening most of them posed no great problem if he saw a handbag or a brief case carelessly exposed, but he did not want to risk challenging an advanced alarm system. They made a lot of noise.

There could be alarms on the houses, too, he

realised; Biff had said that big places often had them and you needed to be careful, but when folk were in, they were often not set, and in any case you had a few minutes before anyone could arrive. In poorer areas, though, there were no alarms and less chance of capture, but also less chance of finding money: Denis, with no outlet here for radios and videos, or jewellery, was only interested in finding cash.

He crept up the short paths to several doorways and slid round the houses in darkness; not everyone had security lights, though he started back in alarm when one came on as he stepped out from behind some shrubs. You didn't find them in poor areas, either.

His eyes had grown accustomed to the darkness, and he began to play a game, testing himself by seeing how close he could get to a building before the light came on. Unable to see where they were positioned, he tried sidling along the wall of a low house with the dim shape of a white-painted conservatory at one side. Voices and laughter came from behind some curtains, beyond which he could see a glimmer of light. People were in there, having a party. He'd tried the door of a blue Viva parked in the road outside, but it was locked. There was no car in the driveway of the house. Brian rode a motor-cycle to his office; their shared estate car, used by Jonathan to get to Chingbury and to transport his pots, was in the garage.

Denis managed to reach the back of the house

without being exposed by a halogen beam. If he could get through an upstairs window, he might strike lucky.

Then a bright light shone and in a flash Denis was out of its range and hiding behind a bush. He saw a tabby cat walk delicately across the paved area at the back of the house, and smiled, safe from discovery. No one came to see what had made the light come on because nobody had noticed; the light was to deter as well as to reveal, and Denis drew nearer, able to look through a lighted window between slats in the blind. Beyond was a kitchen, large and scrupulously neat, with some plates on a drainer beside the sink but no debris of the meal Brian had just cooked; he cleared up as he went along and left only what would be stacked in the dishwasher. As Denis stared at what seemed to him the utmost in luxury, a man came in, carrying a tray laden with dishes. Denis shrank back but stood where he could still see in: the blind would screen him unless the man looked directly at him, and then he'd be off as fast as the cat, which had streaked away when he moved near it.

The man was old – quite as old as Phil – with neat grey hair and a calm face. He set the tray down on the table and began to unload the dishes from it. As he did so, another figure came into the kitchen, a girl. She held a glass and went over to the sink to fill it. Her grandmother had requested plain water as she had already enjoyed one glass of wine and would have no more because of driving home.

Denis, watching, saw the man lift a green bottle from the table and say something to the girl, but he barely registered their actions because he knew the girl.

It was Jet.

19

HE COULDN'T BELIEVE it.

Denis forgot about being observed himself as he stared through the glass at the small girl with the short dark hair. If it wasn't her, it was her double. He almost knocked on the window to attract her attention but, just in time, thought better of it. He'd no right to be out there, loitering with intent – for that was what he was doing.

She left the kitchen, carrying the bottle, and soon afterwards the man followed.

Did she live here? He thought she was a student in London. Steve was her boyfriend and the two of them were friends of Orlando's, just as Biff was – and Denis himself, in a way. Gingerly, he tried the handle of the back door and it yielded. Scarcely knowing what he was doing, heart thumping, Denis opened it and stood inside the room. He heard voices and laughter coming from close by, and the chink of cutlery on glass. They were eating somewhere else: you would, in a place this size, he supposed, though the pine kitchen table was big enough to sit a family of ten around it, he decided wistfully.

Prudently, he retreated. If someone returned, it might be the man, not Jet. Was he her father? He looked the right age. Lucky girl to live here, with no worries about how to pay for the next meal, or the increasing cold. At this thought, Denis shivered and withdrew from his vantage point, out of range of the security light. He slipped round to the front of the house and hid behind a laurestinus, watching. When they'd all gone to bed, he might discover which was Jet's room and visit her. She wouldn't be scared – she'd know who he was straight away, Denis reasoned optimistically.

Brian had tried to prevent Charlotte from fetching the bottle of mineral water which, he said, should have been already on the table. Jonathan had forgotten it.

'The table's his job. The cooking's mine,' Brian had said, and had smiled affectionately at his friend who had murmured, '*Mea culpa*.'

Charlotte had visited the house before, with Frances. She knew that the two men had been together for about eight years. Brian, with his own good position, had given Jonathan the courage and security to start a new life as a potter, and he had done well enough to rent his own workshop in Chingbury. Until then he had used the garage at their house, but they had been refused planning permission to turn it into a proper studio, or to build one in the garden.

Charlotte, beset by her anxieties, had accepted a glass of wine before the meal and drank more during it. The effect was to give her a sense of being in a dream as she sat, rather quietly, in the long drawing-room with its beamed ceiling and pale walls adorned with original water colours which the two men collected. Vaguely she noticed how they dovetailed their activities, one taking her and Frances's coats, the other pouring drinks, never getting in one another's way. They were, she sensed, a team, and there was no aura of tension, as there often was at home between her parents, though she knew their marriage was a success. They sharpened their wits on one another and had spiky arguments which they found stimulating but which were often alarming to their offspring, who frequently, also, quarrelled among themselves.

Frances was dressed in a black wool skirt printed with tiny red flowers, and a red silk blouse. Charlotte had packed only jeans, leggings, and a change of underclothes. Frances had produced a peacock blue shirt which she had suggested, mildly, might be more appropriate for their evening out than Charlotte's bulky sweater. She wore it with black leggings, and she looked, thought her grandmother, rather like Peter Pan.

When she was out of the room with Brian, Jonathan quirked an eyebrow at Frances and asked, 'Trouble with Charlotte?'

Frances nodded.

'I don't know what it is,' she said. 'I may never be told.'

She always enjoyed her evenings with Brian and Jonathan. They often invited her on her own, and the three would discuss art, education, finance, and the state of the world – all subjects of interest to them – and sometimes, when they gave dinner parties, they asked her to make up the numbers. Among their friends were Guy and Amanda Frost. His research was of great importance, Frances knew, and it was dreadful that, misguidedly, his records had been destroyed.

It was she who raised the subject, over the pudding – a mousse containing apricots and almonds, gingered up with amaretto.

'How's Guy?' she asked. 'Have you heard from him?'

'I asked him round this evening,' Brian said. 'I knew that Amanda and the children have gone away. He said he's still too busy trying to retrieve his files.'

'I expect most of his stuff is duplicated at the lab,' said Jonathan.

'Guy Frost is a research scientist who lives up the hill,' Brian told Charlotte. 'He does – or did – a lot of work at home, in a glorified garden shed, but a pack of weirdos set it alight a few weeks ago and shot his children's pet rabbits.'

Some reaction from Charlotte was clearly expected.

'Gran told me,' she managed. She was suddenly unable to face the rest of her delicious, creamy pudding, and began pushing it around her plate while her hair fell forward in two half moons, partly obscuring her face. 'It's dreadful.'

'It could have been murder,' said Jonathan. 'If Guy or the family had been there. They might have been burned.'

'Or shot,' said Brian.

'It was murder of the rabbits, wasn't it?' said Charlotte, in a faint voice quite unlike her normal cool tone.

'Well – in a way, yes,' said Jonathan. 'You could say so, yes,' he added.

Why was he being so emphatic, wondered Frances, who was enjoying her meal. She never made exotic or romantic puddings. Even when people came to dinner, what they got was a flan, fruit salad or a fruit fool; sometimes summer pudding.

'It's wrong to torture animals,' said Charlotte.

'Yes, it is,' agreed Brian.

Frances waited. What was coming next?

'Wasn't that what it was about?' asked Charlotte. 'I mean, that man – your friend – he tortures animals, in his experiments.'

'He doesn't, Charlotte,' Jonathan answered gently. 'He has to use them for tests, yes, but they don't suffer.'

'How do you know?'

'For one thing, what he does is strictly controlled,

so that the rats, or whatever he uses, are sedated so as not to feel pain.' Jonathan felt certain that what he told her was the truth. 'And anyway, since Guy's experiments are to do with nervous diseases, I doubt if pain's involved.'

'But he must paralyse them. The rats. To reproduce the symptoms,' Charlotte argued, her voice rising, sounding angry.

'Maybe, but if humans can be cured as a result, isn't that worthwhile?'

'I didn't know you were a vegetarian, Charlotte,' Brian interposed. 'It was nice of you to eat the lamb, considering your scruples.'

'But I'm not,' said Charlotte. She picked up her fork and began prodding at her pudding once again.

'There are eggs in that,' Brian told her.

Frances was listening to this exchange. More was being said than seemed apparent on the surface.

'So?' Now Charlotte's tone was hostile.

'If you think rats shouldn't be used for medical research, you must be against eating meat, and that includes eggs, from which come chickens,' Brian said. He spoke calmly, looking at her across the table, and did not mention battery hens, but Charlotte couldn't meet his gaze.

'I'm sorry Guy couldn't come tonight. He could have explained things better than we can,' said Jonathan. 'He could have told you exactly what he's doing and what's involved. In fact, why don't we arrange that, Frances?' He turned to her. 'If Charlotte's staying on, I'm sure Guy would show her round the lab and she could see the situation for herself.'

'I – I won't be here long enough,' said Charlotte. 'I've got to get back to college.' She dabbed at her lips with the fine lawn napkin. 'I – er – I – would you excuse me, please?' she gasped, and got up from the table.

'You know where the bathroom is,' said Jonathan smoothly, ushering her from the room.

Brian looked at Frances.

'A confused young woman,' he said. 'Not unusual at her age. I hope our suggestion isn't going to drive her away.'

'She may be hiding here from a problem that she's got to face,' said Frances, as Jonathan returned.

'Love?' he asked. 'Or something?'

'Or something, I suspect,' said Frances.

Upstairs in the bathroom, Charlotte poured cold water into the basin and splashed her hot, angry face. She'd had several glasses of wine, otherwise she knew she would not have been so rude, whatever her convictions. Besides, she wasn't really convinced, only bewildered. One person's truth was another's terror, she could see. Steve, in abandoning the protests, had been right.

She opened the bathroom window and leaned out, inhaling the cool night air, casting a beam of light across the front garden. Suddenly a figure emerged from a large bush and as it crossed the sensor, the porch light came on.

'Jet! Hi, Jet!' came a shrill whisper. 'Down here. It's me – Denis. Can I come in and meet your folks?'

'God!' Charlotte, horrified, recognised him in the brilliance of the light – at least, it looked enough like Denis to make it seem probable that it was really him. 'What are you doing here?' she hissed, praying that her elders were busy talking round the dinner table.

'Came down with Biff, but he's gone,' said Denis. 'Are you going to let me in?' He spoke more loudly now.

'It's not my house,' she said. 'Meet you in the library tomorrow morning. Eleven o'clock,' she said, and closed the window.

What was he doing, skulking in the garden? Up to no good, she thought.

Charlotte took some deep breaths, dabbed at her grandmother's blouse, which she had splashed when trying to cool her face, and went downstairs again.

Both men rose as she entered. They had such good manners; it was rather sweet, thought Charlotte, used to more casual conduct from her siblings and her peers. Some of those old ways were really great.

'I'll make the coffee,' Jonathan said, and, as he passed her, gave her a gentle hug.

'Yes – let's go into the other room,' said Brian, and he shepherded them back into the drawing-room.

Her mind still in a daze, Charlotte allowed herself to be guided to a large armchair.

'I'm sorry – I think I was rude earlier,' she said, looking sheepish.

'No, dear. Just outspoken,' Brian said. 'I like that. I like a person to feel free to give her views.' He smiled at her and produced a box of Bendick's peppermint creams.

Charlotte, accepting one, had the feeling that they were treating her as if she were a penitent child, now forgiven. Perhaps that's what she was, she thought – penitent for her bad manners, and for any part she'd had in causing damage to that man's house and his children's rabbits.

'I think I'd like to meet Dr Frost and see his work, if you really meant it, and if Gran can keep me for another day or two,' she said.

Charlotte should be back at college. Did her parents know where she was? Weren't the authorities wondering why she wasn't at her classes? Had she no essays to deliver? And what was the subtext of her exchange with Brian and Jonathan about animals?

Such thoughts ran through Frances's head as she lay in bed that night.

She had parted from Charlotte on the landing, exchanging a light kiss on the cheek, then Frances had returned downstairs to check the doors and windows once again. She had yielded to the advice of the police fingerprint officer to call in his colleague who would recommend security measures

259

she should take. It would mean special locks on the windows, and the loss of various freedoms which, out here in the country, Frances had taken for granted, even now, when mobile criminals could travel any distance very easily and be miles away in minutes.

Something like that must explain the escape of those who had attacked Guy Frost's house. How oddly Charlotte had reacted when the subject arose at dinner. It was most unlike her to be so abrupt, and it was not as though she had been dragged to the house as an unwilling guest; she liked the two men and had been eager to go, telling her grandmother that the pair gave out 'good vibes'.

'You feel everything's all right when they're there,' she had said. 'They seem strong.'

'They trust each other. They are sure of one another's affection,' Frances said.

Brian had told her of his great joy when he and Jonathan joined forces. Life had been lonely before, he said. He had not proclaimed his sexual orientation to the world: such things were private, he had felt: kiss and tell was never right and why make such a fuss? Meeting Jonathan had seemed, to both of them, a miracle, and neither sought outside excitement nor felt any need to proselytise.

'All this "outing",' Brian had said. 'So noisy and upsetting. Heterosexuals don't feel the need to boast about it; why should we?'

Some do, unfortunately, Frances thought, but let the subject drop. The business with Guy had been linked to public clamour, too. People needed interests, causes to pursue, but did they have to be so confrontational? Why was not more heard of the many good souls who turned their energies towards charitable work, helping the starving overseas, or even here at home? Because it wasn't news. Good news did not titillate; scandal and drama did.

As Charlotte was confused about the rights of animals, a trip to Guy's laboratory and a meeting with that dedicated man might be of benefit. Meanwhile, she was safe; if Arabella were anxious about her, she would telephone to see if she had been in touch with Frances. If the college was concerned, they would contact the parents, in due course. Frances decided to adopt a course of masterly inactivity.

She slept at last, and so did Charlotte, unaware that Denis had slipped into Brian and Jonathan's house while they were out in the road seeing the two women off. Hurrying from his cover behind a bush, Denis had nipped in through the unlocked kitchen door, run upstairs and into the first room at the top. It was a bedroom, and a wallet, Jonathan's, was on a tallboy where he had put it when he came home and hurried to do his share of the evening's preparations. Denis took the banknotes from it, replaced it, and ran back the way he had come just as the Viva drove away.

There'd been only twenty pounds in this one: not as lucky a hit as the other, in that village. Still, it was something.

* * *

Jonathan, like Frances, did not discover the theft for some time. In his case, it was the next morning when he stopped for petrol on the way to Chingbury and found the note section of his wallet empty. He paid with his credit card, but was unnerved. He knew there were two ten-pound notes left in it the previous evening after he had stopped on the way home to buy a bottle of whisky. Frances liked a nip, and they'd run out. He had paid with a twenty, and the change had all been in coins which had weighed down his pocket. He'd put them in a bowl he'd made, an early effort, somewhat flawed. The thief had not taken them: too bulky, perhaps. It had to be Charlotte who had stolen the money; she, alone, had spent time upstairs, after her little drama at the dinner table.

He didn't want to believe it, but what other explanation was there?

20

ORLANDO HAD NOT been able to observe the result of his venture with the kissogram, nor to check that it had been delivered, but he rang Sandra that Tuesday night to invite her out the following evening.

Would she accept? If she did, would she tell him about the kissogram?

He rang her from a public call box. She did not know his real name, nor his address, and he meant to preserve this anonymity until his game with her was over. How long would it last? He couldn't continue it indefinitely. It was expensive, for one thing, and so far, beyond irritating her, he had not accomplished the restoration of Philip Winter's reputation. In any case, the unfortunate man was almost certainly dead.

Sandra had been grievously humiliated by the advent of the kissogram policeman. It was the first of the unpleasant happenings which had been witnessed by others, and those who were present were women she was anxious to impress. At first she'd suspected that one of them could have been responsible: after all, who else knew where she would be that afternoon? But their reactions – though one of them, Meriel, had sniggered surreptitiously for several seconds – had disarmed her: they thought it shocking and in dreadful taste.

After she had gone, the other three decided that her grand manner had irritated someone.

'She's very insecure,' said the hostess. 'It's because her husband left her, I suppose.'

'Wounded pride, not wounded heart,' said Meriel. 'It was a hoot, though.' She laughed openly now, and the other two smiled.

They couldn't drop her from their four; her game was good, and she had time to play whenever they suggested. Besides, she was to partner Meriel in a major contest soon.

Because of this bad experience, Sandra felt an extra glow of pleasure when Orlando – 'Bobby' – telephoned her. Here was a genuine admirer. It did not matter that he was so much younger. Age differences did not signify these days. She wove a fantasy in which they went to bed, but sexual gratification was not her prime aim; she sought reassurance, proof of her desirability, and her power. By conferring her favours upon Bobby, she would demonstrate her generosity.

He must want her: otherwise, why would he seek her company? She'd quite forgotten telling him where her bridge game would be that afternoon, but even if she had remembered, she would never have imagined him to be the prankster.

When she agreed to meet him, he suggested a restaurant near Covent Garden and said he would be there at eight. So he wasn't going to pick her up in that nice car of his. What a pity. She wondered if he was married and did not want his wife to know where he was going. Somehow he didn't act like a married man, but then, which of them did, when out with another woman? Her husband had not advertised his married state, she was certain.

Just in case, she laid her bedroom out attractively, with a nightdress spread upon the turned-down sheets and a soft light burning. It had worked before, but no one ever came a second time.

He was waiting when she wafted into the restaurant on a cloud of Chanel, dressed in a narrow cream dress, high-heeled black shoes, handing her cream coat to the waiter as she entered.

Orlando did not touch her. He was never going to touch her. Ramrod stiff, yet smiling, he greeted her and saw her seated opposite him: no cosy banquette snuggling for him.

'How have you been?' he asked her, and wondered if she would tell him what had happened the afternoon before.

If he asked her about bridge, she might remember that he had known where she was going and begin to doubt him. He must be very careful.

How was this going to end? How could he

somehow bring her to submission, make her admit what she had done to that poor chap? Orlando had rather lost sight of this goal during his campaign of dirty tricks. As a boy, he'd never been one for practical jokes, but he was only too well aware of the pain of humiliation, for he suffered it often enough from Tessa. He had at last caught her in her office, where he was not supposed to ring her unless it was urgent, but she had left him so many messages to get in touch. He was to have a van ready on Friday evening: no troops this time, just himself and the transport, meeting at the usual place.

'Nine o'clock,' she'd said. 'And don't be late.'

What if he didn't go? He wasn't her slave, and he'd lost his enthusiasm for protecting animals.

But he would be there: he knew he would. He'd do her bidding, meekly, and he'd hope to find himself in bed with her afterwards. Even Tessa sometimes needed consolation, if that was what it was.

Meanwhile, here was Sandra, and though, when he asked her what she had been doing since their last meeting, she said she'd played bridge the day before, she mentioned nothing about the kissogram except to say they'd broken up earlier than usual because there had been a small disturbance.

'What sort of disturbance?' he had asked.

'It wasn't interesting,' she said, and would not enlarge.

At any rate, this indicated that it had happened: the kissogram had arrived.

He found a taxi after dinner, and she thought he would get in it with her, but he didn't. He gave the driver ten pounds and told him her address, then waved her away from the kerb.

Sandra found it most frustrating and, when she reached her flat, shed some bitter, angry tears.

Walking home, Orlando's mind turned to Jet, or Charlotte, which he knew was her real name. He hoped she was none the worse for her weekend's experience. She wasn't a trouble-maker, just a sweet girl whose principles had overcome her common sense. He was neither innocent nor sweet, and he had let himself be led along a violent path by Tessa. The episode in Darsingford had been inexcusable on any grounds. After this next venture, he would tell her she could count on him no longer.

He could say it, but would he stick to it?

He ought to talk it through with her, ask her why she was jeopardising her own career; if she were caught for what she'd done, she'd go to prison. It was arson, after all. And she'd shot those rabbits. What good had that done?

He knew she got a buzz from it: that was what she craved; the danger. She might as well take up bungee jumping.

He shouldn't even go with her this weekend. He should drop out now. But he wouldn't. He'd help her just one more time.

He went to yet another rental firm for the van, using his false name. What was Biff doing, he wondered, making the arrangements: Biff, the provider of the false driving licence.

Biff was, in fact, packing up after a night's begging not two streets from the restaurant where Orlando and Sandra had just dined.

Denis found it difficult to go to sleep. He wasn't used to being in a bed, with sheets, and was reluctant to take his clothes off, but old Phil had said he was to wash all over before dossing down.

He didn't go as far as that, but he scrubbed his hands and face, and then, seeing how grimed they were, and balancing on one leg at a time, his feet. After that, he put his singlet and his sweatshirt on again, but left his jeans off; they were filthy and they'd mark the sheets, which Phil would want to sleep in the next day. Then he lay down, pulling the bedclothes over him.

He was warm, and it was peaceful. The traffic had slackened outside and this was a strange sort of quiet: he felt the walls of the room were drawing close to him, pressing on him, and jumped out of bed to draw back the thin curtains, so that the street lights would shine into the room.

He'd liked the dark skies on that first trip with Orlando and Tessa; but he hadn't been alone then. In the woods the other night, the sounds of animals and then the storm had frightened him. Now, the enclosed feeling made him uncomfortable. He'd seldom been alone like this: really not since his sixteenth birthday when he was thrust, rudderless, into the world, and soon the shifting population of other young people had supplied him with company. Now, he wished for morning and old Phil's return.

Seeing Jet like that was a turn up. Denis's world was small, and once he'd recognised her, the surprise was not so great. It'd be good to see her in the morning. She might have news of Biff. He'd keep quiet about nipping into the house and taking that money; she wouldn't approve of him thieving from friends of hers, though she'd understand that he'd got to have some cash to live on. It was all right for her, with her student grant and that: she must be rich, visiting such a grand house. He'd had time to notice how different it was from any other house he'd been in. He hadn't seen much of the one where he'd found the purse, just the kitchen.

He allowed the idea of houses and those who occupied them to pass through his mind. What would it be like to spend all your life in the same one? Or even several years, with a mother and father there, while you were young? He'd never known that sort of life except for the brief spells in foster care, and he couldn't imagine experiencing it again.

He still remembered clearly the day of his abandonment. Until then, he'd lived high up in a tower block with his mother and a series of dads. She'd got another baby now, a girl, and the new dad had taken to bashing Denis, hitting him hard and once throwing him across the room. He was four.

There were rows between his mum and this dad, who even hit the baby. Then one day his mum had taken him on the bus to a shopping centre quite a long ride from where they lived. She'd led him into a shop, and then she'd disappeared. She'd given him a kiss, and gone.

He'd bawled, of course, though not at first. He was used to being left in shops, and in the flat alone, or with the baby. Years later, thinking about it, he guessed the baby had been left on her own that day.

His mother hadn't wanted him. She'd dumped him.

The kiss was strange, though.

He thought about it, lying on the sagging mattress, until sleep came. He was woken up by Phil returning. He'd arrived as another lodger left.

'We must get another key cut,' Philip said. This obvious solution to their admittance problem had struck him as he walked up the road, sure that Denis wouldn't be awake to let him in. He wasn't convinced the boy would be there at all.

'Oh!' Denis supposed it would be simple enough.

'I suppose there's somewhere in Darsingford where it can be done,' said Philip. He could ask at the library, or look in the Yellow Pages.

In spite of Denis's gestures with soap and water, the room smelt frowsty and of sweat. Philip flung the window open and in swirled chilly, damp, winter air.

'Ouch – it's cold,' said Denis, clutching the bedding round him.

'My turn for the bed,' said Philip. He wondered if any effort would be made to clean the room. He was the one who had better be there if it was attempted. Clean sheets would be most welcome; goodness knew what Denis had deposited in these, apart from any lurking parasites that might cling to his hair.

'Yeah – great,' said Denis, dragging his limbs out of their warm nest. His legs were painfully thin and scrawny, Philip noticed. 'Want some breakfast?' Denis added, waving towards the side table where a pack of sandwiches reposed.

He was a good-hearted lad, Philip thought. He shared what little he had, and it was he who had made the renting of the room possible.

'Thanks,' he said, and sat on the edge of the bed to eat a wedge of ham sandwich.

Denis ate the other one. A cup of hot tea would be nice, thought Philip, while Denis fancied a can of Coca-Cola.

'I'd best get out, then,' Denis said, though he spoke wistfully. 'You'll want to grab a bit of kip.'

'I'm dropping,' Philip said, with truth. 'Shall we meet during the afternoon, Denis? Or would you rather be free? You might pick up a job. You could ask at the supermarket.'

They had wanted shelf packers, but would they hire Denis, with his inability to read? How could he stack shelves when he could not tell what he was handling, except by the pictures on the tins or packets?

'I'll have a look around,' said Denis.

'We could have a meal before I go to work,' said Philip. 'I'll pay – I've got enough. Shall we meet at Pandora's Box, where we ate before, at about four?'

'OK,' said Denis. That was good. He didn't want to spend the day without seeing Phil.

Don't get into trouble, Philip wanted to say, as Denis pulled on his jeans and put on his trainers. He wore no socks, Philip noticed, and longed to go and buy him some, and some new trainers, for those he wore had cracks across the toes and the soles were very worn.

After Denis had gone, Philip took the sheets and blankets from the bed and shook them out of the window, then made it up again. Beggars can't be choosers, was his last thought, before he fell asleep.

21

AFTER BREAKFAST, CHARLOTTE told her grandmother that she wanted to go into Darsingford that morning.

She remembered her older sister saying that you needn't always give a reason for your actions: just do it, she would say, dying her hair blue and wearing a nose ring, and failing to provoke her mother into remonstration.

Charlotte had rarely expressed open rebellion at home; she liked to keep out of trouble and avoid the sharp arguments and bursts of temper indulged in by her siblings. Protesting on behalf of animals appealed to her because it was impersonal, and it protected her from having to take part in some other group activity which fellow students found attractive. Steve was a quiet, gentle creature who did not scare her and again her relationship with him protected her from other men. The incident in

273

Darsingford, however, followed by her own later arrest, had shaken her.

What if Tessa went on throwing firebombs and shooting children's pets? Had she tipped over into a form of madness? Charlotte did not know what her surname was, or even if Tessa was her real name, or where she lived. Orlando must know all these things, she thought: he had seemed on very familiar terms with her. The fact that she knew who was responsible for shooting the rabbits and the fire attack weighed heavily on Charlotte and she wondered what to do about it. Should she, for fear that Tessa might really hurt somebody on another raid, telephone the police anonymously, tip them off? Though what could she really tell them? She could say that Tessa drove a black VW Golf – she hadn't noticed even the registration initial – and had left it at that particular service station while the raid was carried out. That might be enough information to enable them to track her down. It would mean trouble for Orlando, though: what did he feel about it all?

She had fled to her grandmother's in order to have peace and space in which to think it out. When the police had arrived at Badger's End on Tuesday afternoon, she had instantly decided that they already knew what had happened and about her part in that night's activities.

She hadn't talked it over with her grandmother: Frances would tell her she must make up her own mind about what to do. Now it turned out that she knew the man whose house had been attacked, and Denis had appeared in the area. What was he doing here? He said he'd come with Biff. Why? Had they had another go at Dr Frost's house?

'You can take the car,' said Frances. She had got Charlotte through her driving test the year before, during a long summer visit. Arabella had not thought it important for her to learn; Frances did, and they had driven out together, practising, between the lessons Frances paid for. From gratitude, Charlotte had determined to pass first time, and she had done so, but she had few opportunities to gain experience.

'I haven't driven for ages,' Charlotte said.

'Take extra care, then,' Frances said, and did not ask why Charlotte wanted to go into town.

After she had gone, Frances walked down to the pottery to thank Jonathan for the pleasant evening.

She found him stacking up the kiln with a new batch of pots, and when he had finished this, he put the kettle on, making coffee for them both.

'It was such a good evening; I don't know what got into Charlotte,' she said. 'She's not usually so irritating. I don't know why she's come here. If she doesn't tell me soon, I may try to prise it out of her, but it's better if she does it on her own.'

'Is she short of money?' Jonathan asked.

'I don't think so — well, no more than any student. They're all hard up,' said Frances. 'Why?'

He shrugged. He couldn't tell her about his missing money.

'It's the usual thing, isn't it?' he said.

'Well – she might need it for a reason, like a sudden expense or having got seriously into debt, but I think she'd ask to borrow some, if that were the case,' said Frances.

'It sounded a bit as if she was into animal rights,' said Jonathan. 'Maybe she's got to pay a fine.'

'Oh dear! Oh, I don't think so,' said Frances. Yet it could be worse, more damaging. 'She's gone into Darsingford this morning. She didn't say why.'

Perhaps she had had an attack of conscience and gone to the bank. When he got home he might find twenty pounds pushed through the door, thought Jonathan, glad that he had not told Frances about the theft. Perhaps she need never know.

'Brian's going to ring Guy today and see about taking her round the lab,' he said. 'It'll make her think, at least. You're often full of doubts and uncertainties at her age, after all.'

'True.' Frances sighed. 'Things change so fast,' she said. 'If you think about it, in the lifetime of my own parents, the car was invented and men flew into space. In Charlotte's lifetime, who knows what other unimaginable feats will become commonplace. Holidays on Mars, for instance.'

Jonathan shuddered.

'Not for me,' he said. 'I think about Napoleon. The Battle of Waterloo was not really so long ago, taking it by generations.'

'And America, so young and yet so powerful,' Frances said. 'Jonathan, I didn't tell you – I had a burglary the other day. It may have happened at the weekend. Someone came into the house and took the money from my purse. The police think it could have been one of the rent-a-mob rabble who came with the hunt saboteurs on Saturday. I didn't discover it till Monday, when I went into Darsingford.'

'Was Charlotte here then?' asked Jonathan.

'No. She came on Monday afternoon – she was here when I got back,' said Frances, puzzled by the apparent *non sequitur*. 'She was here when the police came to test for fingerprints. They had to eliminate hers and mine, and they did find another rather blurred one, on the door, not good enough for matching purposes. I'd been in and out a few times myself, you see, and covered it.'

Jonathan supposed he could tell the police about his own theft and let them test upstairs, but it was only twenty pounds, and he didn't want to discover that Charlotte was the culprit. Besides, depending on who called, the investigating officer might have an attitude about him and Brian: why court hostility?

'How very upsetting for you,' he said. 'I'm sorry.'

'Yes. I've ordered a security light,' said Frances. 'It seemed a good idea.'

'We're well alarmed here,' said Jonathan. 'Have to be, for the insurance. I've never fitted security lights, though. Doesn't seem necessary. We've got them at the house, of course. Scares people off, one hopes.' But doesn't prevent inside jobs, he thought.

It had to be Charlotte who had robbed him; no one else could have done it, and it was just coincidence that Frances had been burgled, too. Perhaps that was what had given Charlotte the idea: yes, that made sense.

He seemed a bit distracted, Frances thought, walking home. He and Brian couldn't have had a tiff after she and Charlotte had left, surely? But why not? Lovers did, and, often enough, made up. However, they were a pair who never seemed out of harmony and had certainly been playing as a team the previous evening.

Her thoughts returned to Charlotte when she reached Badger's End. Maybe she'd wanted to do some personal shopping in the town. It was the simplest explanation for her trip, and often the simple explanation was the right one.

Frances decided to make a cake for tea. Probably Charlotte would be back by then. She'd said she wasn't sure about lunch and not to cater for her.

Would he be there?

Charlotte had not decided what to say to Denis when she saw him. Why was he in the area, knowing what Tessa had done here? Of course she and Denis had had nothing to do with the arson attack but they had taken part in the raid at the research station, abortive though it had been. Stuck in the back of the van, she hadn't recognised the local roads, and the research complex was in a part of the town she did not know. Denis wouldn't have realised where they were. Tessa should be stopped from doing anything as serious again. Orlando might be able to prevent her; why hadn't she talked to him about it?

Because she hadn't been thinking straight herself, was the answer, and it was Brian and Jonathan last night, so kind and courteous when she, on the defensive, had behaved like a spoilt brat, who had made her see the light.

She parked in the yard behind the supermarket and walked down the street to the library. Denis was already there, sitting at a table, poring intently over a book, mouthing words out to himself. He didn't look up as she took the chair next to his, so intent was he. Charlotte wondered what was holding him so spellbound and saw it was a children's book, with large illustrations on each page. She was about to make a smart remark about what a kid he must be when some instinct made her bite back the words. He couldn't really read.

He had felt her presence.

'Jet – listen to this,' he said, and began to read a passage out to her. 'It's great,' he enthused. 'This kid – it's all a dream really. See?' and he showed her the book, *Alexander and the Magic Boat*. 'I read it all,' he said, proudly. 'Well, there was a word here and there I couldn't manage,' he added. 'The kid's name.' He pointed to it and tried to sound it out.

'It's a bit long, isn't it?' said Charlotte calmly. 'A good dodge is to break big words into smaller bits and work them out in stages. *Alex, and, er,*' she said, pointing to the sections. 'The Alex bit's the hardest, I suppose.' He might not know the name. Poor Denis. But it was great that he had cracked it.

'There's this guy, you see,' he said. 'Phil's his name. He's been teaching me, but it didn't take long. He's great, is Phil. Old, though. He's sleeping now.'

'Is he?' Charlotte wasn't really interested.

'Yes. He works nights,' said Denis. 'I'll tell you about it.'

'We'd better go somewhere else,' said Charlotte. 'It's not good to make too much noise in here. Had you better put the book back?'

'Oh – er, yes. But now me and Phil's got an address, maybe I can join,' said Denis with enthusiasm.

'I expect you can,' said Charlotte. 'But leave it now, eh?'

'Yeah – right,' said Denis.

He took the book back to the children's section, then couldn't see where to replace it.

'It'll be OK to leave it on the table,' Charlotte suggested, and so Denis put it on a low table where a pile of books lay, and a small girl instantly picked it up.

'It's really good,' Denis told her.

'Come on,' said Charlotte, taking his sleeve.

She led him away. His face seemed clean enough but his clothes were very grubby. He looked as if he'd been sleeping out, yet he said he'd got an address.

'Let's walk,' she said. 'Then you can tell me what you were doing last night.'

He wouldn't tell her about the money he had taken after she had gone.

'I was just having a look around,' he said, defensively. 'It's a nice place, that. Know them, do you? Those guys?'

'They're friends of my grandmother's,' said Charlotte. 'I'm spending a few days with her. She lives in a village a few miles away. When did you get here?'

'On Saturday. Biff took me to a hunt. It was great. I liked it. I don't see why they shouldn't enjoy theirselves.'

'He went back to London afterwards?' she asked.

'I suppose so. I decided to stay for a bit,' said Denis. 'Then I met this geezer, I told you. He's learning me to read.' He grinned at her, delighted with himself. 'Wait till I show him what I can do.' He pulled the Little Bear book out of his pocket. 'Listen,' he said, opening it at the first page. He had to stand still in order to concentrate, and Charlotte drew him against a shop front so that he was not blocking the pavement. He began to declaim the first page, slowly, hesitating, finding the word *Mother* difficult.

'Well done,' said Charlotte, and her eyes pricked with tears. Poor Denis, product of an education system that had failed him. He hadn't been with this Phil long, so he must have been on the brink of the breakthrough into comprehension which she remembered making, aged five or six, when the sounds for which she had learned the symbols stood suddenly fused. Her grandmother had spent a lot of time with her, she remembered, reading to her and encouraging her.

Denis was slowly deciphering the next page. It was hard work, but he persevered. Charlotte wondered if they would have to remain in the doorway till he finished the book, but he soon gave up, a little deflated because he was not fluent.

'You have to practise. It'll get easier,' she assured him. 'Come on, Denis, let's walk. It's cold standing about.'

Denis stuffed the book back in his pocket and they went on towards the crossroads leading to the bridge.

'You staying long?' he asked her.

'I don't know. No, I suppose I must go back to college,' she replied. 'Let's go to the river.'

They turned towards it, and were soon walking down the steps, as Philip had done when he found his sleeping spot under the bridge.

'Old Phil spent the night here,' Denis chuckled, waving a hand. 'Poor guy, he's not used to it. He's OK now, though, thanks to me.'

'Why you?'

'Oh – you know,' said Denis vaguely, deciding that it might not be wise to tell Jet how he had acquired funds. Last night's haul, after all, was from her friends.

Charlotte was picturing some ancient down-and-out, though Denis had said that this Phil had a job.

'Denis, you know that trip we went on, with Tessa, when she set that place on fire – it's here. In Darsingford, on the far side of the bridge. I didn't know that at the time, only later when it was in the paper.'

'Yeah – I didn't realise, not when I came here,' Denis said. 'I went up there, though, trying for some cash – you know, knocking on doors, looking starving.'

'Begging, you mean,' said Charlotte sternly. Wasn't it against the law? And so was arson.

'Sort of,' said Denis, not about to tell her that he was looking for a chance to steal. 'He came to the door – the man did. The one Tessa meant to shoot.'

'She didn't mean to shoot him. She knew he wasn't there,' said Charlotte.

But was that true? Scientists had received bomb threats and even bombs, by post, and sometimes they were opened by people who were not the intended targets.

Charlotte could not tell this ignorant, immature young man about her own battle with her conscience. He would have no better idea than she about what to do.

'It was wrong,' she said.

'Yeah – them rabbits,' said Denis. 'Poor little kids. I expect they was upset.'

'Let's do some reading, Denis,' Charlotte suggested. 'Get out your book and I'll help you.' It would give her time to think about how to inform on Tessa while protecting the rest of them: herself, Steve, Biff and Denis, and, of course, Orlando.

She worked hard at getting into Denis's head some of the sounds made by two consonants together: he had problems with CH, TH and SH, not to mention GH, the bane of foreigners learning English.

After a while it grew too cold for them.

'Let's go and have some lunch,' said Charlotte.

Where could she take him? He was too scruffy for Pandora's Box and there was no McDonald's in the town.

'You going to pay?' he asked her.

'Yes,' said Charlotte, only too anxious to do anything she could to help him. They could do some more reading, later. She'd get a notebook and some coloured pencils, and see if he was any good at writing.

'There's this place,' said Denis. 'I don't know what it's called. Me and Phil go there. I'll show you.'

He set off briskly, Charlotte struggling to keep up, and soon they were approaching the café.

'You've been in here with Phil?' she asked, astonished, as she realised where he was heading.

Charlotte supposed that, providing they could pay, they could not legally be turned away, just for being dirty and unkempt. She, after all, was not dressed in the height of chic, in her jeans, big sweater, velvet hat and padded jacket, but she and her clothes were clean.

'Yeah,' said Denis. 'What's it called, Jet?' and he began to sound out the letters. B and O were relatively easy but he was troubled by the X and said it meant a kiss. At last the matter was resolved, and they went in.

22

DENIS HAD GOT their keys.

Philip could not settle to a long, healing sleep. He woke after three hours, heart pounding, worrying. What if Denis disappeared? He, Philip, was the one who had rented the room; he could plead careless loss and pay for a new lock.

If he didn't sleep, he'd be useless tonight at work; he might drop off and be caught literally napping by his employers trying to surprise him; worse still, genuine malefactors might come along and get past his guard. But it was no good: in the end he had to get up, dress, and go out. Perhaps he could sleep again later. He'd go for a long walk; exercise might calm him down and tire his muscles.

He set off towards the river bank and walked for over half an hour along the path from the spot where he had first met Denis. For a while he thought about his future; what lay ahead of him from this point? Could he gradually improve his lot, get a better job, start again? People did. How did they do it? Did they need luck, cunning or guts? He did not think he had ever had much of any of these qualities. Hard work had raised him to a modest rung on the Lavery's ladder; luck and cunning might have moved him higher. He'd been lucky in his family, his calm, uneventful upbringing and his unadventurous marriage. Perhaps less good fortune early in his life would have developed his courage so that he could have been more venturesome as an adult.

He couldn't go on like this, working at night as a watchman, with no prospects, but if he moved to another town, somewhere larger, as he had already contemplated, would he stand a better chance? It could be more anonymous; soon, in Darsingford, he would become a recognisable figure, a bearded man who visited the library and Pandora's Box, and who lived in digs into which he took a scruffy youth.

But he'd done nothing wrong, unless renting a single room and letting Denis doss down there was a crime. He'd stolen nothing. But he'd supplied false references. Was that serious? He must give his employers his new address. He ought to do it tonight – leave a note in the office. That would remove one possible cause of difficulty, but there would be more. He needed forms. You couldn't live today without forms and documents. How easy would it be to go to the social security offices saying he had lost all his and wanted new ones? Could he use an assumed name, writing to himself and producing the envelope as proof of identity? If he gave his real name, wouldn't they put it into a computer and come up with his true particulars, thus revealing that he hadn't disappeared at all?

How did people who vanished for years manage? How did they acquire new driving licences? Maybe you could get by without one if you kept out of trouble on the road: after all, people were arrested all the time for driving without a licence. You needed it only if you were challenged, and perhaps if applying for a driving job.

He liked the idea of driving a van around. It was a pity he hadn't got that earlier position. Maybe there'd be more vacancies advertised in the new edition of the weekly paper. If he kept moving round from job to job, his documentation need never catch up with him as he would be a casual worker.

Eventually, he turned around and began to walk back to town. His head felt clearer and his rapidly beating heart had settled to a steady pace. He'd look for a day job. He'd pay for his own room, refund Denis and send the boy on his way. But where was his way? Illiterate, unkempt, with probably a history of petty crime behind him – though that, Philip acknowledged, was an unfair judgement, just because the boy was a drifter – what lay ahead for him?

Returning, Philip went to Pandora's Box. He'd have his meal, and make a cup of coffee last him until Denis arrived. He'd got his book; that would keep him company.

As he approached the doors of the café he saw a girl emerge, a young girl not much older than his own daughter, with a hat on, and a big loose jacket: with her was Denis.

He couldn't have picked her up.

She couldn't have picked him up, for his appearance was so unappealing.

But they were together. Seeing him, Denis's face lit up with a beaming smile.

'Here he is,' he said, grabbing the girl's sleeve. 'Here's Phil. I told you about him. This here's Jet,' he added, to Philip.

Charlotte did nothing to correct him about her proper name: to Denis she was Jet, and that was how it should remain.

'Hi,' she said, regarding Philip in surprise.

She saw a man, who, in appearance, was not unlike her father, with dark greying hair and sad eyes, and a grey beard, though this man's beard was wispy and her father's was luxuriant. It had not occurred to her until this moment that her father's eyes were sad. Why?

There was no time to follow up this thought.

'I'm going back with Jet to see where her gran lives,' Denis said. 'I'll see you, Phil.' Then he added, with shy pride, 'I've been reading, Phil. Jet helped me, too.'

'The key,' said Philip, coldly. 'May I have the key please, Denis?'

'Yeah – right.' Denis fumbled in his jacket and produced the two keys on their string. 'Right, Phil,' he said. 'How'll I get in, though, if you've gone before I'm back?'

How much did this girl know about their arrangements? What was she thinking?

Philip spoke directly to her.

'We need a second set of keys. Could you possibly wait while I get them cut? I saw a locksmith's place in a street near The Swan.'

'Oh yes – they'll do them in a tick,' said the girl blithely. 'All right – let's go there. Or, if you're going to eat, why don't we get them done and bring you the other set?' She held her hand out to receive them.

Philip could not argue. Silently, he handed them over, and she and Denis walked on down the road.

Now it was Charlotte who was pensive as she took Denis to the locksmith's, stood there with him while the keys were cut, then paid. Phil wore a thick donkey jacket and was shabby, but his voice was educated and he was clean. What had happened to reduce him to becoming a wanderer, as she thought he must be?

'What do you know about him?' she asked Denis as they walked back to the café with the keys.

'Not a lot. What is there to know?' asked Denis reasonably. 'He's a good bloke who's lost his wife and kids. That's all.'

'He's not gay? You're not— ?' She let the question hang. What did it matter, after all?

Denis laughed.

'I don't know about old Phil. I'm not interested,'

he said, and it was true. He'd had it off with a few girls but even that hadn't meant a lot; take it or leave it, that was his view. He wasn't bothered.

She waited outside the café while he took the keys in for Philip, who by now was just finishing his portion of the meal of the day: beef stew.

'See you later, Phil,' said Denis, not giving Philip time to ask how much the keys had cost. Jet had paid; why sting old Phil, unless she noticed? Her gran must be loaded, having friends like those two poofters where he'd been so lucky the night before.

Even so, when he discovered just where Jet's grandmother lived, Denis had a shock. Then he rallied. The old girl wouldn't know he was the one who'd ripped her off. Keep calm, look around, cadge some food and stuff: then she might even, out of charity, give him a donation.

Charlotte's motives in taking Denis to Chingbury were confused. She felt he was a danger to them — to her, to Orlando, Biff, Steve and himself. And Tessa. He might, however unintentionally, reveal what they had done, perhaps to Phil or to someone else. He'd admitted trying to beg at the Frosts' house. What she really wanted to do was to persuade him to leave the area, perhaps find him his fare to go back to London. If she decided to leave too, would he go with her?

She'd forget the matter of the raid. No one, after all, had been hurt; only the rabbits. If she went on no more demonstrations, she would be safe. Tessa must decide for herself what she wanted to do and take the consequences; the same went for Orlando. Denis on his own — she didn't count Phil as a restraint — was a loose cannon. She'd tell him that if he went back with her, she'd go on teaching him to read, or find him someone else who'd do it. She knew there were various schemes to aid illiterates; she'd find out about them, get him into one, at least see him started. And she'd return to her own studies, concentrate, do well. She'd go on no more protest marches or demonstrations. Not for ages, if ever.

When they arrived at Badger's End, Frances was out. Charlotte found the spare key which her grandmother kept in the greenhouse and let them into the house. There was a note on the kitchen table, saying that Frances had gone down to the Wares.

'Read it,' she said to Denis. Her grandmother's clear handwriting was not difficult to read; here was a test for him.

He tried hard — her name in full at the top, Charlotte — defeated him, and she told him to ignore that and try the next line.

I have he managed, but was stumped by *gone*, rhyming it with stone, and the connected letters added to his problems. He was discouraged, but Charlotte, enthused, told him to take off his jacket, wash his hands, and wait. Then she went to the room which her grandmother used as a study and fetched rough paper and some coloured pencils.

They were sitting together at the kitchen table

when Frances came home. Charlotte had drawn an apple; Denis had coloured it in. He had learned the sounds made by all the letters which it formed, and he had written it below. They'd done *bottle*, too, and *cat*; Charlotte was no great artist but she had not set herself a project that was beyond her powers.

Frances showed no surprise at seeing Denis there.

'It's Denis. I know him from London,' Charlotte introduced them. 'Mrs Dixon, Denis,' she added, and waited for him to make some response.

'Yeah – right,' said Denis.

While they worked, Charlotte had suggested he should return to Biff. She'd promised him some money. She'd buy his ticket, she insisted, and she'd give him twenty pounds if he would agree to go to the classes she would find for him.

It was easy for him to say yes. He could always change his mind. They'd leave on Saturday, she'd said.

Frances suggested he should stay to supper, and while she prepared it, he and Charlotte went on with their reading. Frances was pleased and touched as she noted their activities, while cooking mince and boiling spaghetti; she put in a lot of pasta, for Denis looked half starved.

'Where are you living, Denis?' she asked him, as they ate. He dangled the spaghetti above his mouth and sucked it in, while she and Charlotte twirled theirs round the forks with expertise.

'I'm staying with a friend in Darsingford,' said Denis, smoothly.

'Ah,' said Frances. Charlotte would have to take him back.

'I like the country,' Denis said. 'There's so much air and that.'

'Yes,' agreed his hostess. She wondered what his story was and how Charlotte and he had met; perhaps she was involved with some scheme for helping out of work young people. No doubt Charlotte would tell her later. It was surprising, though, to hear Denis call her 'Jet'. Before Frances could say so, Charlotte forestalled her by saying it was a nickname used by some of her friends. Frances accepted the explanation.

After they had gone, she saw the spare key on the kitchen sideboard. She must remember to replace it in the greenhouse.

Charlotte had given Denis some paper. She'd written several page headings for him to copy – his name, the words he'd learned. He must practise writing them, she said. He could do a bit more work before he went to bed.

She dropped him at the bridge. He said he'd make his own way to his room from there.

She hoped he would. She hoped he wouldn't get himself into any trouble. She'd given him no money, in case he spent it in a pub. She'd got to get him back to London.

Going back to Badger's End, she felt happier. She'd made a few decisions.

When she returned, Frances asked no questions. It was her way, though this time Charlotte wished that she would. She must give her an explanation, however sketchy.

'Denis has never had a proper job,' she said. 'As you could see, he can't really read, nor write properly. He'd soon learn though, if he'd stick at it.'

'I'm sure that's true,' said Frances, who had seen that the youth was keen to learn.

'He came down here with a friend of his,' she said.

'So I gathered,' said Frances, assuming that this was the one with whom Denis was staying.

'Sorry he was so dirty. He is a bit smelly,' Charlotte said. 'I thought of suggesting he had a bath, but he might have been insulted.'

'Yes, he might,' Frances agreed, wondering why he couldn't have one at his friend's.

'I've sorted out my mind,' Charlotte told her then. 'I just needed to get away. Soon I'll be going home for Christmas.'

'Yes, of course.' Frances waited, in case she would be told more, and when Charlotte did not add anything, she asked if she was all right for money.

'Yes, thanks, Gran – same as usual. I'm not in debt or anything. Just ordinary student poverty,' she said, smiling. Then light dawned. 'You thought I might be pregnant. I might need quite a bit of money, if I wanted an abortion,' she said.

'It had occurred to me to wonder,' Frances said. 'In my girlhood, an unwanted pregnancy, one outside marriage, was the ultimate disaster.'

'It wasn't that,' said Charlotte. 'I've broken up with Steven, you see – I was a bit confused about it all.'

'Not heartbroken?'

'No. Just a bit sad,' was the answer.

Frances had not met Steven.

'There'll be someone else,' she said. 'Best not be too serious too young.' Easy advice to give: harder to follow.

'I expect that's true,' said Charlotte. Then she said, 'I'll go back on Saturday, if that's all right. Denis is coming with me. I mean to get him into some sort of educational programme. I'm sure it will be possible.'

Frances thought so, too.

'It's worth doing. Or at least, trying to get him started,' Charlotte said. She'd told him to meet her at the station.

'Yes, it is.' Frances still had not learned how they had met.

While he was being discussed, Denis had found an open window at a house not far from the rented room. He'd picked up thirty pounds and a small portable radio. He was happy when he went to bed that night.

Philip had not expected to be paid until his Friday night shift was over. So he was surprised and pleased when, just as he went off duty on Friday morning, he was handed his pay packet, the amount in full because he had had no P45.

Now he could pay his debts, and he could move on; head north, as had been his original plan. But it would be better to amass more money first, do another week at the job. It was peaceful; no one bothered him, and last night no one had come to make sure he was not asleep. He had been undisturbed until his pay packet arrived. He had agreed to work every night, weekends included, for the present; the firm planned to engage a second man with the idea of the two of them working shifts, but this solved their immediate problem. It also meant better pay for Philip, and concealment. He'd seen no more about himself in the paper; Lesley couldn't be pressing the police to hunt for him and they wouldn't feel any sense of urgency, though he might be listed in some file or other.

He must offload Denis somehow: he could not go on sharing his room with an unwashed lad of uncertain habits, yet he felt a sense of responsibility towards the boy who, after all, had generously shared his food with Philip when they met, and who had paid for the room.

Denis was still asleep when he returned to the room. He lay sprawled, one hand flung above his head, his chest covered in a grey singlet, the rest of his clothes flung on the floor. He never washed a garment, but then he had no spares.

Philip saw the small radio on the night table. Beside it were some banknotes. His heart sank: where had Denis got hold of the money and the radio? That girl – Jet – had hardly bought him a radio. Where had he found her? In some pub? She was clearly local, for Denis had gone with her to see her grandmother.

Denis had not stirred at Philip's entrance, and, remembering how difficult it had been to sleep the day before, Philip decided not to wake him. He'd postpone a conversation which might lead to explanations he did not want to hear. He was in funds; he'd go out and have breakfast. If Denis still wasn't up when he returned, he'd rouse him then.

Philip tucked twenty-five pounds inside the Little Bear book which was also on the table, more than repaying his debt, and went out, locking the room so that the maid, if there was one, wouldn't walk in on Denis. So far their room had not been cleaned; it probably wasn't part of the service, but he'd have to ask about that and about clean sheets, when he paid for the week ahead.

He went off to Pandora's Box, which had just opened. It was good to have eggs and bacon and coffee, all hot and freshly prepared, and to be able to pay. He enjoyed it.

When he returned to the room, Denis had gone. So had the cash and the radio. And the Little Bear book.

23

WHEN SANDRA WHITE received the dog turd in the post, the police had to take her complaints of harassment more seriously. This was a nastier mail shot than those she had received before. Small and dry though it was, it was stinking and she said it had made her sick.

The offending specimen, with its wrapping paper, was removed, and quite soon Philip Winter's prints were detected on the inner paper which surrounded it. None of his had been found on the anonymous letters she had received, but the assumption was that all must have come from him; possibly the reason for his disappearance was to leave him free to wage his war against her.

Detective Sergeant Sykes went to see Lesley.

'You'll be relieved to hear we've got proof your husband is alive,' he said. He did not tell her where they thought he was; postmarks could be misleading. The earlier mailings had come from London, but the pizzas could have been ordered by telephone from anywhere. Doubtless he was staying nowhere long.

Sykes explained to Lesley that Philip's finger-prints had been found on two communications sent to Sandra White. He did not reveal the malicious turn the harassment had taken. When he had gone, Lesley felt emotionally bewildered. She discovered that she was relieved he wasn't dead and some sense of her own guilt lifted with that realisation. But was he really capable of conducting a hate campaign by post? It was too bad of him to cause them all this extra misery. Her anger grew as she thought about his heartlessness.

Sandra and his plans for her downfall had been filed away at the back of Orlando's mind because now he had the more urgent problem of Tessa to confront.

She wanted to set off on this next – and his last, he had resolved – expedition on Friday night, which was unusual. Normally she campaigned on Satur-days, with Sunday for repose and restoration – and rewards, when he was lucky. His own office closed promptly on Fridays; city men with weekend cottages liked to head out to the country in good time. He'd decided to be very careful, wearing gloves throughout so that he left no trace in the hired van. He put on a baseball cap and his dark anorak, and when he collected the transport he wore tinted glasses.

Driving westwards, he contemplated asking for a

transfer to an overseas branch of the bank. Removing himself from Tessa might be the only way to overcome his addiction to her. She was like a drug, and cold turkey was the remedy. He wouldn't be going back with her to her parents' house tonight because he would have to return the van, but if she had nothing better to do, she might ask him down tomorrow.

The traffic was heavy, much heavier than on a Saturday, with all the weekend travellers speeding out of town. Tessa would be furious if he was late, but she must be driving through it too. What did she do with that shotgun, between raids, he wondered, and the other stuff she took with them?

This wasn't love, not really; what he felt for her was surely lust because she was so physically exciting. He'd had other sexual encounters, even thought himself in love before, but he had never known anything like Tessa's wild, abandoned passion. She was always the controller; she never used his name; he sometimes wondered if she knew who was with her in these moments. Any other man would have suited her as well as he, he thought, but he was safe. She trusted him.

But if he didn't love her, why did he do all this for her and put himself at risk, breaking the law? Perhaps it was a special sort of love, he told himself forlornly.

There were other girls: Jet – or Charlotte – for instance. But she was so young, so inexperienced, and maybe she'd get back with Steve eventually, or some other fellow student. He ought to look around for someone kind and sweet; someone to marry.

While Orlando was driving unhappily to meet her, Tessa was also on the road, having just concluded a successful piece of litigation. She'd gained huge compensation and costs for her client and now, elated, she was going to finish off some private business which had been her aim for months, even years. She'd learned last Sunday, from her parents, that Guy Frost's wife had left him, taking the children.

'It's only temporary, because of that awful business at their house,' Millicent had said. 'It must have terrified her.'

'But they weren't hurt. They weren't there,' said Tessa. 'Or so the papers said.'

'The rabbits were. That was sick,' said Millicent.

Was she sick?

Tessa asked herself that question as she drove along. She'd shot the rabbits on an impulse, wanting to cause misery to Guy and his family. All her work with the animal protest movement had been geared to that: to hurt Guy, by association, wreck his work and upset his domestic life. She didn't give a fig for animals, alive or dead, though she'd been fond of her pony and had liked the Jack Russell terrier her mother had when they first moved to the country. It had died and never been replaced.

When Guy, whom she had known at university, got married, she had thought that she would die of jealousy and pain. She identified her emotions even though she tried to think of them as grief. He had been her first lover, and she had never loved another, though she had been to bed with more than she could count.

How could he have preferred that milksop Amanda to her? It must be like drinking Ribena after tasting vintage claret.

Their ways had separated when she went to London and he to a research position in Edinburgh, but they had met at frequent intervals, Tessa becoming a regular on the shuttle flight. He'd travelled down less often, but they had gone on holiday together, always to exotic places like the Himalayas and Brazil. Guy's work had broadened; he was interested in parasitic diseases and viruses that attacked the nervous system. Tessa, bored by his dedication, constantly provoked quarrels and said he loved his bugs more than her.

Eventually he'd turned on her, accused her of having other lovers, which was true, and there was a blazing row which led to the end of their relationship. For over a year, Guy had wanted to finish it, but because they did not live together, he had let it drift, still revelling in its sexual aspect. Like Orlando later, when he was alone with her, he could think of nothing else, but her demands for more frequent meetings, and their constant quarrels, were exhausting; they'd separated mentally, and sex alone was not enough to bind them.

Then he met Amanda, and saw that there could

be a different sort of love – gentler, deeper, and worthwhile. Now he had a reason to break away from Tessa.

There had been a dreadful scene. She had screamed at him and pounded him with her fists. He'd gone to London intending to avoid being with her in a place where she could weaken his resolve by arousing him sexually. They'd had dinner in a restaurant where they had often been before – Tessa did not care for cooking – and she'd talked about her work, and her new flat, which she would show him later.

'You'll love it, Guy,' she'd said. 'It's got a view over the river.'

He was never going there. He had determined that in advance. He made some non-committal reply and, over coffee, had told her so.

'I'm not hearing this,' she said, putting down her coffee cup and staring at him in disbelief. She'd been expecting him to suggest they marry, and had been ready to discuss it, for of course they would when the right time came, but she was not prepared to go to Scotland. He would have to move south.

He made a little speech about their conflicting ambitions and opposing locations. They'd drifted apart, he said.

'Whose fault is that?' she demanded, accusing him of making excuses to postpone their meetings.

He'd pleaded work pressure, not mentioning Amanda until she asked him if there was someone else. Then he'd admitted it, repeating that he knew she was seeing other men. At this, she began hitting him, causing an uproar in the restaurant.

Two waiters caught her by each arm and marched her to the door, with Guy following. He flung money at one of the waiters, almost all he had in cash; there was no time for the credit-card routine. Then he rushed after her but she had vanished. A waiter said she had caught a passing taxi.

He telephoned her an hour later but there was no answer. He decided she was too angry to attempt to hurt herself, and fled back to Scotland without seeing her again.

When his project ended, he had obtained another post with a pharmaceutical company based in the south, nearer Amanda's parents. Her father was in poor health, his illness one that interested Guy, and his research could embrace its possible causes. Until the recent attack on them, things had run happily for Guy and his new family.

Tessa had kept tabs on his movements. While he and Amanda remained in Scotland, she had let them alone, trying to forget him, but when he moved, she tracked him down, parking in the road near their house, and watched the dull-looking woman, as Tessa thought of Amanda, taking the children off in her car. Once, she'd followed her to a supermarket and walked round the store behind her, hearing her talking to the boy and girl. The girl looked just like Guy.

Why should that goody-goody prig have Guy? He must be bored with her by now. Tessa had told herself that the marriage would not last; he'd tire of bland Amanda and domesticity and long for fireworks. He'd seek her out again.

It hadn't happened.

Some adversity would split them up, she had decided, and when none seemed to do so, she'd determined to provide a dose of it.

As her parents lived little more than an hour's drive from Darsingford, it had been easy enough to stalk Guy and make enquiries about his work. She did not plan to harm Amanda or the children, merely to drive a wedge between him and his wife and then she'd dry Guy's penitential tears. She'd wreck his work, so that his life and marriage would collapse. That whey-faced girl would be no comfort to him; he'd need Tessa.

She had become an animal rights activist in order to adopt their methods. They had attacked other scientists; she would attack Guy and bring terror to his life.

When she went to his house she had two plans, one to use if the children were there, and another if they were out. If they'd been there, she could not have done so much: petrol bombs in the garden would have been the limit. But Biff had found the place deserted, and so she did not care how much damage she did. When she saw the computer in his workshop she was delighted. Breaking that up would really hurt him. Owning the unlicensed gun gave her a sense of power and she shot the rabbits on an impulse. She was a good shot. One of her lovers, who farmed in Yorkshire, had taught her. She had gone potting vermin with him on his land. He'd wanted her to marry him, but after Guy, she found him very dull.

Orlando was a useful smokescreen. Tessa was fully aware of her charismatic hold on him; it had worked with every man she played with, and her powers had increased rather than diminished in her thirties. They'd work again with Guy if that woman could be removed, and now it had happened. What a spineless creature she had turned out to be: as if Tessa would be frightened off by a mere fire. Knowing nothing about Denis's visit to the Frosts' house, Tessa had admitted to herself that Amanda had lasted for a while after the attack, but imagined tears and tantrums had occupied the interval.

She had no suspicion of the heart-searchings that had compelled Amanda, in the end, to put the children's safety first, and, after leaving them on their own for two days with her parents, to join them.

Tessa's own parents had no idea that she had ever met Guy Frost; they knew only that she had had a boyfriend dating back to Cambridge who had gone to Scotland, and that after some years the romance had died.

'You're to follow me,' she told Orlando.

She had said he was to meet her in the cafeteria, and this surprised him because before his instructions always were to drive about until he found her car, then make the switch and load up as fast as possible. He was even more surprised when he saw that she was not in combat clothes but was wearing a long black skirt made of some woollen fabric, and a hip-length fleecy jacket, also black. Her hair stood out round her head like a brilliant halo, and her eyes were shining. She had never looked more beautiful, and even in these surroundings she attracted glances.

'What's this?' he asked, stooping to kiss her.

Tessa offered him a cool cheek, and he felt dismay at this chilly response.

'We've got a different plan tonight. I may need my own car,' she said. 'Come on. There's no time to lose.'

She walked briskly off, skirt swinging, feet in high-heeled shoes, but he knew she'd drive shoeless, or in pumps.

On the slip road back to the motorway she stopped the car and waited while he took from it the familiar holdall containing her equipment. To Orlando's relief, she did not hand him the shotgun, but there was a length of plastic piping and a long package wrapped in brown paper. Meekly, he stowed them in the van.

Soon she was back in her car and, instructing Orlando to follow her, she drove off. Orlando settled down behind her, wishing she would not go so fast, as the van was not as finely tuned as the Golf and lacked its acceleration. When she turned off for Darsingford, he was astonished. Surely she couldn't be returning to the scene of what he now thought of, quite spontaneously, as her crime?

She stopped not far from the research station, in a side road, and when he drew up close to her, berated him for not keeping on her tail.

Useless to protest. He waited for her next instruction.

'Come on,' she said, getting in beside him.

Orlando saw that she now had on a pair of flat-heeled shoes. He started up the engine, driving on to join the wider road where the research depot stood in its large plot, near some other factories and warehouses. She told him to stop outside a much smaller block whose name was painted on a board attached to the wire fencing by the gates.

'They pack cosmetics here,' she said, getting out of the van. 'Who knows what poor beasts they test them on. Bring the package and the tube.'

He obeyed, and she lifted out the holdall herself. Tessa gestured to him to unwrap the package and he did so, disclosing, to his astonishment, three large expensive firework rockets. Meanwhile Tessa had taken some wire cutters from the holdall and begun cutting the wire fence about a foot from the ground, opposite the building. He moved to help her, then drew back. He did not want to be involved with this.

Tessa slid the stick of one rocket into the pipe and poked it through the hole she had made, resting the end on the ground at a low angle.

'Light it,' she commanded. 'Then stand clear.'

The matches were in the holdall. Slowly, Orlando took them out. He had to remove his gloves to strike one. The first match flickered in the air and then went out, and Tessa, impatiently, told him to get a move on.

The first rocket went off with a whoosh, directly towards the shadowed building, and in seconds Tessa had placed another in the pipe. Orlando had already heard a crashing sound as the first one hit a window. The second went off, angled only slightly higher than the first.

'I'll do it,' he said, when Tessa loaded the last one, and he took the pipe from her, shoving it through the wire, resting it so that its trajectory would send the firework upwards. Tessa, packing up the wrappings, did not realise what he had done until it was too late and the rocket had exploded in the sky, sending out a shower of stars and small reports. Orlando had remained quite near it, wanting to conceal it from her, and he felt his face scorch as it soared away.

'What did you do that for?' Tessa said angrily. 'Come on, you idiot, let's get out of here.' She pulled something from the holdall and lobbed it over the fence. Then she thrust the bag and wrappings at him. 'Drive to the park where we stopped before, above the bridge,' she said. 'Wait there for me. I've got something else to do. Mind you wait, though. If I'm not back after an hour, then go back to London and get rid of the van.'

As she started up the Golf, he contemplated

abandoning her, leaving her to carry out alone whatever desperate scheme she had in mind, but he couldn't do it.

He bent to pick up the piece of piping which she had ignored. It would have his fingerprints on it. He put it in the van, then, with a heavy heart, he followed her into the town and across the bridge to the park, where he stopped.

Tessa had already reached Guy Frost's house.

24

DENIS HAD AGREED with Jet's plan to go back to London on Saturday because it was what she wanted to hear, and he liked keeping people happy. She'd said she'd pay his fare, but what a waste of money when you could travel free on the road. Waking on Friday morning, he looked round the room and saw Phil's plastic bag on the chair. So he'd been back after work. Denis yawned, stretched, and got out of bed. The old guy'd need to get his head down. He glanced at the night table, anxious about his money, but Phil wouldn't touch it: not old Phil, who was so keen on repaying Denis for the rent, as if it mattered between mates who shared what luck came their way, the good and the bad. His small pile of loot was safe, and then he saw the other money, stuck between the pages of the Little Bear book.

He could go, then. Denis wasn't one to turn his back on handouts and this was the repayment of a debt. Now he could leave old Phil to get on with it. He'd manage, as he'd found a job. It was all right for him; guys like Phil could get them, but the likes of Denis couldn't. He wasn't sure he wanted one, but he would like someone to look out for him, as Biff had done, yet he wasn't sure he wanted to go back to London. There was something about the space round here that still appealed to him, and yesterday with Jet had been just great.

He might go and look for Jet, try to spend the day out there, in that big house. Maybe the old girl would cook another meal. She was all right; she'd not been at all nosey.

Stuffing his few possessions into his pockets, Denis left his temporary lodgings. He kept his keys; he might decide to come back, and all trifles had their uses. He started walking out of Darsingford in the direction of Chingbury, passing the research establishment which Tessa had attacked. There were still signs of their slogans on the walls. Spraying paint was great; he'd liked that, but he hadn't written any words. Tessa had made them pick up all their paint tins afterwards. He'd laughed at that, as they'd shoved them into the bag she held. Biff had said something about litter, and Orlando had said they must keep Britain tidy. There'd be prints on those tins; his and Biff's prints were on file as they'd been nabbed by the police more than once so it was just as well she'd removed the evidence against them, not that they were likely to be connected with that affray. Was that what it was?

Had they caused an affray? Denis's grasp of legalese was limited.

Even so, Tessa had gone too far at that house. Fancy shooting little kids' rabbits! Denis had gone off her a bit after that but Biff had made excuses, said the animals might be being kept as pets as a cover for using them for secret experiments. Even so, why kill them?

He hadn't come this way with Jet; she'd driven in by another road. He mustn't get lost. Would he be able to read the road signs? Her gran's village was called Chingbury, that was CH, which Jet had said stood for CHOCOLATE, a long and difficult word, but she had broken it up into some small bits, just like an actual bar of *choc-o-late*, she'd said, and made him write it later. She was good, was Jet. A few more lessons and he'd read as well as she did.

Denis got a lift in a workman's van. The man was going to Swindon, but he dropped Denis on the main road, where he'd soon pick up another ride.

At first he was unlucky, trudging along, looking around him, still admiring the wide sky and the fields on either side, a light rain falling now. An old bus passed him, going the other way. It was travelling at some forty miles an hour, not capable of going faster, and the driver waved cheerily as Denis paused to look at it. Behind it came a camper van in rather better condition, but still shabby, with swirls of colour, faded now, ornamenting its once cream sides. Maybe he could get a van like that one day, take his house with him.

He walked on, and eventually was picked up by a student from a local college of technology who drove him the last few miles.

The rain was coming down harder. Denis thought some shelter would be nice. Jet's gran would welcome him, he decided. Soon he'd be in that big warm kitchen with a plate of something hot before him.

He rang the bell, but there was no answer. Walking round the house, he looked through the garage window and saw that it was empty. Since the burglary, Frances shut the garage when she went out, though before that she had never bothered. He tried the doors and windows. They wouldn't mind him waiting inside till they returned. Everything was tightly locked, however.

But not the greenhouse. He went over to it, opened the door, and stepped inside. It was not very warm but it was dry, and soon the rain began to slacken.

After a while, he remembered where Jet had found the key to let them into the house, the day before.

Frances was a volunteer worker in a hospital shop on alternate Fridays, and before she set off that morning, she asked Charlotte if she wanted to come along.

'I don't think so,' Charlotte answered. 'I'll do some work.'

Though she had left London in a hurry, she had brought some books and files with her. Now she was anxious to make up lost ground, and she should have handed in an essay this week. After Frances had gone, she settled down and concentrated for a while, then, restless, went out for a walk, ending up at the pottery when it began to rain.

Jonathan seemed preoccupied, not particularly pleased to see her, and she was put out. She'd always had a welcome before. Was he still annoyed with her because she'd been so rude on Wednesday evening?

'I'll sweep up, shall I?' she said, seeing that the studio floor was rather messy, with dried clay particles lying about and some dead leaves which must have blown in when the doors were opened.

'I don't want a lot of dust, Charlotte,' Jonathan answered curtly.

'Oh – right.' She felt at a loss. 'I'm going back tomorrow,' she told him.

'Oh?' He did not look at her, concentrating on the lump of clay he was turning into a tall urn-shaped vase.

Charlotte, who had always been fascinated by his skill, moved nearer.

'I should have gone today, really,' she said.

'Why didn't you?'

'What's another day?' she said lightly.

'A wasted opportunity,' he said.

'But I'm not wasting today. I've been working on my essay. Am I wasting your day by being here?' she asked sharply. 'Sorry, but you've never seemed to mind before.'

'Things were different. You were different,' Jonathan stated.

'It's because of the other night. You've gone off me,' Charlotte said.

'That's not the reason, though you weren't over civil,' he responded. 'But we welcome discussion at our table and you're entitled to your views. You didn't seem to have thought them out very clearly. That's all.'

'Well, if it isn't that, what is it?' she demanded.

'You went upstairs to cool down. What did you do besides?' he asked, pausing in his work to look at her. His pale wispy hair stood on end and he had a streak of clay down one cheek. She almost moved to wipe it away, but drew back.

'I washed my face and took in some fresh air through the bathroom window,' she replied. And saw Denis down below.

'You went into another room,' he charged her. 'My bedroom.'

'Oh Jonathan, I didn't! Why do you think I did?' she asked.

'You might have been curious about our arrangements,' he said. 'But now you know we don't share a room.'

'I don't. I didn't – oh!' She had turned quite pale. 'That's very private to you,' she said. 'How could you think so?'

'After you'd gone, twenty pounds were missing from my wallet,' he said. 'No one else went up there. Only you.'

'Oh Jonathan! As if I would!' she wailed. 'How could you think that of me?'

'I found it difficult,' he admitted. 'And I've said nothing to Brian. Nor Frances, naturally. I thought you might have an attack of conscience and take steps to put things right yourself.'

It was Denis. It had to be Denis, hanging about below and coming in either during the evening while they were eating, or later, perhaps while Brian and Jonathan were clearing up. And he could have burgled Frances: he and Biff had come with the hunt saboteurs. He'd told her so.

'But Frances was robbed too, before that,' she said. 'Before I came down. Couldn't it have been the same thief? It wasn't me, Jonathan. How could you think I'd do anything like that?'

'I found it very difficult to believe,' he repeated. Her dismay and shock were evident. 'If I'm wrong, I apologise, Charlotte,' he said, stiffly.

'I'll make it up. I'll give you twenty pounds,' she said. 'I'll have to get it from the bank.'

'Don't be silly. It's not the money – it's the principle,' he said. 'And it seemed the only explanation. The money was there when I got whisky on the way home and missing the next morning.'

'Nothing else went? Not your credit cards or driving licence?'

'No.'

'Only notes went from Frances's purse, too,' she said.

'That doesn't mean the same person took them.'

'No,' she agreed. 'Are you going to tell the police? Frances has.'

'I wasn't, because I blamed you,' he said. 'Now I'm not so sure.' He paused, then continued, 'No, I won't, because they'll enquire about the evening and they'll suspect you, too. It would mean too much trouble.'

'But the real thief will get away with it,' she said. Unless she did something about it: made Denis confess. But he'd have spent the money by this time, and would arresting him do any good? It would involve her, too. She'd tell him what she thought of him, however. If it was him. Fancy coming to Badger's End and being made welcome, fed, taught reading, and taken back to Darsingford after ripping off her grandmother and Jonathan.

'He'll get caught on some other job,' said Jonathan. 'I don't want to drag you into it, Charlotte. I'm sorry, my dear.' He put out a clay-covered hand and, with the back of it, lightly touched her cheek. 'Forgive me. I'm glad we got it sorted out. Like to make a pot or two?'

She couldn't refuse, and while Denis enjoyed the warmth of Badger's End, she stayed to lunch with Jonathan – bread and cheese – and spent the afternoon as his assistant, their amity restored.

25

PHILIP KNEW BETTER than to be convinced that Denis had left for good. He'd taken the money and his book, and the radio he must have liberated from its rightful owner, but had he really departed, moved on? Philip knew nothing about him. Curiosity had seemed out of place, and Philip was too concerned with his own problems to show much interest in Denis's past. In the strange, gipsy life he'd lived lately, the present was what mattered. People had secrets better not disclosed, and food and shelter became the most important items in a drop-out's life.

Philip did not like thinking of himself as a drop-out, but he'd become one, and if he hadn't met Denis, who was generous, his difficulties would have been much greater.

The money which had paid for this room had probably been stolen. Still, that was no affair of

Philip's, now that he had repaid Denis for his share, with interest.

Undisturbed, Philip slept soundly right through the day until it was time to prepare for another working shift.

He might move on. He could simply leave, after tonight.

When he reached the works, he did his rounds, going through the storerooms with their waiting packages, the vats of face cream, the jars and the conveyor belts, where the day workers supervised their filling and their final stacking in protective cartons. Two daytime shifts operated, which was why his hours were not longer; they covered the gap between the shifts, though he clocked on before the last shift left. He already felt quite settled in, even after so short a time, master of his video screens and his quiet empire of idle workrooms and stores. His previous existence – Lavery's, his home – seemed to belong to a different person, one always striving anxiously to please.

Philip thought about the scrap of dried-up dog dirt which he'd sent to Sandra White. That had been a silly, childish gesture, but it would have disgusted her. Anyone would have been nauseated at receiving that in the morning's mail. He'd do no more of that sort of thing. Now feeling rested, he'd given up on vengeance, though that woman was contemptible.

When all was quiet, he washed his clothes. He'd wash himself later on, nearer morning; that wasn't so important now that he could bath at the digs. The bathroom was far from inviting, but he cleaned the tub before he used it.

He was reading, drinking a cup of coffee, when the first rocket went off. He heard a crash as it struck an upstairs window, breaking the glass. Its impetus was halted but it exploded in the store-room above and sparks landed among piles of shredded paper waiting to be packed round pots of face cream in their cartons. Almost at once the smoke alarms sounded but there were no sprinklers in the building. Philip stared at his screens and saw where the trouble was. As he reached for the telephone, another rocket hit the building, then a third burst overhead. Philip heard the noise, like machine-gun fire, as the explosive shattered into stars.

There was no hot line or panic button in his office, though there was talk of having both installed. A major security firm had advised more precautions than were yet in force, and the insurance company also wanted them, but they were expensive. These allergen-free products were a new brand, launched recently, not yet breaking even financially. Balanced judgements of expenditure were important. No testing went on here, but demonstrations, like so much that was good or bad, had a knock-on effect and copy-cat protests could easily follow the earlier incident.

Having telephoned for the emergency services, Philip went to the area where the rocket had expired. Tessa could not have picked a better spot to start a conflagration; three or four small fires had already caught light. He snatched up a fire extinguisher from the outside corridor, and, after a short struggle, got it going, deploying it on the flames. As the fire caught hold, he sprayed foam round, moving to face each separate blaze as the last died down under his ministrations.

He was still up there, doing what he could, when the fire brigade arrived. As they wound out their hoses and their ladders, he knocked against a stack of boxes and they toppled over, sending him off balance so that he tripped and fell, and a sudden spurt of flame gushed out towards him.

When she left the house, Charlotte had taken the back door key with her. She put it in her pocket and, on her return, used it to let herself back into Badger's End.

Her grandmother had seen badgers in the garden snuffling round at night, large beasts, their sett in the spinney beyond her boundary, but Charlotte had never been there when they were seeking food so near to humans. She was thinking about that as she walked up the road from the pottery, a more comfortable line of reflection than her talk with Jonathan. Thank goodness they had sorted it out; obviously he and Brian were sensitive about their situation, possibly too quick to take offence, but how could he have thought that she would steal from anyone, much less him? They were friends.

Denis, in the kitchen, never saw her come up the path and did not hear her opening the door. He was listening for the car, the blue Viva which, though he did not realise it, Tessa had so nearly crashed into on that first raid.

Charlotte, in her rubber-soled boots, closed the door quietly and walked through into the hall. She heard a movement from the kitchen and the hairs on the back of her neck seemed to rise up on their own. It wasn't Frances; she would not be back until much later. Charlotte looked around for a weapon, and was on the point of opening the door so that she could run out again and save herself when she saw the umbrella stand in which, along with two umbrellas, was a walking stick. She grabbed it and advanced.

Denis had heard her now, and there was nowhere for him to flee to since she blocked the doorway. His mind worked slowly and he did not reason that the new arrival was one of the two women; he suspected another intruder, like himself, and grabbed the knife with which he'd been cutting bread. Charlotte stepped forward, thinking she could close the kitchen door on the burglar, though he might escape through the window. Very frightened, she advanced to stand on the threshold of the room and saw who was facing her, his back to the fridge, the knife wavering, looking more terrified than she was. It would be him, of course.

'Oh God, Denis! Put that knife down,' she said in a weary tone, walking in. 'What are you doing now?'

'Ah, it's you Jet,' said Denis, much relieved and smiling cheerfully. 'I thought it might be some thief.'

'How did you get in?' she asked, but she knew. If she'd taken the key from the greenhouse instead of the back door key, he could not have entered without breaking in, and even Denis might have had second thoughts about that. 'What have you stolen?' she added, angrily.

'Nothing. I was just having a bite,' said Denis. He picked up the hunk of bread he had hacked off a homemade loaf and laid butter on it, in chunks, because it had just come out of the fridge and was too cold to spread. He'd got the cheese out, too, she saw, and the piece of ham which they'd had hot for supper on Tuesday evening. He hadn't cut that yet.

Charlotte muttered under her breath. She went into the hall to replace the walking stick, then pulled off her coat. She still had on her velvet hat. Returning, she began packing away the food.

'Hey – Jet—' Denis objected. 'I'm just eating. Your gran wouldn't mind me having a snack. I'm starving.'

'Too bad,' said Charlotte. 'I think she'd mind a lot if she knew you'd stolen her pension and ripped off her friend in Darsingford, while we were having dinner there. You did it. Don't deny it.'

'It was only twenty quid,' Denis protested. 'Those poofters are loaded.'

'Those gentlemen—' she emphasised the word – 'might have given you some money if they'd seen you begging in the street. I'm sure they give to worthwhile charities that help people like you. My grandmother certainly does.'

'She shouldn't have left the place open,' Denis said. 'I was just passing. It was easy.'

'What have you taken this time?' Charlotte repeated her question.

'Nothing – only the food,' he said.

'Is that true?' she demanded. 'You haven't been upstairs and pinched her jewellery? She's got her purse with her today.'

'I haven't been upstairs,' he said. Not yet: he'd planned to poke about and see what he could find without trashing the place. He wouldn't do that to Jet's nice old gran, not after she'd fed him the other evening, but he'd not be above nicking a ring or pearls or something. You could sell those.

'Hm.' Charlotte wasn't sure if she could believe him. 'Take off your coat,' she ordered. 'Give it here,' and she held out her hand.

Meekly, he obeyed, and she searched his pockets, finding his wad of money, the small radio, and the Little Bear book.

'There. I told you,' he said, and pulled out the empty side pockets of his jeans.

'This is my grandmother's money,' she said. 'And Jonathan's.'

'What's left of it,' he said, and added, 'I paid for the room what me and Phil had, and our food.' He spoke proudly. 'Course, Phil's got a job now – nightwatchman at some factory near where we went with Tess that night. He paid me back his share.'

Charlotte was wondering what to do. Justice demanded that she took his money and returned it to her grandmother and Jonathan, but that could end in difficult explanations and might lead to revelations about their part in the attack on Dr Frost. Charlotte had no illusions about what their fate would be if this was discovered: both of them would be locked up. She, now, was known to the police, marked down as a demonstrator and disturber of the peace; very likely Denis had a record, and there was Orlando to consider. And Steve.

No. Denis must be allowed to get away with it, this time, and to put miles between himself and Darsingford.

'You've got to go, Denis. Go, and don't come back. Get right away from here. If you were ever connected with what happened at that house that night, you'd go to prison for a long time.'

'Prison'd be OK, in the winter,' Denis said. 'Food and that. Things to do.'

'Don't you believe it,' Charlotte said. 'You get going now, Denis, and don't ever come back to this house or this district. I'll turn you in, next time.' She stood glowering at him. 'Take that bread you've got and go,' she repeated. 'If I don't get this cleared up before my grandmother comes back, I'll have some explaining to do. And where's that key?'

He gave it to her. It was in his hip pocket with two more.

'What are those?' she asked, and then she

recognised them. 'They're the keys to your lodgings, aren't they? Give them here. You're not to go back there and make things difficult for that poor man who was good to you.'

Denis handed them over without a word. Jet was all fired up. What a great little girl she was! He felt like saying so, but this was not the moment for any such sweet talk.

'I'll go,' he said.

'Go the other way,' she ordered. 'You're not to go to Darsingford. If I hear of any other burglaries, I'll drop you right in it.'

She wouldn't, of course, because it could rebound on her, but he might believe her threat.

'Cor – I'm terrified,' he said, laughing at her.

But he left, and she watched him walk down the path and along the road away from the village. Then she set about clearing up after him. He'd eaten so much that she thought she might have to tell her grandmother he'd been here and she'd fed him. What else ought she to reveal?

She'd suggest keeping the spare key in some new hiding place.

26

THE JUDGE AND his wife were discussing Christmas plans. Court had risen in time to let him get down to the country before it grew dark, and he had enjoyed a cup of tea by the fire in the drawing-room.

'Tessa hasn't mentioned anything. Perhaps she'll grace us with her presence,' said Millicent. 'It would be so nice if she'd plan ahead a little.'

'We could,' said the judge. 'We could close up the house and go on a cruise somewhere warm.'

They smiled at one another and Millicent rose to stir up the fire, a real one of logs in a wide hearth where the pile of accumulated ash glowed red.

'There's Clive,' she said. 'What's he going to do, I wonder? He might want to come here with the children, if he's allowed to have them for part of the time.'

'I suppose so,' James sighed. 'We always have to fit in with them, don't we? Shall we ever be permitted to please ourselves? It's what they do, after all.'

'It's what Tessa does,' said Tessa's mother. 'Clive is in a bit of a hole. Obviously if he brings the children here, it's easier at a time like Christmas. Space, and so on.' Clive was at present living in a small flat.

'True,' said the judge.

'Perhaps for the New Year? The cruise, I mean,' said Millicent. 'We could see what's available.'

'Or, at the last minute, flee to Sidmouth,' he said, and they both laughed.

'Flee from our children, you mean. Otherwise why not stay here, where it's warm and we've got our books and some good old films on tape,' said Millicent.

'They'll expect to be fed and housed, if it suits them,' said James. 'And they'll think they're doing us a favour by granting us the blessing of their company.'

'It would be nice to see the grandchildren,' Millicent said. 'They are so sweet.' She doted on them, and so, in his restrained way, did James. Both thought that stable grandparents in the background might reduce the damage of their parents' divorce.

'What will Orlando do? Poor fellow, his family seems to have cast him aside and he's got no future with Tessa. I'm afraid she's playing with him,' said the judge. Like a cat with a mouse, he thought. 'Milly, I'm worried about our Tessa.'

'In a new way?' asked Millicent. They had been

anxious for some time: proud of her successful career but aware that she was growing ever more brittle and dissatisfied.

'Yes – yes, in a new way,' the judge admitted. 'You know all that business with the arson attack in Darsingford, where Jenny works?'

'Yes.'

'Guy Frost, the scientist involved, whose rabbits were shot —' he hesitated, fearful of putting into words his dread.

'Yes? What about him?'

'He was at Cambridge during Tessa's time there,' James said.

'So were hundreds of other men,' said Millicent. 'What are you trying to say?' Suddenly her whole inside seemed to lurch. 'James, if she knew him, she'd have said so after the raid.'

'Would she?' asked the judge. 'Can you be sure of that?'

She couldn't. Tessa had always been very secretive.

'I looked him up. He was in Scotland for quite a while. He moved to Darsingford two years ago,' he said.

'She was always going up there.' Millicent spoke slowly, then added, 'To Scotland. More than once a month, for years. To see friends, she used to say.'

'You thought it was one particular friend. A man. A lover, probably,' said James.

'I did,' Millicent remembered. 'I might have been wrong. Anyway, there's Orlando now.'

331

'He's a blind. A smokescreen. He's for show to hide what's really going on,' said James. 'I'm sure of it, Milly.'

'How can you know?' asked Millicent.

'Call it the result of a lifetime spent among the criminal classes,' said the judge. 'I can smell deception.'

'But you have to rely on evidence. And this is your daughter – a lawyer, too.'

'I have no evidence, only my instinct,' said James.

'Well – even if you're right, and she did know this Guy Frost years ago, that's when it was – years ago,' said Millicent.

'Yes.'

'Why is it worrying you, James?' asked Millicent.

'I don't know. That attack – so potentially lethal – there was something about it that didn't fit,' he said. 'Perhaps it was the rabbits. I'm being stupid. Tessa must have forgotten about the man long ago, if she ever knew him.'

'You can't really suspect her of being mixed up in that raid!' Millicent was aghast.

'Other people – even other judges – have problem children, Milly,' James replied sadly. 'What do we really know about her private life?'

'Not a lot,' his wife agreed. 'She doesn't seem to have many friends.' She used people, thought Millicent; she was using Orlando in some way.

'She's thirty-four years old, with a blossoming career, and she's highly intelligent. I'm telling myself she wouldn't risk all that for some foolish gesture,' said James.

But she had come home very late the night of the incident, and had slept in the next day, when she had been in a happy, even elated mood; he had noticed that. He'd checked the dates to confirm that they tallied. As a child, and in her teens, moods of exhilaration had often followed wrongdoing which, when discovered, was bad enough to require punishment. Once she had locked her brother in the disused hayloft, taking away the ladder, and before he could be found, frightened in the darkness, he'd jumped to the ground, breaking his ankle. Tessa could be merciless; had she gone in for the bar, she would have been a powerful advocate. He did not remind his wife of her past misdemeanours.

'Why should she?' Millicent insisted. 'Oh James, I think you're letting your imagination run away with you.'

'Jealousy is a terrible, destructive thing,' he said. 'But no doubt you're right. I'm just anxious about her. We both are. And, as you've said, there is no evidence.' The gun, for instance; Tessa couldn't own one, could she?

Millicent rose and crossed the room to kiss his cheek, slightly bristly now at the end of the day.

'Do parents ever stop worrying about their children, even when they're so old that the children feel obliged to worry about them?' she asked.

'Probably not,' he said. 'Let's have a drink.'

He went on worrying.

* * *

Orlando waited in the van near the park gates, as instructed. He sat there for a few moments wondering what to do next, and, more to the point, what Tessa was doing.

She couldn't be going to attack that man again, and in normal dress, not combat gear. Or could she? He'd got the holdall; what had she kept in her car that he didn't know about? The shotgun?

He got slowly out of the vehicle and locked it, putting the key in his jacket pocket. Then he inhaled some deep breaths of still, damp, wintry night air. It was cold, but a long way off freezing. A car drove by, then another came towards him, but this was a quiet area, not on the way to anywhere. Sighing deeply, squaring his shoulders, he walked slowly towards Guy Frost's house.

On the way over, a fire engine and several police cars, all with lights flashing and sirens wailing, had torn past travelling in the opposite direction, no doubt going to the scene of Tessa's firework effort. What had she hoped to accomplish? And what had she lobbed over the fence as he left?

Tonight was the end. He didn't really know why he was not driving rapidly back to London, except that he couldn't bring himself to desert her, not in action, so to speak. It would be cowardly, but then he didn't think he was a brave person; someone brave would have stood up to her long ago and walked out of her life.

Someone brave wouldn't go around calling himself Orlando when his name was Roland.

Orlando wasn't sure which was Guy Frost's house, but then he decided it must be the one outside which Tessa's car was parked.

He tried the Golf's door. It was unlocked, and her keys were in the ignition. He took them out. Anyone could steal it, and then where would she be? Putting them in his pocket, with the van keys, he walked up the path towards the house, where bright lights shone out over the driveway.

Where was she? Was she skulking about in the shrubs which bordered the garden? He was now illumined for all to see. If challenged, he'd act the idiot and ask for directions to the rectory. That was a safe enough question anywhere, guaranteed to reduce suspicion. It would create a diversion, too, and give Tessa time for second thoughts.

He walked round to the rear garden, where, according to all the reports, Guy Frost had his workshop. How badly had the shed been damaged? Was it gutted?

It seemed not. He could see it now, quite clearly, lit by a bright security light on the exterior wall. There were lights inside, too.

Orlando advanced, and looked through the window. He saw Tessa there, with her back to him. She was holding her gun, tucked under her right arm, quite casually, but in a position from which she could soon raise it to her shoulder. He could not tell if it was cocked or not. She was talking, but he could not hear her clearly.

Oh God! She'd got the man, and possibly also his family in there! But he could see no one else, not even the scientist.

Orlando moved round, seeking the shed door and trying to think rationally. The children would, by rights, be in bed, of course, but what about their mother? Should he return to the house and, if she was there, get her to phone the police?

There might not be time.

Tessa couldn't intend to shoot this Guy Frost, could she? Why him and not some other scientist? What was this one doing that made him particularly detestable in her view? After the arson attack, the papers had said he was engaged in research into the relief of nervous disorders – not mental breakdown but illnesses which left the victim with impaired or total loss of movement: surely that was a more worthwhile occupation than thwarting such efforts?

If Tessa were to shoot him, that would be plain and unadulterated, violent, pointless murder.

Wavering outside, Orlando could hear the murmur of voices. He was reluctant to leave his vantage point but he must somehow try to stop Tessa, save the man and anyone else who might be in the shed.

He moved round the side of the shed to the door, which was shut. Guy Frost must have been inside, working, when Tessa entered, armed, yet dressed up to the nines. Why so smart when her intent was hostile?

He listened.

* * *

After the fire, the insurance company had insisted on an alarm being installed and Guy was supposed to set it when he was in his workshop, but he wanted Amanda to feel free to enter so he never did this, and although she was away now, he had not locked himself inside.

He did not hear the door open. The first thing he was aware of was a voice behind him saying 'Guy'.

He turned. Though he had not heard her voice for years, and it was only a single syllable, he knew at once who had spoken. There she stood, dressed all in black, her hair a brilliant splash of reddish gold, eyes blazing. At first he did not notice the gun she was holding, barrel pointing down, but cocked.

'Christ, Tessa! What on earth are you doing here?' he gasped.

'I've come to see you, of course,' said Tessa. 'So that milksop's left you. I've been waiting for you to get tired of her.'

'Oh God!' He was standing now, and he rubbed a hand across his forehead. 'Amanda hasn't left me. She's taken the children to stay with her parents. We had some trouble here,' he said.

'I know you did. Those poor rabbits,' Tessa said. 'What a shame. Were the children very sad?'

'Yes, they were.' But now Guy had seen what she was holding. He stared at her, incredulous. 'What are you doing here, Tessa?' he repeated. 'Why have you come?'

'I told you. I knew she'd go, and then you'd

realise just how foolish you'd been, if you hadn't already,' Tessa said.

'But I love Amanda,' Guy declared. 'Tessa, I love her. We have a happy life.'

'Where's the excitement, though?' she asked, her voice almost a hiss. 'I'll bet it's nothing like what we shared.'

'I don't want excitement, Tessa,' Guy insisted. 'You have to let the past go. It's over. It was over long ago.'

'Not for me,' she said. She took a step nearer him. 'Don't you want to kiss me, Guy?'

He didn't, but he could feel the old attraction, all the same, only this time it was tinged with fear.

'No,' he said. 'Go away, Tessa, and we'll forget this ever happened.'

'Forget what? My visit here today, or our love?'

'Everything,' he said.

She couldn't have been behind the raid. It wasn't possible. Or was it? She was quite ruthless: he knew that. Look at her now, marching about with a shotgun which he felt sure was loaded. She was not one for empty threats. Admitting that she could have been responsible, with sickening certainty he knew she was.

'We can't forget,' she said. 'It's our history.'

She must have been brooding about it all this time. Guy tried to think of a way to placate her, make her accept the truth, then leave.

'If you just go, quietly, I won't tell the police you've been, or that you set fire to the place and shot the rabbits,' he said, trying to speak calmly, concentrating on her, not taking his eyes from her. Would she deny it?

She didn't.

'Or Amanda?' she said, head on one side, almost coy. Tessa was never coy. 'You won't tell her?'

'Nor Amanda.' Most of all, not Amanda.

'And you'll entice her back?'

'She'll come willingly, when she's sure the threats to us have gone,' he said.

'Ah, but they won't have gone, will they, Guy?' she said. 'You'll never know when I might appear again, with flaming torches, or explosives.'

'You'll get caught, if you do,' he warned.

But who would suspect her? A judge's daughter: a successful lawyer. There'd be evidence, of course; that gun, for instance.

'I'm not going to let her have you,' Tessa said. 'If you won't send her packing, then it's the end,' and she slowly raised the gun, pointing it right at him.

'Put it down, Tessa,' Guy said. 'Don't do something you'll regret.'

'I won't regret it,' Tessa said. 'I want you, Guy. You've got one last chance.'

Could he bluff her, somehow? Make some conciliatory remark that would calm her down so that he could take the gun away from her? Should he suggest they go into the house?

No. He wasn't going to let Tessa invade Amanda's territory.

'Give me the gun, Tessa,' he said, and then he saw the door behind her open.

For an instant Guy's eyes left her, and Tessa noticed. Turning round, she saw Orlando in the doorway, raised the gun and, as she fired at him, Guy punched her hard in the back so that she stumbled. The sound of the shot was deafening, but both men moved towards her and Guy wrested the gun from her grasp. He pointed it at her. These things had two cartridges in them, didn't they?

Tessa had banged her elbow as she fell. She'd got those high-heeled shoes on, Orlando irrelevantly observed as he held his own arm, which felt as though it was on fire.

'Orlando!' she screamed his name. 'I told you to wait at the park,' she stormed. The pain in her elbow was, briefly, excruciating.

'Tessa, come away,' Orlando said. 'Let me take you out of here before someone gets hurt.' But he was already hurt. She'd shot him, not Guy; but of course the gun had gone off by accident.

'Have you been helping her?' Guy asked him, his voice deep, suspicious.

'Not to attack you, no,' said Orlando. 'I'm another victim, in a way. Come on, Tessa. Let me take you home.'

But could he, with his wounded arm? Was it a serious injury? He touched the painful area below his shoulder and his hand came away covered with blood.

For a moment Tessa looked appalled; Guy saw

the brief horrified expression on her face. Then, in a flash, it had gone. She'd fired on reflex, not with intent to hurt this man.

'Bloody fool, getting in the way,' she said.

'You'll go, Tessa,' said Guy. 'Let him take you, as he said.' But the man was hurt. Guy was a biochemist, not a doctor of medicine; nevertheless, he could not let a wounded man leave untreated. 'We'll have to fix your arm first,' he said, despairingly.

'It's all right. It's only a scratch,' said Orlando, who was sure he had received a serious injury.

Both men were intent on watching Tessa. She had retreated against the window, still rubbing her elbow, but it hurt less now. Hearing them discuss her fate was unendurable; she had to be the one in charge, but she'd lost her weapon. She'd retreat, but only to rethink her strategy.

'I'll drive myself,' she said. 'Let me pass.'

They did, Guy still holding the gun. She stalked past them, out into the darkness, and then Orlando remembered her car keys.

'I've got her keys. She'd left them in the car. I took them for some reason – thieves – anything,' he said.

'Let me have them,' said Guy. 'I'll give them to her. When she's gone I'll have a look at that arm.'

'All right,' said Orlando, who unlike a hero in a film did not feel up to running down the drive and throwing punches. He foraged in his pocket for the keys, handing them over without protest.

Guy put the gun down and went out of the studio, running after Tessa, who had reached her car and was sitting in the driver's seat thumping the steering wheel in frustrated rage. Guy opened the door.

'Tessa. Your keys,' he said, and she looked up, face blotched, mascara running down her cheeks, for once, but only briefly, broken. He dropped them in her lap, closed the door on her and turned away. As he hurried back to his workshop, he heard the car start up.

Orlando was sitting down, still looking dazed.

'She seems to have gone,' said Guy, who had found the sight of Tessa weeping quite unnerving. 'Come on – let's go into the house and see about you.'

While Guy was gone, Orlando had unloaded the gun. Other cartridges and weaponry were in the van. Would Tessa go to it and make a firebomb? She was quite capable of it. Well, he was past protecting her now. He allowed himself to be led into the house, where Guy helped him take off his jacket and inspected his injury. It was a flesh wound in his upper arm. Guy could see some shot there, and very gently, with small tweezers, he extracted several pieces. It was agony.

'You ought to go to hospital, of course,' he said.

'There'd be questions,' said Orlando.

Guy had poured him a large brandy, as an anaesthetic.

'Yes,' he agreed. 'Most of it missed you, I'd say,'

he added. Orlando's skin was badly burnt. 'A proper doctor ought to see it.'

'What are you going to do?' Orlando asked, ignoring his advice. 'Are you going to call the police?' She hadn't really meant to shoot him. Of course not. Why, this chap, Guy, was her real target.

'I don't think so. Not now,' said Guy. 'What do you think she'll do?'

Various possibilities ran through the minds of both men.

'I don't know,' said Orlando. 'It's the end for her, anyway.'

'She's done other things, hasn't she?' said Guy, dabbing away. 'You don't need stitches,' he went on. 'It's mostly scorching from the blast. But I'm not a medic. If it throbs, looks angry, if you get a temperature, you must see a doctor. You ought to anyway,' he repeated. 'Maybe you've got one who's a chum, or who you can string a line to.'

'I'll manage,' said Orlando. 'It was all a lie,' he added. 'All her concern for animals. She was after you all the time. You had an affair, didn't you?'

'Years ago,' said Guy. 'I've been married six years.'

'I don't understand it,' said Orlando, but in a way he did: he'd been obsessed with Tessa, as she was obsessed with Guy, but he had never wished to harm her, and didn't now.

'Where do you live?' asked Guy.

'In London,' said Orlando.

'I could put you on a train,' Guy said doubtfully.

'There's the van. I must deal with that,' said Orlando. 'Usually we leave Tessa's car and go on in the van. Tonight she brought her car. I suppose she thought she was going to make a night of it with you.' He'd have to get rid of all the stuff that was in the van: dump it somewhere. 'What about the gun?' he asked.

'I'll keep it for a bit. Just till we see what happens. It's evidence,' said Guy. She might accuse this poor chap of something, if she were caught.

'All right,' said Orlando, glad to share responsibility. 'I guess you haven't got a licence, though,' he said, and both men laughed.

'I'll be careful,' promised Guy.

'Don't let your wife see it,' said Orlando.

'I won't,' said Guy, who was worrying about Orlando driving, after the stiff brandy he had had, never mind his arm. 'What about a sandwich? Have you had anything to eat tonight?'

He hadn't.

Orlando felt much better after several ham sandwiches and some strong black coffee.

'I'm through with her too,' he said. 'I'd decided that, regardless. Tonight was the last time. I'd made up my mind.'

'Sensible,' said Guy. 'Takes a bit of doing, though.'

'Yes.' The two men, united by their curious link as Tessa's lovers, exchanged wry looks.

'She was quite a girl,' acknowledged Guy. 'Now,

come along. I'll walk you to your transport.'

Together, and in silence, they walked along the road to the park gates, where the van still stood.

'Will you be able to manage the gears?' asked Guy anxiously, as Orlando climbed in. His left arm was the injured one.

'Yes. It'll be all right.' Guy had dressed it very thoroughly. 'Thanks,' said Orlando. 'You could have turned me in,' he added.

'I don't know who you are, do I?' Guy replied. 'Good luck,' and he waited while Orlando started up the van and drove off.

Guy half expected Tessa to have returned when he went back to the house, but there was no sign of her.

27

L EAVING IN THE van, Orlando avoided the area
near the factory which Tessa had selected for
attack. He didn't think the rockets could have done
serious damage; the fire brigade's response was
probably automatic, resulting from some wired-in
alarm. Maybe there were broken windows; the
rockets had travelled fast, and the one that went up
into the sky had been spectacular.

She'd planned it; it was her scheme, but he had
been there and had helped her. He, in law, was also
culpable. But they wouldn't be caught. They'd been
quick. Even so, someone might have seen the
stationary van, and her car. What would happen
now?

What would Guy do? Would he eventually
report Tessa? If he did, it would rake up the past,
expose both Guy and Tessa to intense public
scrutiny. The tabloid press would love such a story.
It could kill Guy's marriage.

Orlando, driving steadily back to London, kept thinking of these possibilities and wondering what to do. He'd got all Tessa's gear except the gun. How should he dispose of it? He must stop drifting, must construct a plan.

His arm was hurting, but not badly; Guy had done a good job, telling him to take pain killers when he reached home, but not while he was driving: not on top of the brandy. The miles went by: no need, tonight, to call in at the service station as was their normal practice after such a trip. He wondered where Tessa was: she could be almost back in London by this time; he had spent at least an hour with Guy, being bandaged and revealing what Tessa had done on earlier raids. He'd said nothing about the attack on the cosmetic packing works earlier that night. The fewer people who knew about that, the better and the safer, though Guy would soon hear about it and realise they had been responsible.

He was feeling very tired. It would be wise to stop, but if he did, he'd never get going again. He opened the van window and let cool air blow in on him. That helped to wake him up. Traffic, on the motorway, was intermittent. It was late now and there wasn't a great deal; there were very few lorries. It was Friday, he remembered; usually the lawless trips took place on Saturdays and afterwards she always wanted sex. He knew that now, and if she didn't turn to him, then she found someone else.

Who would it be tonight?

He tried to think of other things: of Jet, so innocent and sweet, but soon his mind returned to Tessa. What she felt for Guy was not love: love did not seek to destroy its object. Perhaps, in truth, she hated him.

He did not want to destroy Tessa, and nor, he knew, did Guy, but how could she be protected, from herself, if not from justice?

Orlando was still meditating in this fashion when he arrived at the garage from which he had rented the van. He drove past, to the street where he had left his BMW. Even with his injured arm, it took him less than a minute to transfer the holdall, the pipe and the rocket wrappings from the van to the boot of his car. He glanced quickly round the van's interior: there was nothing else, no other trace of where they had been and what they had carried.

He'd forgotten his gloves. Where had he left them? He'd replaced them after lighting the rocket and had been wearing them when he followed Tessa to Guy Frost's house. He must have taken them off after he'd been hurt. They could incriminate him.

It was too late to think of that now.

Guy, however, had taken care of them. He had burnt them and dispersed the ashes in the garden.

Orlando left the van on the hard standing at the garage and, as arranged, put the keys through the door. Then he got into his car and started up the engine. He turned west, his mind already made up before he heard the radio news.

A man employed as a security guard had died in

a fire believed to have been started by animal rights activists at a cosmetic packing firm in Darsingford.

Orlando had to stop on this journey. He pulled up at the first service area he came to, used the washroom, splashing cold water on his face, and had a cup of coffee.

A man had died: an innocent man had perished after Tessa's rockets had started a fire, all because of her unforgiving bitterness towards Guy Frost.

And he, Orlando, had wasted two years of his life hanging around Tessa, fitting in with her moods and whims, and aiding and abetting her criminal activities.

It was nearly four o'clock in the morning when he turned in at the gate of Tessa's parents' house and parked on the gravel sweep opposite the front door. Lights came on as he walked towards it and pressed the bell. Would they hear it? Were they sound sleepers? Must he blow the horn of his car to arouse them? Orlando heard the bell shrilling inside the house as he kept his finger on the button. There was a big, heavy old iron knocker on the door; he banged that, too, and eventually a head poked out of an upstairs window and an irate voice called out, 'All right – all right. I'm coming. Who is that down there?'

'It's Orlando,' James Graham heard.

From the noise, he had been expecting to learn it was the police. James called to his wife as he started down the stairs, and she hurried to follow him, pulling on a dressing-gown as she went.

'What's happened? Has there been an accident?' asked James, opening the door and drawing Orlando into the house. He saw that the younger man was swaying as he stood, almost passing out. 'Where's Tessa?'

'I don't know. I thought she might be here,' said Orlando. 'She's all right – sort of. She was, anyway.'

'You'd better explain,' said James grimly, leading the way towards his study, just like a headmaster, thought Orlando inconsequentially, almost laughing at the notion. He felt a huge sense of relief at being swept along by other people, taken in charge for the second time that dreadful night.

'It's murder – it's murder,' he said, as James gestured to him to sit down.

'What's murder? For God's sake, Orlando, tell us what's happened,' Millicent implored.

So Orlando related the whole story. He described all their raids, mentioning the four other people who had been involved in the earlier exploits. At one point, Millicent went off to make some tea. Orlando was, she saw, severely shocked: tea would be better and more thirst-quenching than coffee. By now she had seen the bandage on his arm and knew that he had been hurt in a tussle over a gun.

James clarified some points in the story while they waited for Millicent's return. Neither had for an instant questioned the truth of his account, Orlando realised; neither had protested that their daughter could not have done such things.

While they were drinking their tea, the judge said, 'You say there is some evidence in your car. A bag of equipment.'

'Yes. And some wrappings and a tube.'

'I think it would be wise to bring that in,' said James Graham. 'And to put your car away, out of sight. May I have the keys?'

'They're in it,' said Orlando.

'I won't be long,' said James, and he went outside, still in his dressing-gown. He took everything out of the boot of the BMW and carried it into the house, then started up the car and drove it into the spare garage which Tessa often used.

While he was gone, Orlando said, 'He thinks she'll come here. That's why he wants to hide my car.'

'Yes,' agreed Millicent. 'Where else could she go?'

Orlando didn't know.

'I've shopped her,' he said sadly.

And yourself, thought Millicent.

'You had no choice,' she said. 'She must be stopped.'

When James returned, he told them he was going upstairs to put some clothes on.

'I'll hear the rest of what you have to say when I'm dressed,' he said.

He was using the time for thought as well, Millicent knew.

'How is your arm?' she asked. 'You ought to see a doctor.'

'It can wait,' Orlando said.

She had poured him out another cup of tea and he drank it gratefully.

'It was brave of you to come here,' she said.

'I'd decided before I heard the radio news,' Orlando replied. 'I was already on my way.'

'Well done,' she said, and wondered if this would earn him some clemency when, eventually, there was a trial, as there must be.

'Where's the gun?' asked James, when he returned, wearing a thick sweater and a pair of corduroy trousers.

'Guy said he'd get rid of it,' Orlando answered. 'I don't think he wants her charged.'

'But he didn't know about the security guard, when he said that,' said Tessa's father.

'I suppose there couldn't have been another incident. Perhaps that guard was at some different factory,' said Millicent.

'Unlikely. They reported it because of the previous attack in the same town,' said James.

They had listened to the news on the hour and heard the same short announcement that Orlando had described. He went on with his story, covering everything he could remember, even his and Jet's adventure the previous weekend.

'It would be a pity to drag those others into this,' he said.

'I agree,' said James. 'It may not be necessary. No one was hurt until today.'

'Except the rabbits,' said Orlando. 'It seems silly,

352

but it was such a pointless, awful thing to do. And the whole argument was about saving animals, yet she shot those pets.'

'She did it to hurt Guy,' said Millicent. She felt rather sick.

'This is awful for you,' said Orlando. 'This is your daughter we're talking about.'

'She can be very cruel,' said her father. Apart from persecuting her brother, there had been bad moments in her childhood: in one instance, she'd bullied another girl, physically tormenting her, setting the end of her plait on fire. Fire, even then, he thought. 'She wanted her own way all the time,' he added. And she got it, usually.

Eventually the tale was over. Orlando had revealed everything he knew.

'You must go to bed,' said Millicent. 'You've had no sleep. And you're in no state to go home,' she added.

'I won't run away,' he said.

But Tessa might. Would she? All of them were wondering that as Millicent took Orlando upstairs, found him a pair of her husband's pyjamas, and turned down the spare room bed.

'I'll go and fill you a hot bottle,' she said. 'Would you like a bath?'

He would, but he was much too tired. He said so.

He managed to undress while she was gone. His arm hurt, and he remembered about the pain killers which Guy had advised him to take. Millicent had thought of those, however, and she brought him some paracetamol with the hot water bottle.

'They're cosier than an electric blanket, I always think,' she said, putting it into his bed. Then she tucked him in. 'I'm so sorry, Orlando,' she added. 'You've been very badly wounded, and I'm not talking about your arm.'

'It was my own fault,' he answered. 'I walked into the line of fire. Each time.'

Downstairs, Millicent found her husband busy at his desk. He was writing down everything that Orlando had told him, while it was still fresh in his memory.

'What will happen to Orlando?' she asked.

'I don't know. We'll have to see,' said James. 'A great deal will depend on Tessa.'

'That poor man. The guard. I suppose he had a family,' she said. 'I wonder who he was.'

While she had been busy with Orlando, the judge had telephoned the chief constable, whom he knew well, saying he had heard about the incident at Darsingford. Was it true? Had the victim been identified?

A call came back some time later to say that an arson attack had involved a death, but the victim's identity had not been confirmed. He had been knocked over by falling boxes and was badly burnt.

'Tessa might get away with manslaughter,' said James. 'With a clever lawyer and some luck.'

'While of unsound mind,' said her mother. 'She must be mad, James.' It was a plea.

'What is madness?' he said. 'Was Hamlet mad?'

'Ophelia was,' said Millicent. 'Blighted in love, and so insane.' Like poor, unhappy Tessa.

'I'm going to ring Edward back,' said James. 'I just wanted to talk it over first with you, my dear. I think we must tell him what we know and let him take what steps he thinks appropriate. We'll try to leave the others out of it and do what we can to minimise Orlando's part in the whole sorry business. I'm afraid he loved not wisely, but too well.'

'It's tragic.'

'Yes. He's shown he has courage, coming here like this. He could have fled, kept quiet, tried to save himself.'

'I suppose so.'

'Self-preservation is a strong impulse,' said the judge.

'Do you think that's what's driving Tessa now?'

'We'll find out,' James replied. 'I think she'll turn up here and behave as if nothing's happened. She won't believe that Orlando, at the last, could grass her up, as the criminal fraternity would describe it.'

'What about Guy?'

'He let her go. She knows that. It shows she still has some power over him.'

'We'd better keep Orlando here,' said Millicent. 'It'll stop him doing something else heroic, like walking in to a police station.'

'Yes. We'll wait a while, and give Tessa time to calm down,' said James. 'The police can easily be brought to her. She may find Edward here, waiting for her, when she arrives.'

'That will flatter her,' said Millicent. 'To be arrested by the chief constable.' They looked at one another sadly.

'She may not know about the dead man. Not yet,' said James. 'She'll have had Wagner playing in the car, and when she reached the flat, if that's where she's gone.'

'We could telephone.'

James shook his head.

'Let's leave her for the moment. She won't do anything else just yet. Guy was her target, and he has the gun.'

'Without a licence.'

'Yes. Without a cartridge, though. Orlando unloaded it and put the second one in his pocket. I daresay there are others in the holdall,' said the judge. 'Maybe in Tessa's pockets, too.' He put his arms out and drew his wife towards him. 'Have courage, my dear. We're going to need it.'

Neither, even for an instant, contemplated trying to shield their daughter from the law.

It would mean the end of James's career. Millicent knew it; this wise, liberal judge would have to retire because the media would tear them all apart.

'I'm going up to shave, and put a tie on,' said James. 'Shall you get dressed, too?'

'Yes – oh yes. I must. One can deal with things better if one's properly clothed,' she said. 'We mustn't wake Orlando, though.'

They were having breakfast in the kitchen when she came. They heard the car: both were listening for it, and were waiting in the hall when she opened the front door.

She was wearing trousers and a reefer jacket. Her eyes were bright, her face beautifully made up.

'I've come to leave my car,' she said. 'I'm going skiing until after the new year. Piers is right behind me. We're taking his car.'

As she spoke, a young man entered the house. He was tall and fair, a younger version of Orlando, someone she had picked up in a club a few weeks before and met occasionally since then.

'Hullo, sir. Hullo,' the young man said, nodding in the direction of the elder pair. 'I've moved the bags into my car,' he added.

'Take them out again,' said James. 'And go away. Get going, if you don't want to end up in court.' He moved between Tessa and the front door. 'Go on, young man,' he said.

'For God's sake. His name's Piers, I told you,' Tessa said, 'Don't listen to him, Piers.'

Inevitably, he would have a name like that, thought James.

'The police will be coming here, Tessa. I'm sure you don't want to be embarrassed in front of – er – Piers, nor to involve him in your problems,' he said.

'What problems?' asked Tessa in an airy tone. 'I was with Piers throughout last night. Wasn't I, Piers?' She turned to her bewildered companion.

'Who has mentioned anything about last night?' said her father. 'But what you've just said is a lie.' He looked at Piers. 'Leave while you are free to do so,' he directed. 'If you swear to something you know to be untrue, you will commit perjury, a very serious offence, and this could be a matter of murder.'

'Murder?' Piers blenched.

'Perhaps my daughter has failed to tell you that I am a judge. Perhaps she has told you a false story about her recent nocturnal activities,' said James. 'I suggest you choose to believe me when I tell you that because of her, a man has died. I suggest you take my advice and go. No one need know that you were here at all.'

With a last desperate look at Tessa, Piers went.

Tessa made to follow, but her father stood in front of her, a burly man, with authority.

'You're going nowhere, Tessa,' he said, and now his voice was sad.

'Orlando hasn't died?' she asked, and added, defensively, 'He was all right. Anyway, it was his own fault.'

'Would you care if he was dead?' James spoke wearily. 'You went to Guy Frost's house with a gun. You went with intent.'

'I wouldn't have shot Guy,' said Tessa.

'Why was your gun loaded, then?'

She shrugged. The fire in her was dying down.

'You said someone was dead.'

'An unknown man. A security guard at the

factory you chose to attack first,' her father said.

'I didn't know there was a guard,' she answered, not denying, otherwise, his accusation. 'How do you know about this?' she demanded. 'I suppose Guy called the police. The shit.'

'There was a guard,' said James. He did not answer her last question.

'No one will know who did it. They'll think it was someone else. Someone with a record,' Tessa said.

'Why should they do that?'

'They might find something at the scene with prints on,' Tessa said, and now a smirk spread across her face. 'I thought of everything.'

'You didn't, Tessa,' said the judge, understanding that she'd planted something to incriminate another person: not Orlando, for he could not have a record, but one of the youngsters she'd taken on the earlier excursions. She'd needed them to form an admiring audience of courtiers, but also as diversions in case she was suspected. 'You forgot about honesty.'

'You've got to let me go, Dad,' said Tessa. 'I'll go away, keep my head down till it's sorted.'

'I will not,' said the judge. 'I will see justice done. I'm going now to telephone the police. They are expecting me to call,' he added. 'Go into the kitchen with your mother. You'd like some coffee, wouldn't you?'

He glanced across at Millicent, who, very pale, gestured to Tessa to precede her. Would she do so?

Both of them waited. Tessa might decide on flight and physically it would be difficult to restrain her. However, the fight had gone out of her, though she still maintained an air of defiance, walking, head held high, out of her father's presence. She allowed her mother to put a cup of coffee before her, and as she sipped it, Millicent wanted to take her in her arms and hug her, but when she moved towards her, Tessa rounded on her.

'Keep away,' she snapped. 'I'm your daughter. How could you do this to me?'

'We have to do what's best for you,' Millicent said. 'You're ill, my dear.'

Tessa did not answer. She sat there with a mulish look on her face until her father entered the room. He poured himself a cup of coffee and sat down to wait for the police.

'How did you know?' she asked again, her voice flat.

'Your car was seen near the factory,' her father said. It was not a lie. Orlando, for one, had seen it there. 'That's why you brought it here, isn't it? To hide it, while you ran away.'

If anyone had noticed it near the scene – and they could have done – it would have been traced to her, in London.

She did not contradict him. She started on her silence then, admitting nothing when the police arrived.

A bag containing lighter fuel, rags, and wrappings which later proved to have been in contact with fireworks, and some cans of spray paint, was found in her car. Oddly, the handle showed no prints: the judge had wiped it very thoroughly, when, after telephoning the police, he put it in the Golf.

He had also wiped a length of piping lying there: the forensic laboratory could find no prints on it, though it bore traces of explosive and they deduced it was used to fire the rockets. James had removed Tessa's waxed jacket. There were spare cartridges in its pocket, and if he had simply taken those away, they would have left traces. Much later, when the car had been taken away, like Guy, he had a bonfire. There was no evidence to connect Tessa with a firearm.

28

CHARLOTTE TOLD HER grandmother that Denis was the thief.

'I came back and found him here,' she said. 'He'd let himself in with the spare key.' She related the whole story, even confessing to her arrest.

'I've been so stupid,' she said.

'Not at all,' said Frances. 'You were right to be concerned about the animals.' She looked at Charlotte, young and passionate, at the beginning of her adult life. 'It's right to feel deeply,' she said. 'It's right to have the courage of your convictions. But it's also right and brave to admit that you may have been mistaken.'

She was concerned about this mysterious Tessa, whose true identity Charlotte did not know. The woman sounded dangerous and fanatical, but as far as Charlotte was concerned, their link was over. Charlotte would not go with her again.

'Concentrate on your degree,' she advised. 'Forget

all this. Tessa will probably do something else that's extreme and be arrested.'

'You don't think I should tell the police about her?'

'Not really.' Frances was thinking of Charlotte, who would be arrested too, if she informed on their leader. 'There are the others to consider.'

'I know,' Charlotte agreed.

She'd decided to go back to London in the morning, not staying for any proposed visit to Guy Frost's laboratory. It might be very interesting, but it could wait.

Poor Denis, Frances was thinking; he wasn't really wicked, just an opportunist thief who would probably be caught one day and locked up. She was content to let him keep what he had stolen from her.

'Put it down to experience,' she said. 'And be less gullible another time. Where do you think Denis has gone?'

'Back to where he came from. Some squat in London, I suppose,' Charlotte said.

But she was wrong.

Denis, leaving Chingbury, was annoyed with Jet. Why had he let her take his keys like that? Now he'd have trouble getting into the room tonight.

But he didn't want to hang about round here. He didn't want to be with Phil so much, getting told to wash and all that boring stuff, though the old geezer had been decent in his way. He'd planned to move on, and so he would. Soon, though, it would be getting dark. He didn't fancy another night in a wood, not with all those animals squeaking near him. He thought about going to demand the keys back from Jet, but if he did, she'd threatened to drop him in it over the money. Better not to risk it, he decided, walking on. If he hurried, he could get back to the room before Phil set off for work; he could be let in, sleep soft and comfortable once more, then leave in the morning.

Reaching the main road, he turned away from London, heading, contrary to Jet's instructions, towards Darsingford, hoping for a lift. Several cars had passed him, with no one slowing down, when a battered van drew up.

'Where you going, then?' a voice asked him.

A girl looked out of the passenger's window. She had long hair and wore a stud in her nose.

'Dunno,' Denis answered. 'Anywhere,' he added, grinning. 'Wherever you are.' After all, why not?

'We're going to save the trees,' the girl told him.

'What trees?' Denis asked, as the man driving leaned past the girl to take a look at him.

'The trees they're chopping down to make space for a road,' said the girl. 'We want to save them. There's crowds of people there already. More are on their way. You could come along.'

'Yeah,' said Denis. 'Good idea.' He liked trees. He'd be keen to save some.

'Get in the back, then,' said the girl, and Denis went to the rear of the van. Another girl was there already. She made room for him. Climbing in beside her, Denis felt a warm, familiar thrill. It was like being with Tessa and Orlando on their trips, but this time they were saving trees.

'It's in the country, then?' he asked. 'Where we're going?'

'Sure – course it is,' said the second girl. 'They just mean to chop them down to make their road. Spoiling the environment.'

Denis settled down to listen while she explained their reasons for protesting. They'd build houses in the trees, she said, so that no one could start sawing. Everything was organised; plenty of others were at the scene but the more there were, the better it would be. It was all about people power, and once they were there, in their tents and tree houses, or sleeping in their vehicles, the social would arrange their money, for they would have an address.

Denis had found a new family. He was happy, soon forgetting all about his former loose attachments.

He was far away when Philip died that night.

At the cosmetic packing factory, remnants of the rockets fired were found. Also discovered at the scene were two cans of spray paint. They were tested for prints but those on them were blurred: so much for Tessa's plans to protect herself by incriminating her former team. The tins had spent too long being tossed around in the holdall with her combat gear and other devices. House to house enquiries in the neighbourhood of the factory were undertaken in the hope — faint, because the area was mostly industrial — that someone would have noticed a parked vehicle or some other suspicious sign.

A police officer went round to Guy Frost's to make sure that he had not been subjected to another attack, since there had been an earlier one on the night his workshop was fired.

'No,' he responded. 'It's been quiet here. Nothing to report.'

When the officer had gone, Guy faced the truth, for Orlando had told him only part of it. As on the first occasion, there had been a diversionary attack before the real one, and this time a man had been found dead in the wreckage of the factory. Orlando would not have known that, however. Guy felt that as a good citizen he should have put the police straight on to Tessa, but he couldn't do it to her. And he couldn't drop the unfortunate Orlando in it, either. The police might trace her on their own. This time Tessa had surpassed herself. She should be apprehended, charged and punished, and prevented from committing further crimes. Was all this really because of him and his rejection of her? Surely there was more to it than that, some innate imbalance in her make-up? Guy did not want to feel responsible for pushing her over the edge, and he did not intend to bring about her downfall. She would do it for herself, or Orlando would act the role of nemesis.

Guy slept badly that night; memories of Tessa rose up in his mind and he felt guilt. He should have ended their relationship long before he did, but until he had the impetus of his deep feelings for Amanda, it was easier to let things drift. In the morning, he locked up carefully before setting off for work, and on the way he made a detour to an isolated spot beside the river. There, he threw the shotgun out into the water, as far from where he stood as possible.

He'd go and see Amanda and the children in the evening. Maybe by then there would be some news about the dead man and the hunt for who had caused his death. It wasn't murder; it was, at worst, manslaughter, because it must have been an accident that he was in the way.

Philip's personal papers were in the office where he had sat before his surveillance screens. His wallet was there, with his credit cards inside, and a cheque book. There was his driver's licence, too.

It took a little time to work out that he was the same Philip Winter who had disappeared. The factory management had not followed up his references because his employment would have been short term, as a regular security firm was soon to be engaged.

'So he'd have been for the chop,' said the investigating officer.

'Oh yes. Probably after next week,' was the answer. 'His hours were excessive but he wanted the job.'

Philip's possessions were all with him, in his

plastic bag. The address he had given soon proved to be the public library; he had never told his employers that it had changed. By the middle of the following morning his identity as Philip Winter, the missing alleged rapist, was determined, though official identification had yet to be established. His wife or some other relative or close associate would have to be brought down to view the body and confirm the findings.

Lesley had to do it.

She could not believe it. What had he been up to, sending poison-pen letters to that woman, and working as a watchman? Where had he been living?

It had better be got over and done with quickly, she decided. She'd soon lose her job if the police kept calling on her at work. She made a call to a friend, asking her to take care of Jackie after school, and left with the police officer who had come to see her, a detective from the force dealing with the case.

They drove in silence, Lesley sitting in the back of the comfortable car, unable to believe what was happening, but when she saw the body, she knew that the dead man was her husband, in spite of the beard he had grown. The fact that it was so grey was what made her cry, but the police officers decided it was grief.

And so it was, but not the sorrow of bereavement.

29

PHILIP WINTER'S FUNERAL took place a fort-
night later, after an inquest had been opened
and adjourned. Lesley, all in black, with a wide-
brimmed hat, looked pale and tense; Jackie wept
throughout. Andrew stood expressionless beside his
mother. There was a scattering of mourners: a few
from Lavery's who had taken a day's leave, and some
neighbours. His frail parents stayed away, still
numb and bewildered by the events leading up to
his death, let alone the death itself, and unable to
face this further ordeal.

An unknown man was in the congregation at the
crematorium, a pale, thin man who looked
extremely sad: Orlando, Philip's avenger, who had
never met the dead man but had indirectly contributed to his death. He thought of speaking to the
widow afterwards, but decided not to.

Another man who was neither friend nor relative
was also there. Lesley recognised him as he stood

apart when she and the children were about to leave in the undertaker's large black limousine. It was Detective Sergeant Sykes. They stared at one another, neither speaking.

Two nights previously, he had called on Lesley.

He'd offered his condolences, asking her to spare him a few minutes, and she had been obliged to let him in.

'I've got something I want you to listen to,' he said. 'A tape recording.'

'What about?' she said, and then, 'It's all right, Andrew and Jackie are at the cinema. It's to take Jackie's mind off things, though it won't work.'

'It may, for a little while,' said Sykes.

He followed her into the comfortable sitting-room, where a fire burned. The chairs and sofa were deep and soft; the room was warm; and that poor bugger had been living rough and in a cheap boarding-house for the last weeks of his life, the victim of a spiteful liar.

Sykes produced a small tape recorder and set it on the coffee table. Then he spoke.

'The very day that Philip Winter died, that final Friday, much about the time he went on duty at the factory, I called on Mrs Sandra White,' he said. 'As I'd told you, we knew he was alive because his fingerprints were found on some anonymous communications that she had recently received.'

They hadn't been on all of them: only the last two mailings, the letter saying 'YOU LIED' and the offering of dog dirt; other prints were on the rest, and that was baffling, yet who else could have sent them unless Philip had a friend who arranged to post them and who had not come forward? The junk mail and the pizzas, even the kissogram, had been easy to organise. Philip's movements, before he went to Darsingford had not been fully traced, but the librarian there had recognised him from a photograph and said he had been with a scruffy youth whom he was teaching to read. Sykes did not tell Lesley this; maybe the Darsingford police had done so, if she was curious about his final days. Sometimes people wanted every detail; often, they preferred not to know things that were distressing.

'I taped my interview with her,' he said. 'My visit was unofficial. I was so certain that the verdict was the right one, that Philip Winter was completely innocent. In my opinion, it should never have come to court. It was a waste of time and public money, and it destroyed him. I planned to prove it, and I did, but then he died, and in such a dreadful way. Making it public after that would have added to the media harassment.' There had been a lot of it, when his identity was revealed.

'Well?' Lesley waited, tapping her foot impatiently.

Sykes had rung Sandra's bell that Friday night, and when she opened the door to him, he had smiled, and said this was an informal call.

'Well, come in, then, Sergeant,' she invited, opening the door wide, making him think of a sly spider luring a fly into its web. But this fly had taken steps to protect himself.

She offered him a drink, and he accepted a glass of mineral water. Alcohol was not going to be admitted to this scene; not by him, at least. Sandra had poured herself some white wine. She sat down on the sofa, patting the space beside her, and Sykes took it. The voice-activated tape recorder would work best at close quarters.

He told her that they were still waiting for the results of tests on the offensive package she had received, though this was untrue. They knew that Philip Winter was the sender.

'You said you had no idea who could hold a grudge against you,' Sykes reminded her. 'But you had some unpleasantness with a man called Philip Winter, whom you alleged had tried to rape you.'

'Yes – it was horrible. But he's dead – the man who attacked me,' Sandra said. 'He killed himself. Guilt, you see,' she added.

'His body hasn't been found. He may have simply left home.'

'Why should he do that? He got off,' she said. 'Quite wrongly.'

'Suppose he felt that he was the one who'd been wronged, and went into hiding with the aim of harassing you,' suggested Sykes.

At this, Sandra White belied her name and blushed a deep and ugly red, almost purple. She shook her head.

Sykes pressed his advantage.

'If so, he's moved from annoying pranks to nastiness,' he said. 'Turds now. What next? It could be much worse, even dangerous.'

'Like what?' Sandra could scarcely get the words out.

'Oh – incendiary devices. Letter bombs,' said Sykes.

'Would he do that? He seemed so feeble,' Sandra said. The colour had now faded from her face, replaced by pallor and a sheen of sweat. To Sykes' relief, she moved away from him.

'He lost his job. He was unemployed,' he pointed out. 'His life was ruined.'

'He was acquitted,' Sandra said.

'But he was publicly disgraced. His wife didn't altogether believe in his innocence,' said Sykes.

'It all got a bit out of hand,' Sandra, now alarmed, reluctantly conceded.

'What did? You mean his attempt to have sex with you?'

'No. My complaint against him. I only meant to teach him a lesson.'

'Because he rejected you? Because, as he said on oath in court, you attempted intimacy and he would not cooperate?'

She shrugged. He wanted her to answer, so that her reaction would be recorded on the tape.

'Was that it?' he pressed her.

'Once it went ahead at the police station, I couldn't back down,' she said, defiantly and clearly.

'I should say he'd got a grievance, then,' said

373

Sykes. 'You seem to be telling me that he was completely blameless.'

'He was insolent,' she said.

'He returned your purse. Did you leave it in Lavery's on purpose?' Would she admit it? If so, he'd got her all sewn up.

'Yes.' Now her tone was that of a sulky child. 'I was unhappy and lonely,' she said. 'I've got no one here to take care of me. I'm so wretched,' and as she began to weep she moved towards Sykes again, but he rose swiftly to his feet.

'You did that to Philip Winter, didn't you? Moved towards him, and when he resisted, you scratched his face,' said Sykes. 'I'm surprised he stops at dog shit.'

'Why you – you— ' Now her face was filled with fury and she flew at him, long nails spread out like talons.

He backed out of range.

'I must warn you, Mrs White, that attacking a police officer is a serious offence,' he said.

She almost gibbered at him, quivering on the spot. Hardened as he was, Sykes found her an alarming sight. No wonder Winter had fled when she made a play for him. She'd got off rather lightly so far, with the kissogram and postal shocks.

'I want you to leave,' she said. 'Now go.'

'You committed perjury,' said Sykes, and spelled it out for her. 'You lied in court.'

'You can't prove it,' Sandra muttered. 'It was my word against his.'

'But the court were not convinced,' he pointed out. 'And now I have the evidence to clear his name and give him grounds for bringing a civil case against you. He'll get colossal damages.' As he spoke, Sykes withdrew the tape recorder from his pocket, praying it had worked. Even if he were to be disciplined for this, it was worth it. 'We'll trace Winter,' he told her. 'We know where he's been, but we may not find him before he carries out some other hoax or trick against you. You'd better think about how to stop him. Like making an official statement,' and he turned to go. 'I'll see myself out,' he said.

But that night, Philip Winter died.

Lesley listened in silence till the tape stopped.

'I don't know what to say,' she said.

'No,' said Sykes. 'I don't suppose you do.' He took the tape out of the machine. 'It's yours,' he said. 'You may care to play it to your children.'

He'd kept a copy, just in case Sandra White tried the same trick in future.

'His death was really an accident,' said Lesley.

'It will probably be recorded as manslaughter,' Sykes replied. 'It wasn't an accident that he was in that factory. It was because he had been disgraced – dishonoured.' That was the word.

'She's the true killer, then. That woman – Sandra White,' said Lesley.

'Is she?' Sykes asked, as he rose to leave. 'I'll see myself out,' he said.

* * *

Orlando had been named by no one as an accessory to Tessa's crimes. She invoked her right to silence, however that would be interpreted by the time the case came to court. Martyrdom was now to be her role: she admitted the attacks in Darsingford but revealed nothing about her past relationship with Guy and he, apprehensive, hoped that no one would expose the truth.

Her father had stated that an unknown man had told him Tessa was responsible for the death of Philip Winter.

'It's quite true,' he'd told Orlando. 'You've now said your real name's Roland. Just keep quiet, because if you don't, those others may be dragged down too.'

His arm had almost healed. Guy had done an expert job on what was not a very serious wound. Orlando maintained his belief that the gun had gone off by accident.

He had applied for a post in Singapore and, if he were appointed, would be leaving long before Tessa's trial. Once there, sending Sandra postal presents could be difficult, but he would try. Meanwhile, he'd arrange for more surprises: manure, he thought, a rich and steaming load to be delivered, and coal. He'd devise other teases in the time that remained.

He tried not to think of Tessa, who had been remanded to a psychiatric hospital, but she came to him in dreams, taunting, cruel, beautiful. And mad?

☐ Almost the Truth	Margaret Yorke	£5.99
☐ The Cost of Silence	Margaret Yorke	£4.99
☐ No Medals for the Major	Margaret Yorke	£4.99
☐ Pieces of Justice	Margaret Yorke	£5.99
☐ The Point of Murder	Margaret Yorke	£4.99
☐ Safely to the Grave	Margaret Yorke	£5.99
☐ Serious Intent	Margaret Yorke	£5.99
☐ The Small Hours of the Morning	Margaret Yorke	£4.99

Warner Books now offers an exciting range of quality titles by both established and new authors. All of the books in this series are available from:

Little, Brown and Company (UK),
P.O. Box 11,
Falmouth,
Cornwall TR10 9EN.

Telephone No: 01326 317200
Fax No: 01326 317444
E-mail: books@barni.avel.co.uk

Payments can be made as follows: cheque, postal order (payable to Little, Brown and Company) or by credit cards, Visa/Access. Do not send cash or currency. UK customers and B.F.P.O. please allow £1.00 for postage and packing for the first book, plus 50p for the second book, plus 30p for each additional book up to a maximum charge of £3.00 (7 books plus).

Overseas customers including Ireland, please allow £2.00 for the first book plus £1.00 for the second book, plus 50p for each additional book.

NAME (Block Letters) ....

....

ADDRESS ....

....

....

☐ I enclose my remittance for ....

☐ I wish to pay by Access/Visa Card

Number ☐☐☐☐☐☐☐☐☐☐☐☐☐☐☐☐☐☐☐

Card Expiry Date ☐☐☐☐